OPERATI
SOVEREI

Further Titles by Clive Egleton from Severn House

THE ALSOS MISSION
THE ROMMEL PLOT

OPERATION SOVEREIGN

Clive Egleton

07426195

This title first published in Great Britain 1998 by
SEVERN HOUSE PUBLISHERS LTD of
9–15 High Street, Sutton, Surrey SM1 1DF.
Originally published 1982 in Great Britain under the
title *China Gold* and pseudonym of *John Tarrant*.

This book is for Dickie and John

British Library Cataloguing in Publication Data

Egleton, Clive

    Operation sovereign
    1.   Larceny – Hong Kong – Fiction
    2.   World War, 1939-1945 – Hong Kong – Fiction
    3.   Thrillers
    I.   Title
    II.   Tarrant, John, 1927-. China gold
    823.9'14 [F]

    ISBN 0 7278 5312 0

Typeset by Hewer Text Composition Services Limited,
Edinburgh, Scotland.
Printed and bound in Great Britain by
MPG Books Ltd, Bodmin, Cornwall.

WEDNESDAY
3rd DECEMBER 1941

CHAPTER ONE

Waldron leaned both elbows on the sill and stared through the window. The bungalow was high up on the hillside and way down below he could see tiny ant-like figures sunning themselves on the beach fronting The Repulse Bay, the most expensive and most luxurious hotel in Hong Kong. A mile of golden sands between pine-covered, razor-back peaks, the azure ocean calm as a millpond and the temperature in the mid-seventies; the guide books had got it right for once when they'd described the bay as a slice of heaven by the sea. So far as Waldron was concerned though, heaven was spoilt by the steel bars set in the window frame and the barbed-wire fence surrounding the bungalow.

Less than a month ago, the bungalow had been occupied by the Mother Superior in charge of St Theresa's, and the two-storey building next to it had housed a hundred-and-seventy-five Chinese orphans. Then, almost overnight, the nuns and the children had been evacuated to alternative accommodation on the north side of the island, the orphanage had become a barracks for two infantry companies and the bungalow had been converted into a guardroom. One closed and disciplined society had replaced another, and all because of a requisition order, signed and dated 9th November 1941.

Waldron heard the sound of heavy footsteps in the corridor outside his cell and moved away from the window. Moments later, the key turned in the lock, the door opened outwards and Ogden, the tall Canadian provost sergeant from Grand Rapids walked into the room and dumped a large valise on the bed.

'Hope you like it, Frank,' he said.

'What?'

'The valise; it's part of your going away present. The army

finally got things straightened out. They're sending you home.'

Waldron felt his stomach lurch. Right now, home was the last place he wanted to go. 'You've got to be kidding,' he said in a husky voice.

Ogden shook his head. 'You sail tomorrow afternoon at three o'clock on the US *Warren Harding*, flagship of the President Line. Manilla, Honolulu, then San Francisco three weeks from now; that's some luxury cruise.'

'Terrific.'

'You don't seem very happy about it.'

There was nothing to be happy about. In three weeks' time, some stranger would find him lying in a dark alleyway with a bullet hole in his head. Waldron had lived with that supposition from the day the army had placed him under close arrest pending repatriation to the States.

'I guess I'm a little stunned by the news,' he said flatly.

'In your shoes, I'd be over the moon.' Ogden undid the valise and began to lay the contents out on the bed. 'One grey two-piece suit, three brand new shirts, four pairs of socks, one tie, vests, underpants, and a pair of black lace-up shoes, size ten.' He grinned at Waldron. 'The suit's off the peg, but it should fit you okay.'

Waldron grimaced. He didn't need to ask Ogden why the army was providing him with civilian clothes free of charge. For all that Congress had passed the Lend-Lease Bill, America was still technically a neutral country, and the captain of the *Warren Harding* would never allow him to embark in uniform.

'You're getting your discharge, Frank.'

'Honourable or dishonourable?'

'The Canadian army doesn't hand out good conduct medals for fraudulent enlistment.' Ogden lit two cigarettes and gave one to Waldron. 'After you've handed your kit into the stores, we'll run you over to Murray Barracks.'

'The Detention Centre?'

'Yeah. That's where you'll spend your last night in Hong Kong.'

Waldron nodded. Murray Barracks was on the north side of

the island within easy distance of the Star Ferry terminal in Victoria. Sometime tomorrow morning, the military police would escort him across the bay to Kowloon on the mainland and put him on board the liner. If his memory served him right, it was usual for ships of the President Line to be allocated a berth on the Number 2 Pier, which was only a stone's throw from the ferry terminal in Kowloon.

'When do we leave here?' he asked.

'Five-thirty, right after dinner. We'll be travelling on the mail truck.'

Murray Barracks was a good eight miles from Repulse Bay, and the road twisted and turned through the hills like a black serpent. With any luck, Waldron thought, it would be pitch dark long before they reached the Wongnei Chung Gap, half-way to Victoria.

'You're not going to give us any trouble, are you, Frank?'

'Of course I'm not.' Waldron dropped his cigarette on to the floor and crushed it under the heel of his boot. 'I've been a model prisoner up till now, haven't I?'

'Sure you have,' said Ogden. 'Just keep it that way.'

George Ramsay glared at the office intercom, then picked up the paper knife and stabbed the point deep into his desk. 'My office on the double.' Ramsay scowled. Who the hell did Kellerman think he was talking to? He was a Detective Chief Inspector, for Christ's sake, not some bloody office boy. Kellerman might be the Assistant Commissioner in charge of the Kowloon Division, but there was such a word as please and it wouldn't hurt him to use it once in a while.

Ramsay glanced at the occurrence report for the previous twenty-four hours, which was lying in his pending tray. Kellerman hadn't said why he wanted to have a word with him, but no doubt the Assistant Commissioner would have something to say about the increase in the number of indictable offences which had occurred since he'd been in charge of the Criminal Investigation Department.

The statistics looked bad, and they were bad, but the detective squad's lack of success in recent months was in no way attributable to inefficiency on his part. The CID was simply going through a sticky patch – and the Vice Squad weren't helping matters, either. When he'd arrived at police headquarters this morning, a small army of prostitutes, pimps and drug addicts had been lined up in the yard, waiting to be ferried down to the Magistrate's Court on Gascoigne Road. An occasional crackdown was all very well, but this sustained campaign which the Vice Squad had launched against the streetwalkers and their hangers-on was counter-productive. For every conviction obtained in the courts, the detective squad ended up with one less informer, and the job of serious crime prevention became that much more difficult.

Just why Kellerman couldn't see that the activities of the Vice Squad were hampering the CID was beyond his understanding, but he figured it would do no harm to make the point again. In a somewhat calmer frame of mind than he had been a few minutes ago, Ramsay made his way up to the Assistant Commissioner's office on the landing above and obeying the notice on his door, knocked twice before entering.

Kellerman had abandoned his desk at the far end of the room and was seated at the head of the conference table in the window. Ralph Cottis, the G2 Intelligence officer from Fortress Headquarters, was on his right and next to him, a neatly attired fair-haired civilian whom Ramsay had never seen before. He didn't know why the other two men were present, but at least he didn't have to explain now what his squad were doing about the assault with a deadly weapon, the three burglaries and the attempted rape that had been committed in Kowloon yesterday.

'Good afternoon, George.' Kellerman managed a brief smile that flicked on and then off like a neon sign. 'I don't think you've met Mr Hammond of the Hong Kong and Shanghai Bank?'

The civilian stood up and leaned across the table to shake hands. 'David Hammond,' he said. 'I'm in charge of security.'

Hammond was a shade over six foot, and lean with it. His face was tanned, unlined and strong, like his firm handshake. Sizing him up, Ramsay thought he'd be between twenty-six and twenty-eight, which meant he had to be a high flyer. The Hong Kong and Shanghai was the largest banking corporation in the Far East and the board would never have chosen a man of his age to be their Chief Security Officer unless he was outstanding. Ramsay also found it hard to picture him behind a desk; Hammond looked the type who would be more at home on the athletic track or chasing a ball around the tennis court.

'And of course there's no need to introduce you to Major Cottis,' Kellerman continued. 'You two know each other rather well.'

Ramsay nodded, said, 'Hullo Ralph, nice to see you again,' and pulled out a chair. Special Branch formed part of the CID in Kowloon, and he and Cottis were in the habit of meeting once a fortnight to exchange information.

'Major Cottis has some rather disturbing news for us, George.' Kellerman took out a handkerchief and mopped his face. It was pleasantly warm, the temperature only in the mid-seventies, but Kellerman was fat and even though the two electric fans in the ceiling were creating a draught, he still dripped with perspiration. 'Very disturbing news,' he repeated.

'We had an unexpected visitor on Monday night.' Cottis leaned forward, elbows on the table, his thin shoulders hunched. 'Private second-class Shoji Doi, a deserter from the Imperial Japanese Army.'

'We don't get too many of his ilk,' Ramsay said dryly.

'Doi is something of a rarity amongst Nipponese soldiers; it seems he'd taken all the discipline he could stomach from face-slapping NCOs. Whatever his motives for deserting, the fact remains that Doi crossed the border near the police post at Lo Wu and surrendered himself to 'C' company of the 2/14th Punjabis up at Fanling. I spent most of yesterday interrogating him.'

'That must have been quite a change for you, Ralph.'

'It certainly was.' Cottis smiled. 'Cocktail parties and official receptions at Government House are usually more in my line.'

Ramsay thought he sounded bitter. If he was, he had good reason to be. Despite the Military Cross and bar he'd won in the 1914–18 War, Cottis would never make Lieutenant Colonel. Ever since he'd arrived in the Colony way back in August '38, he had consistently voiced the opinion that war with Japan was inevitable, a prediction which had made him highly unpopular with just about everybody who was anybody from Hong Kong to Whitehall.

'What did you get from this deserter of yours?' Ramsay asked him.

'I learned where he came from and the names of both his regimental and divisional commanders – Colonel Tanaka Ryosabura and Major General Ito Sano.'

'And that's significant?'

'It was enough to convince me that the Japanese have moved the 38th Division to a concentration area near To Kat, eight miles north of the border. There are also elements of two other divisions within easy striking distance of the frontier that I know of. This means that the build-up in South China is now approaching sixty thousand combat-ready troops, with supporting artillery.'

Ramsay shook his head. Sixty thousand men, and all they had to oppose them were two British, two Canadian and two Indian infantry battalions, plus the two thousand part-time soldiers of the Hong Kong Volunteer Defence Corps. And the RAF was in an even more parlous state to fight a war. Their total front line strength at Kai Tak consisted of two Walrus amphibians and three Wildebeeste dive-bombers, ancient biplanes that had a top speed of one hundred miles an hour.

'What have you heard on your grapevine, George?'

'I had a phone call from Bill Donovan yesterday,' Ramsay said slowly. 'He's been in charge of the border post at Sha Tau Kok since the beginning of April and is on pretty good terms with Captain Tanaka Saki, his opposite number. Saki used to be the Assistant Military Attaché at the Japanese embassy in London a few years back and he likes to practise his English on Bill. They meet for dinner once a week, turn and turn about.'

'Do you mind getting to the point, Chief Inspector?' Keller-man said irritably. 'We haven't got all day.'

There was an embarrassed silence. Hammond raised an expressive eyebrow, while Cottis looked up at the ceiling as if suddenly fascinated by the electric fan.

Ramsay gritted his teeth and silently counted up to ten, waiting for his anger to subside. 'The point is,' he said tightly, 'Saki told Bill that he would be unable to repay his hospitality this coming weekend. He also suggested Bill should take a few days' leave with effect from the fifth of December.'

'You couldn't ask for a broader hint than that,' Hammond said, frowning. 'And I certainly wouldn't care to be in Dono-van's shoes when the invasion starts.'

Too bloody right, Ramsay thought. Sha Tau Kok was out on a limb, a tiny village half in China, half in the New Territories, with Mirs Bay to the south and a range of hills stiff with Jap troops immediately to the north. There was only one road in and out, and that ran parallel with the frontier.

'It was probably only meant as a joke.' Kellerman looked at Cottis, seeking his support. 'I mean, surely the Japanese High Command wouldn't take a junior officer like Captain Saki into their confidence?'

'I doubt if they gave him the date of the invasion, but Saki was probably shrewd enough to make an educated guess.' Cottis dragged his eyes away from the electric fan in the ceiling. 'Donovan?' he said idly. 'Does he have a namesake in the CID?'

'Inspector Donovan was transferred to the uniform branch eight months ago.' Kellerman mopped his face again with the silk handkerchief, then smiled uneasily. 'It's our policy to rotate officers in order to broaden their experience.'

'Quite,' said Cottis. 'I was just curious, that's all.'

Ramsay lit a cigarette and leaned back in his chair. Donovan would never have been rotated had Superintendent Challinor still been in charge of the CID, but he'd died of cancer back in February. From the day Kellerman had been promoted to Assistant Commissioner, he'd had his beady eyes on the detective squad. Everybody knew that he was determined to clean up the

CID, and Challinor's death was exactly the opportunity he'd been waiting for. Ramsay was afraid he would be the first victim of the purge, but Kellerman had chosen a more devious approach. Instead of appointing a new man, he had allowed him to take over from Challinor and had then proceeded to lumber him with his own blue-eyed boys, men like Sub Inspector Pascoe.

'Donovan's a good officer, but sometimes he's too impatient and apt to jump to conclusions.' Kellerman cleared his throat. 'Personally, I'm inclined to take this so-called warning he received from Saki with a large pinch of salt.'

'That's your prerogative,' Hammond told him brusquely. 'I can't afford to be quite so sanguine about the situation, especially in the light of Major Cottis's information. I'm going to put "Sovereign" into effect.'

'Are you empowered to do that?' Kellerman asked judiciously.

'I wouldn't be here if I wasn't.' Hammond turned to Ramsay. 'I don't suppose "Sovereign" means a great deal to you, does it, Chief Inspector?'

'Not a damn thing,' said Ramsay.

'"Sovereign" is a contingency plan to safeguard the gold reserves of the Hong Kong and Shanghai Bank in the event of hostilities with Japan.' Hammond reached inside his jacket and took out a small notebook about the size of a pocket diary. After consulting it briefly, he looked up and said, 'The SS *Delphic Star* is due to arrive on Friday afternoon. She'll then spend two and a half days in port before departing for Sydney on Monday the eighth.'

'With your gold reserves on board?'

'Right first time.'

'That doesn't seem a very satisfactory arrangement to me. Why not entrust the bullion to the Royal Navy?'

'We'd like to,' said Hammond. 'Unfortunately, apart from two elderly gunboats and a flotilla of motor torpedo boats, the Navy only has one "S" Class destroyer on station and she can't be spared. That being the case, we'll have to transfer the reserves to our Kowloon branch and from there to Number 3 Pier, where the *Delphic Star* will be berthed.'

'I don't get it,' said Ramsay. 'Why take two bites at the cherry when the docks are less than half a mile from the Kowloon branch? Wouldn't it be easier to run the bullion straight on to the wharfside?'

'That would be just a little too obvious. The bullion must be transferred to the *Delphic Star* under cover of darkness a few hours before she leaves harbour. The last thing we want is a run on the bank.'

Hammond didn't have to spell it out for him. They could well have a major riot on their hands if word got around that the vaults of the Hong Kong and Shanghai Bank were empty.

'I can appreciate the need for secrecy.' Ramsay leaned forward and stubbed out his cigarette in a glass ashtray. 'But how do we go about it?'

'We've given a considerable amount of thought to that problem, haven't we, Commissioner?'

Kellerman nodded and pushed his chair back. Leaving the table, he crossed the room and opened the wall safe behind his desk. Moments later, he returned with a slim file which he handed to Ramsay. 'This will tell you exactly what's involved,' he said tersely.

The file was graded Most Secret and contained two sheets of foolscap. According to the distribution list inside the cover, copies number two and three were held by the Central Police Station in Victoria and Fortress Headquarters, while the fourth was retained by Hammond in his capacity as Chief Security Officer. The actual operation appeared straightforward enough, but to Ramsay's way of thinking, there was a curious lack of urgency about its execution.

'How come the transfer is spread over two days?' he asked.

'Because we intend to utilize the existing daily shuttle between Head Office and the branch in Kowloon. It's the only way we can effect the transfer in secrecy.'

Hammond was right. Every morning, six days a week, an armoured truck left the Head Office in Victoria and proceeded

to the vehicular ferry on Connaught Road. Even though the
route and time of departure was never the same two days
running, it was so much a part of a familiar pattern of events
that very few people spared the truck a second glance.

'Two trips, eh?' Ramsay smiled, looking up from the file.
'You must have an awful lot of gold in that vault of yours.'

Hammond nodded. 'The bullion weighs six tons. At current
market rates our gold reserves are worth two point five million
pounds.'

Two and a half million. Ramsay's eyes glittered; a man could
live like a king on that kind of money. Avoiding Kellerman's
speculative gaze, he studied the plans for "Sovereign" with
new-found interest.

CHAPTER TWO

Waldron heard the mail truck grind to a halt outside the
bungalow and smiled grimly. After six and a half months, the
last nineteen days of which had been spent in close arrest,
Private Frank Waldron of the Winnipeg Grenadiers was about
to become a civilian again. One lousy phone call; that's all it had
taken to blow his cover. One lousy phone call to his sister's
house in Yonkers the night before the battalion had sailed from
Vancouver, and the Hong Kong police had been waiting for
him on the wharf-side when their troopship had docked at
Kowloon. The only thing he had to be thankful for, he thought
grudgingly, was that the Canadian Army had refused to hand
him over to the civilian authorities; had they done so, he would
have ended up in Stanley Prison, where the security was really
tight.

The key turned in the lock for the last time and he waited for
the cell door to swing open; cool, relaxed and subservient, the

model prisoner who never gave anybody any trouble.

Ogden said, 'Time to go, Frank.'

Waldron nodded. He noticed that the provost sergeant had brought an escort with him, a boyish-looking private he'd never seen before.

'You want to put your jacket on?'

'I might as well.' Waldron picked up the jacket from the bed and slipped his arms into the sleeves. 'How do I look in civilian clothes?' he asked brightly.

'Presentable,' said Ogden. 'Now hold out your arms, wrists close together.'

'What for?'

'Because I've got to handcuff you, that's why.'

'Oh no.' Waldron shook his head vehemently. 'I was discharged from the Canadian Army at exactly three forty-five this afternoon. As of now, I'm an American citizen, and you've absolutely no jurisdiction over me. As a matter of fact, you have no legal right to hold me overnight at Murray Barracks.'

'You're talking like a goddamned lawyer.'

'I used to be one, remember?'

'I've got my orders,' Ogden said stubbornly.

'I know you have, but don't count on the brass standing by you when the shit starts flying. It wouldn't take much to spark off a major diplomatic row between my government and yours – and you could find yourself in the centre of it.'

'Are you threatening me, Frank?'

'No. I was just offering you some friendly advice.' Waldron smiled. 'Now, why don't we call it quits and get out of here?'

Ogden stared at the handcuffs he was holding, his black eyebrows drawn together in a perplexed frown. Finally he shrugged his shoulders, tossed the handcuffs on to the bed and grinned at Waldron. 'What the hell,' he said, 'I'm not looking for trouble, and you've got enough of it already.'

Easy does it, Waldron told himself, you've won the first round, but there's still a long way to go. His face expressionless, he picked up his valise and followed Ogden out of the cell, the escort a few paces behind him.

The mail truck was a museum piece, a 1934 Fordson three-quarter-ton load-carrier with a top speed of thirty-five on the flat. Waldron reckoned it would take the driver about half an hour to cover the eight miles or so between Repulse Bay and Victoria, and on some of the inclines the truck would need to be in bottom gear to make it to the top. There was also another point in his favour: the sun was below the horizon now and the parade ground in front of the orphanage was already deep in shadow.

'Get in, Frank,' said Ogden. 'You've got Corporal Dobson for company.'

'So I see.' Waldron heaved the valise over the tailgate and climbed in after it.

'Move right up to the back, near the cab.'

'Anything you say.'

Waldron edged his way past the postal NCO, stepped over a mailbag and sat down on his valise. The escort scrambled in after him and squatted on the floor near the tailgate, facing Dobson. Ogden then walked round to the front and got in beside the driver. Moments later, and shuddering as if it had the ague, the Fordson pulled slowly away from the bungalow and down the hill to the main road below.

'We're breaking King's Regulations,' Dobson said plaintively. 'The mail truck's not supposed to carry passengers.'

'Tell that to Sergeant Ogden,' said the escort.

'I already have. He said the Transport Officer had okayed it.'

Waldron eyed the two men, sizing them up. The private was nineteen or twenty, around five ten and seemed in pretty good shape, if a little underweight for his height. He wasn't exactly brimming over with self-confidence, and the perpetual half-smile on his mouth suggested he wasn't altogether sure of his role. Dobson, on the other hand, was soft and flabby, in his mid-thirties and renowned throughout the battalion for his aversion to any form of physical exercise. It was alleged, with some justification, that the hundred-and-fifty-yard walk between the mail room and the tented mess hall three times a day was his idea of a route march.

'When do you reckon our Christmas mail will arrive?'

Dobson gave the question some serious thought, then said, 'With any luck, it should be here by Easter.'

'You're joking.'

'How long have you been in the army, son?'

'The name's Frazer,' said the private. 'I joined the battalion straight from recruit training, just before we shipped out.'

'Well, that explains it; you've still got a lot to learn. We were stationed in the West Indies before they sent us over here.'

'So?'

'So that's where our mail will end up. Ain't that right, Waldron?'

'You can bet your shirt on it.'

'Goddamn right,' Dobson said with feeling. 'This man's army is one big foul-up.'

Waldron stood up and flexed his leg muscles, moving the valise nearer the two Canadians in the process. 'Any chance of bumming a cigarette from you guys?' he asked.

'Sure.' Frazer unbuttoned the left pocket of his drill shirt and took out a packet of Sweet Caporal. 'Here, have one of these.'

'Thanks.' Waldron took a cigarette, then went through the pockets of his pants and jacket looking for a box of matches. 'Got a light?' he said presently.

Frazer produced a slim lighter from his other shirt pocket. 'A guy in the transport section made this for me,' he volunteered.

'Yeah?'

'Out of a .303 cartridge case.'

'Does it work?'

'Like a flame thrower.' Frazer thumbed the wheel against the flint. 'See?'

'Very impressive.' Waldron took a light, once more easing the valise nearer the tailgate with his foot before he sat down again. 'How do you put it out?'

'You blow on it,' said Frazer.

'I might have known.'

'You'd think they'd have better things to do with their time,' Dobson grumbled.

'Who?' Frazer demanded.

'The MT section. This truck could do with a thorough overhaul for a start.'

Waldron reckoned he had a point. Black smoke trailed from the exhaust, a sign the engine was burning oil, and the tappets sounded like a kettledrum. The resultant lack of power had been evident from the moment they'd started to climb the hill above Repulse Bay.

'Any idea where we are now?' Frazer asked, peering into the darkness.

Dobson sucked on his teeth. 'How long have we been on the road?'

'Close on fifteen minutes.'

'Then we're about a couple of miles from the Wongnei Chung Gap.'

The driver changed down from second into first and their speed dropped below ten miles an hour. Although unfamiliar with the terrain, Waldron figured it could only be a matter of minutes before they reached the summit and started on the downhill stretch to the pass. Suddenly leaning forward, he flicked his cigarette at Frazer and followed through with a short right-arm job that landed on the side of his jaw and knocked him cold. Still crouching, Waldron swung round and clapped the palm of his left hand over Dobson's mouth. Then he hit the corporal twice in the belly, driving his fist deep into the solar plexus. The Canadian gagged, went limp and keeled over sideways, his head striking the floor as he slid off the mailbag.

His pulse racing, Waldron grabbed the canopy bars above his head, stood on the tailgate and launched himself into space. He landed on the grass verge with a spine-jarring thump, lost his balance and pitching forward, rolled on down the hillside. Twenty feet below the road, he tumbled into a hollow and came to a dead stop. Winded and bruised by the fall, Waldron lay there for some moments to catch his breath, before crawling painfully out of the dip.

There was no sign of the truck, but a faint breeze carried the distant throb of its engine as it continued to grind on up the hill.

Smiling to himself, Waldron got to his feet and began to make his way down to the valley below.

Hammond carried his gin and tonic out on to the balcony. The white stucco house which he owned in Macdonnel Road near the Botanic Gardens was halfway up The Peak above Victoria, a location that accurately reflected his present position in society. Junior civil servants, trainee managers and middle-rank officers of the armed services occupied rented bungalows and flats below Government House, while the 'Taipans', the men who ran the giant export-import corporations like Jardine Mathesons, lived in gracious homes in Lugar Road, right at the very top of The Peak. To have climbed halfway up the ladder by the age of twenty-eight was a considerable achievement. But Hammond knew that his wife Jill would never be satisfied until she too had a house on Lugar Road.

They already had five Chinese servants to look after the two of them, but Jill wanted more. They already led an active social life, sometimes dining out five nights a week, but Jill wouldn't be happy until the invitation cards were stacked two deep on the mantelpiece. He rarely used the drophead sports coupé in the garage, but although she was free to use it whenever she wanted, the full measure of Jill's ambition was to have a chauffeur-driven limousine at her disposal. She couldn't see that their life together was artificial, as unreal as the twinkling coloured lights of Victoria below; that reality lay twenty-six miles north of Kowloon across the harbour at To Kat, where the Japanese 38th Division was concentrated within easy striking distance of the frontier. There was nothing to stop the Japs except the 'Maginot' fortifications stretching from Gin Drinkers Bay across the hills to the Tolo inlet by Sha Tin. The Gin Drinkers Line; he hoped that wasn't an accurate assessment of the three infantry battalions who would man the concrete bunkers and shallow underground galleries when the invasion started.

'How much longer are you going to stay out there on the balcony, David?'

Why was it that Jill seldom spoke to him these days without that plaintive whine in her voice? Sighing, he turned his back on the view and faced the french windows of their bedroom. 'Until I've finished my drink,' he said patiently.

'We're going to be late unless you get a move on.'

'Who are we dining with tonight?'

'The Blakeneys. How many more times do I have to tell you?'

There was really no answer to that. Jill had reminded him once over breakfast, before he left for the bank, and again on his return only a few minutes ago.

'What's the matter with you, David?' she complained. 'You don't seem to listen to a thing I say.'

Hammond swallowed the rest of his gin and tonic and went back inside. There was nothing wrong with him; it was just that the social whirl bored him, and he had other, more important things to think about. Right now there was one very important matter he had to talk over with Jill and he was still debating how to broach the subject.

'I had a long meeting with Ralph Cottis today,' Hammond said, feeling his way carefully.

'Oh yes?' Jill frowned at her reflection in the dressing-table mirror, then applied a touch more lipstick to her mouth.

'He said that we can expect the Japs to invade any day now.'

'Ralph has been saying that ever since he arrived in Hong Kong.'

'This time he happens to be right.'

'I'll believe that when the Japs cross the frontier. Until they do, it's just another rumour.'

Hammond placed his empty glass on the chest of drawers. There were influential people he could name who didn't share his wife's scepticism; the Chairman of the Hong Kong and Shanghai Bank for one, Detective Chief Inspector Ramsay for another. Of course, Ralph Cottis had been preaching to the converted; Ramsay had his own intelligence sources and knew which way the wind was blowing. He hadn't said much in front of Kellerman, but later, when they were checking out the vaults of the Kowloon branch in Nathan Road, Ramsay had told him the Japs had a considerable number of sympathizers amongst the local Chinese population – Fifth Columnists who were prepared to carry out acts of sabotage on their behalf. All the same, Hammond knew it was no use quoting Ramsay at Jill; two summonses for speeding in the space of nine weeks had left her with a very jaundiced opinion of the police. The news that the bank was about to transfer the gold reserves to Australia might have convinced her, but unfortunately that was something he was obliged to keep to himself.

There was, however, one other item of information he could impart which might just open her eyes and make her see reason.

'I shan't be needing my civilian clothes after Friday,' he said.

'What do you mean?'

'The Hong Kong Volunteer Defence Corps is to be mobilized on the sixth of December. That's official, darling.'

'I expect it's just another practice alert.' Jill turned away from the mirror and looked up at him, searching his face for the reassuring smile that would confirm her supposition.

'I only wish it was.' Hammond watched the expression on her face slowly darken, and felt a sudden urge to comfort her, give her the reassurance she craved. 'I really think you should get out of Hong Kong while there's still time,' he said quietly. 'It'll mean pulling a few strings, but I can get you a berth on the *Delphic Star* before she departs for Sydney on Monday.'

'I'm not going to Australia, David, and that's final. My place is here with you and doing the job I've been trained to do. I happen to be a member of the Auxiliary Nursing Service, or had you forgotten?'

The Florence Nightingale act struck a false note. Like many of her friends, Jill's decision to join the Auxiliary Nursing Service in June 1940 had not been occasioned by a sense of duty or patriotism. On the contrary, it had been prompted by the news that the government intended to evacuate all non-essential civilians. A passage to Australia on the *Empress of Asia* was something she had been determined to avoid at all costs.

'I still think you should go.'

'You just want to get rid of me, don't you?'

'Why on earth should I want to do that?'

'Because you've got a girlfriend tucked away somewhere. I wouldn't be surprised if it wasn't your pretty little Chinese secretary.'

'Now you're being ridiculous.'

'Am I?' Jill stood up and moved slowly towards him, her lips parted, a predatory gleam in her eyes.

'You know you are.'

'If you say so, darling,' she murmured.

One slender arm encircled his neck and her knees brushed deliberately against his. Tall, dark-haired, her skin tanned to a golden brown, Jill was unquestionably the most attractive and desirable European woman on the island. She could also twist him round her little finger, a power she had exercised with unfailing success right from the moment he had been introduced to her at Government House during the official reception in honour of the King's birthday four years ago.

'You're not being very sensible. The *Delphic Star* could well be the last ship to leave Hong Kong.'

'You know something, David? I'm not in the mood to be sensible.' Fastening her mouth on his, she kissed him passionately. 'End of discussion, darling,' she whispered, and then moved her body against his, gently caressing him until he erected.

Ramsay emptied his ashtray into the waste bin and then lit another cigarette. Two and a half million in gold bullion. If he didn't lift it, the Japs would; that thought had entered his head the moment he saw the contingency plan. But there was another, even stronger motive. Kellerman already suspected he had been on the take and was determined to break him. If the Assistant Commissioner had his way, there'd be no pension to look forward to in five years' time; instead, he'd be out on his ear and back where he'd started in the slums of Glasgow. The motivation was there all right; the trick lay in stealing the bullion without getting caught in the process. And he was no closer to finding a solution to the problem now than he had been when he'd first started to examine it, shortly after returning from the Kowloon branch of the Hong Kong and Shanghai Bank three long, gruelling hours ago.

No plan was foolproof, but "Sovereign" came very close to it. Every possible contingency had been looked at. It was impossible to fault the arrangements for safeguarding the bullion while it was in transit from the Head Office in Victoria to the branch in Nathan Road. The only potential weakness Ramsay could see was the fact that the gold would lie in the vaults for more than thirty-six hours before it was transferred to the *Delphic Star*. Even so, the bank would be a tough nut to crack for anybody who was so inclined. Apart from the usual burglar alarms, and photo-electric beam, any intruder would find four heavily-armed policemen waiting for him. There were three shifts, each consisting of four men, which meant that he had to find a total of twelve officers from the detective squad and Special Branch – a simple enough task at first sight, but one that was proving extraordinarily difficult to execute. Six months ago, it would have taken him less than ten minutes to work out the duty roster, but not any more. Thanks to Kellerman's clean-up operation, most of the men he could trust had been transferred from his department to the uniformed branch.

Ramsay stared at the provisional roster he'd drafted. Of the twelve officers on the list, there were only two who would be prepared to go all the way with him. Had he been available, Bill Donovan would have been a useful man to have around, but of course he was running the police post out at Sha Tau Kok, a victim of Kellerman's purge. Detaching the roster from his clipboard, Ramsay folded the sheet of scrap paper in half and slipped it into the inside pocket of his jacket. It was after nine o'clock and for all the good he was doing, he might just as well call it a day and go home. In the event, a sudden knock on the door and the entrance of Sub Inspector Pascoe delayed his departure.

So far as Ramsay was concerned, Pascoe was bad news. A slim young man of twenty-four with sleek black hair and a face that reminded him of a ferret, he was one of Kellerman's blue-eyed boys. The spy on the inside? Maybe that was stretching it a bit, but you needed to watch your step when Pascoe was around.

'Yes?' Ramsay gazed at the teletype Pascoe was holding. 'What have you got there in your hot little hand?' he asked curtly.

'An APB on Frank Waldron, the Yank who enlisted in the Canadian army. He's just escaped from military custody.'

'Wouldn't you just know it.' Ramsay scowled. 'I always said he should have been locked up in Stanley Prison.'

Until the FBI had contacted the Royal Canadian Mounted Police on the 10th November, nobody in Hong Kong had ever heard of Frank Waldron. A former Assistant District Attorney, he had dropped out of sight in June 1941, a few days after being sub-pœnæd to appear before a Congressional committee investigating the activities of the 'America First' organization. Just how the FBI had learned that he'd enlisted in the Canadian army had never been disclosed, but they'd provided enough information for Ottawa to discover that he was serving with the Winnipeg Grenadiers and was on a troopship bound for Hong Kong.

'When did he break out?' Ramsay asked.

'About four hours ago,' said Pascoe. 'Waldron overpowered his two guards and then jumped out of the unit mail truck halfway between Repulse Bay and Victoria.'

'I thought the Winnipeg Grenadiers were stationed in Shamshuipo barracks up the road from here?'

'Most of them are, but they also have two companies on the island.' Pascoe laid the APB on Ramsay's desk. 'For what it's worth, I reckon Waldron has gone to ground in Victoria.'

'Maybe.' Ramsay scanned the APB. It was a somewhat stereotyped description of Waldron; age – twenty-six; height – five eleven; weight – one-seventy-three; grey-blue eyes; light brown hair parted on left, and a small mole on right side of chin. 'Get on to Fortress Headquarters,' he said crisply. 'Ask them if we can have a photograph of him.'

'Yes, sir.' Pascoe stretched his mouth in what was meant to

be an ingratiating smile. 'Perhaps they can also tell us what he was wearing?'

'Don't waste your breath. Waldron will have been in uniform.'

'I don't think so. I have a hunch he was issued with civilian clothes.'

'Why?' Ramsay asked, and immediately regretted it.

'Because he was due to embark on the US *Warren Harding* and America is still a neutral country.'

'That's good thinking.' Somehow Ramsay contrived to sound as if he meant it. 'Give yourself a pat on the back.'

'Thank you, sir.' Pascoe moved towards the door, then hesitated. 'I suppose you've heard the other piece of news?' he said diffidently.

'What news?'

'About the border posts; they're being evacuated tomorrow with effect from twelve hundred hours.'

'About time,' said Ramsay.

'Yes, sir, that's what I thought,' Pascoe said and left the office, closing the door quietly behind him.

Ramsay allowed himself a brief smile. Suddenly the problem that had been exercising him was no longer insuperable; suddenly everything was looking good. All he had to do was remove Pascoe and then there would be an opening for Donovan.

THURSDAY
4th DECEMBER 1941

CHAPTER THREE

Ramsay turned right in Fanling and headed towards Sha Tau Kok. In the course of the half-hour journey from Kowloon, he had seen only two other vehicles, a country bus and a Pontiac station wagon, both of which had been travelling in the opposite direction. Five miles back down the road, the usually busy market place of Tai Po had been practically deserted, and not one fishing boat had been tied up at the quayside. Although it was after eight-thirty, there were no signs of activity in the paddy fields on either side of the road. He wondered if the local farmers had heard of the impending invasion and fled the countryside.

A sullen, brooding atmosphere gripped the land, a sensation so intense that he could feel the hairs rising on the back of his neck. At any moment he expected to hear the staccato rattle of machine-gun fire in the hills to his left. Reacting instinctively, he pushed his foot hard down on the accelerator and inside a quarter of a mile the speedometer climbed from a sedate thirty-five to close on seventy. Tyres drumming on the uneven surface, the steering wheel shuddering in his hands, Ramsay didn't let up until he saw the Union Jack hanging limply from the flagpole near the border post in Sha Tau Kok. Then, rapidly easing his foot on the pedal as he approached the village, he shifted into third and slewed to a halt outside the police station. Conscious that a mere twenty yards away, a Japanese infantryman was watching his every move, Ramsay got out of the Chevrolet sedan and walked into the building.

The small muster room on the ground floor resembled a left luggage office, with suitcases, holdalls and brown paper parcels stacked untidily in one corner. Of the sixteen policemen on strength, only the desk sergeant and one constable remained;

the rest, Ramsay gathered, were in the café across the road, killing time until the truck arrived to collect them.

Moving upstairs, he found Donovan in the duty inspector's quarters at the far end of the landing overlooking the main street. The Irishman was standing in the window, both hands stuffed deep in the pockets of his khaki drill shorts, his back towards him.

Ramsay said, 'Taking a last look at your patch, Bill?'

Donovan turned slowly about, his full mouth creasing into a smile. 'Hullo, George,' he said in a faint brogue. 'What brings you to this neck of the woods?'

'Curiosity.'

Ramsay moved to the window and stood there, gazing down at the Nipponese sentry manning the border crossing-point, a diminutive figure armed with an ancient-looking 6.5 mm Ariska rifle and dressed in an ill-fitting uniform. Ramsay thought he would have gladdened the hearts of those pundits in the Far East Intelligence Bureau down in Singapore, who fondly believed that all Japanese infantrymen had bandy legs, were short-sighted and puny.

'According to Fortress Headquarters, the Japs are poised to attack us with sixty thousand crack troops. If the rest of them are anything like him, I don't see what the army's so worried about.'

'Appearances can be very deceptive,' Donovan said wryly. 'He may not intimidate you, George, but he scares the hell out of my police constables. Two of them did a bunk last night – decided they couldn't wait for the transport to pick them up this morning. I'll probably lose a few more when we get to Kowloon.'

'It's like that, is it?' Ramsay said quietly.

'Nobody's feeling on top of the world, George. As a matter of fact, I shan't be sorry to leave this place – even if I end up on point duty in Kowloon.'

Ramsay laughed. 'Somehow I can't see you directing traffic.'

'I can, knowing how Kellerman feels about me. That bastard

tried hard enough to put me away for five years. Bribery and corruption.' Donovan pushed a hand through his short, jet-black hair that was here and there flecked with grey. 'Why did he have to pick on me? The whole damned squad was on the take.'

'Because you were living too high,' said Ramsay. 'And of course, Challinor was no longer around to protect you.'

Donovan boasted a flat in Waterloo Road, an Eurasian mistress with expensive tastes and a souped-up Alfa Romeo sports car; tell-tale signs of a lifestyle way beyond the means of an inspector in the Hong Kong Police. Two things had saved his neck; not one cent of the backhanders he'd received had ever passed through his bank account; and more importantly, every-body on the force knew that he liked to back the horses. Thanks to a little arm-twisting here and there by the rest of the detective squad, Kellerman's investigators had found themselves con-fronted with a score of Chinese bookmakers who were prepared to swear on their ancestors' graves that Donovan was one of the luckiest gamblers they'd ever encountered.

'I doubt if Challinor could have done more for me than you did, George. I'm not likely to forget that.'

Ramsay smiled. If Donovan did but know it, it had been a case of enlightened self-interest. The whole squad had known that if Donovan went down, it would only be a matter of time before they followed. 'How long have we known each other, Bill?'

'Sixteen years,' said Donovan. 'I joined the force in 1925, a year after you did.'

'An excellent opportunity for an adventurous young man,' Ramsay said acidly, quoting the recruiting literature from bitter memory. 'A secure future and every prospect of rapid promo-tion. That's what they told us.'

'Bullshit.' Donovan went through his pockets, found a packet of Gold Flake and offered Ramsay a cigarette. 'I joined as a sub inspector, and in sixteen years all I've collected is one extra star on my shoulder.'

'And a few black marks on your record sheet.'

'Some of them were there before I came out here, only I didn't know it at the time.'

They were two of a kind. Both of them had been in the trenches during the 1914–18 War and had known the misery of the dole queue after being demobbed. The press advertisement appealing for men prepared to face 'a rough and dangerous task' could have been aimed straight at them. Both had walked into the nearest recruiting office and joined the Royal Irish Constabulary, Donovan signing on in Liverpool, while Ramsay had taken the oath in Glasgow. One week later, they'd been posted to Tipperary and County Clare respectively, destined to become part of Irish history and legend as members of the hated Black and Tans.

'We've got a lot in common,' said Ramsay. 'Neither of us has much of a future.'

'You can say that again.'

'Unless we're prepared to take a chance.'

'What sort of chance?'

'Your police constables are not the only ones who've got the wind up. The Hong Kong and Shanghai Bank is about to send its gold reserves to Australia – all two and a half million pounds' worth.' Ramsay blew a smoke ring towards the ceiling. 'I'm thinking of helping myself to a few bars, once the bullion's been transferred to the Kowloon branch.'

'You've got to be joking.'

Ramsay shook his head. 'I've never been more serious in my life. Do you want in?'

Donovan mulled it over. As far as he could see, there was nothing you could do with a gold ingot except admire the damned thing. On the other hand, George Ramsay was a shrewd operator; he would have considered all the angles and figured out some way of converting the bullion into cash.

'Have you got a buyer in mind?' he asked.

'Li Ho Chung. I reckon he'd be interested, don't you? Especially if we offered him bullion at twenty per cent of the market value.'

Donovan nodded. Li Ho Chung; now there was a man to be

reckoned with. The biggest building contractor in the New Territories. He had a finger in every pie – the Canton Kowloon Railway, the Macao Steamship Company, hotels, casinos and a floating restaurant off Aberdeen on the south side of the island. A steward of the Hong Kong Jockey Club and in line for a knighthood, Li Ho Chung also controlled the Red Spears, the most powerful Triad in the colony. Of course, nobody could prove his connection with the Chinese secret society, because half the policemen in the Kowloon division were on his payroll. And besides, the legislative council weren't exactly keen for anybody to rock the boat, for apart from being a respectable member of the local business community, Li Ho Chung had helped to raise more than ten million Hong Kong dollars for various charities, not to mention the war effort.

'Maybe twenty per cent is a knock-down price, but diamonds can appreciate in value.' Ramsay patted his stomach. 'You can also carry half a million pounds' worth in a money belt without anyone noticing it.'

'All the diamonds in the world won't help us if we end up in a Jap POW camp, George.'

'You think I don't know that?' Ramsay opened the window and tossed his cigarette stub into the street below. 'No little man from the Land of the Rising Sun is going to stick you and me behind barbed wire, Bill. By the time they're holding their victory parade through the streets of Victoria, we'll be on the high seas, neutral citizens on a neutral ship bound for a neutral country in Europe.'

Spain and Portugal were not among the leading maritime nations, but the Swedes had a sizeable merchant fleet, and while Donovan rarely bothered to read the shipping news in the *South China Morning Post*, he knew that the Olsen cargo line regularly plied to and fro between Gothenburg and Hong Kong. They'd need a change of identity and false passports, but with Ramsay in charge of the Special Branch, that was unlikely to be much of a problem. And if by chance their papers weren't quite up to standard, a little folding money would soon silence any ship's captain who seemed a mite inquisitive.

'So who else have you got lined up for this job?' Donovan smiled lopsidedly. 'Somehow I don't see you and me pulling it off on our ownsome.'

'The bullion will be guarded day and night by four CID officers. All I've got to do is juggle the shift roster.'

'You're ducking the question, George.'

'Adams and Thirsk,' Ramsay said calmly. 'They're all that's left of the original squad.' He neglected to add that he hadn't approached either man yet, but that was a minor detail. Both officers had been on the take for years and would go along with the idea, provided he convinced them the risks were negligible. Twenty-five thousand US dollars cash in advance would be the final sweetener that would kill any lingering doubts they might have.

'How are you going to fix it with Kellerman?' Donovan tossed his cigarette end out of the open window. 'I mean, he's never going to allow me to work with the squad again.'

'He won't have any choice, Bill. Halfway through the operation, he'll be faced with a manpower shortage.'

The way Ramsay saw it, Sub Inspector Pascoe would end up in hospital, the victim of a hit-and-run driver. The accident would happen early on Saturday morning before the armoured truck left the Hong Kong and Shanghai Bank in Victoria with the second and final load of bullion. By the time he was through, the remaining CID officers would be fully committed elsewhere and Kellerman would discover that Donovan was the only man available.

'You've got it all figured out, haven't you, George?'

'You know me.'

Donovan nodded, then grinned. 'All right,' he said cheerfully. 'Who do I have to lean on?'

'A man called Hammond,' said Ramsay. 'You're going to steal his wife.'

Waldron stared at the bungalow some two hundred feet below him. Located on the outskirts of Victoria and close to the race course at Happy Valley, its secluded position was certainly a plus factor so far as he was concerned. There was one other advantage; the bungalow was obviously occupied by three single men, trainee business executives whom he'd observed some hours back leaving for their respective offices down-town. On the other hand, he'd no idea how many servants he was likely to encounter if he broke into the house. So far, after watching the place for more than five hours, he'd only seen one gardener. The gardener had now moved round to the back and the houseboy had left the bungalow a good twenty minutes ago, carrying a shopping basket. Two servants between three? Somehow he couldn't see them getting by with less than two houseboys, a cook and a gardener.

Waldron rubbed his face, feeling the stubble and the rash of prickly heat that had come up on his throat. It didn't matter how many servants there were; he badly needed a shave and a change of clothes and it was too late in the day to think of looking elsewhere. Backing out of the clump of bushes where he'd been hiding since dawn, Waldron moved crabwise to his right and scrambled into the monsoon ditch that ran downhill towards the road fronting the bungalow.

A few more hours and he'd be safe; a few more hours and the *Warren Harding*, flagship of the President Line, would leave Kowloon for Manilla, Honolulu and San Francisco. Of course, it wouldn't end there; other American ships were bound to call at Hong Kong, but he would deal with that problem when it arose. He'd learned to live a day at a time; it was a way of life that he'd been forced to adopt shortly after Roosevelt had been re-elected for a third term in December 1940. That had been the final straw for some of the people behind the 'America First' organization, the biter bit; now it seemed only a man armed with a high-power rifle fitted with a telescopic sight could stop the President dragging America into a war nobody wanted. That, at least, was the opinion of Joe Lamont, the genial Vice Chairman of the New York caucus; Waldron had heard him say so on the night the polls had closed, when everyone in the 'America First' committee rooms on East Fifty-six Street had suddenly realized that Wilkie wasn't going to make it to the

White House. Only a joke, Lamont had explained to him afterwards – but his broad smile had been at odds with the hard glint in his eyes. And that determined look had started the whole lousy business, and set Waldron to work as an amateur detective, following the trail that had led him into the arms of the FBI and a place in the firing line.

Waldron halted a few yards short of the road and crouched down low. He would have to leave the monsoon ditch and cross a wide expanse of lawn to reach the bungalow, but at least he'd have no difficulty in effecting an entrance. Even though he was still some distance from the house, he could see that two of the windows at the far end of the verandah were wide open. He glanced left and right to make sure no one else was about; then, removing his shoes, he climbed out of the ditch and slipped across the road in his stockinged feet.

Five months in the Canadian army had taught him it was no use pussy-footing around when you were confronted with an open stretch of ground in broad daylight. Sprinting over the lawn, he made it to the verandah and pressed his back against the wall. Then, keeping in the shadow, he edged his way to the nearest open window at the far end and climbed stealthily into the room.

He froze like a statue and looked about him, his ears attuned to catch the slightest sound of movement elsewhere in the house. There was a single bed in one corner, neatly made up with a mosquito net suspended from a steel frame and tucked under the mattress. A mahogany chest of drawers was positioned against the cream-distempered wall some three feet from the door, and immediately to his right and near the window was a large matching wardrobe. Around a twelve-by-nine Indian carpet the exposed floor-boards had been stained a slightly darker hue than the mahogany furniture. The only personal touch was a small, amateurish oil painting of a thatched-roof cottage festooned with ivy and surrounded by brightly coloured flowers.

A bachelor's den, Waldron thought; stark, functional and depressing as any barrack room. Moving to the wardrobe, he unlocked it and opened both doors. Four suits were hanging on the rail and next to them, a khaki shirt, the sleeves rolled up to the elbows and pressed flat. The cloth shoulder boards showed that the owner was a Second Lieutenant in the Hong Kong Volunteer Defence Corps. On the shelf above, he saw a web belt and pistol holder.

The door opened behind him and a cool feminine voice said, 'It's not there; I've got it.' Then he heard the hammer click back and realized what she meant.

CHAPTER FOUR

Waldron turned slowly about and tried a friendly, disarming smile. The girl facing him was around five foot seven, had dark brown hair with an auburn tinge, prominent cheekbones and a wide, generous mouth which probably turned up at the corners when it wasn't set, as it was now, in a hard, determined line. His eyes travelled downwards and centred on the revolver, held at hip level in a slender hand with long, tapering fingers. A Webley .455 double action, with a kick like a mule and the impact of a sledgehammer – except he could see that five of the six cylinders were empty.

'I'm impressed,' Waldron said. 'I'd be even more impressed if you'd remembered to load that thing.'

Her finger tightened on the trigger, taking up the slack. 'What makes you think I haven't?'

Waldron raised both hands above his head. It seemed only sensible to do so. The girl was very self-assured, and as he stared at the barrel, it occurred to him that there just might be a soft-nosed .455 calibre round seated in the chamber, dead in line with the firing pin.

'Take it easy,' he warned.

'Oh, I will,' said the girl. 'I suggest you do the same.'

'Right.' His smile was fast becoming a grimace that was difficult to hold. 'My name's Waldron,' he said. 'Frank Waldron.'

'I see.' She nodded gravely. 'Where do you come from, Mr Waldron? Canada?'

'No, I was born in Yonkers; that's about fifteen miles north of New York City. Until yesterday I was a soldier in the Winnipeg Grenadiers.'

'And now you're a fugitive?'

'You could say that. Truth is, the British were planning to send me home on the US *Warren Harding* this afternoon and I didn't want to go.' He lowered his arms a fraction; then, meeting with no reaction, he slowly dropped them to his side. 'What happens now?' he asked quietly.

'We wait.'

For what? he wondered. For the police to show up? She had obviously spotted him early on when he was coming down the hill-side, but even so, it was hard to believe that she'd found the revolver, loaded it and called the police all in the space of a few minutes. No, she must be waiting for one of the young trainee executives he'd seen.

'What time does he get back from the office?' Waldron said abruptly.

'What?'

'The man we're both hanging on for.'

'He'll be here soon enough.'

Waldron doubted it. The girl had been a shade too eager to latch on to his suggestion, and that meant she hadn't phoned the police either. Furthermore, he was prepared to bet they were alone in the house, otherwise she would have called out to one of the servants.

'Why don't you put that revolver down?' he said and moved a pace towards her.

'Don't come any nearer.'

The revolver weighed close on two and a half pounds and he

could tell from the way the barrel was wavering that it was beginning to make her wrist ache.

'One more step and I'll shoot.' She raised the Webley, supporting her wrist with the left hand.

'Go ahead.' Waldron managed another tight smile. 'Of course, as a lawyer, I should point out that you'll be in serious trouble if you do.'

'You're a lawyer?' she said, her eyebrows meeting in a frown.

Waldron nodded. 'I used to be an Assistant District Attorney before the "America First" organization hired me as a legal counsellor.' He was only a few paces from the girl now. Or eternity, if his luck ran out. 'Representing that crowd is the reason I'm here now.'

'Why?'

'Because, in the end, I knew too much about their activities. A lot of people want to see me dead.'

Waldron suddenly shot out his left hand, grabbed the barrel and shoved his thumb between the cocked hammer and the cylinder. Then, twisting the Webley, he wrenched it from her grasp, holding her at arm's length while he eased the hammer forward and made the revolver safe.

'You bastard,' she panted. 'Let go of me.'

Fingernails raked his face and a lunging foot caught him a glancing blow on the left shin. Dropping the revolver, Waldron pinioned her arms and wrestled her towards the bed in the corner. Crashing into it, she went over backwards and brought the mosquito net down on top of them. She twisted and turned, sank her teeth into the sleeve of his jacket in a vain attempt to bite his arm and tried repeatedly to knee him in the groin. Then gradually she ceased struggling and lay passive beneath him, her face and hair damp with perspiration.

'You won't enjoy it,' she said presently.

'Enjoy what?'

'Raping me.'

'Oh, for Christ's sake, nothing could be further from my mind.'

'You expect me to believe that?'

'What do you think I was looking for in the wardrobe? A naked woman?' Waldron released her, stood up and moved back several paces. 'Take a good look at me,' he invited. 'I need a shave and a change of clothes. Right?'

She glanced at him briefly, then quickly pulled the beige linen skirt down over her knees and tucked the silk blouse back inside the waistband where it had come adrift. A nice figure, Waldron noted in passing; long shapely legs, a narrow waist and breasts that didn't need the artificial support of a bra.

'It's a relief to know you're only a thief,' she said acidly. 'Now why don't you take what you want and get out of here?'

But it was no longer that simple; the girl was a complication he hadn't bargained for, an eye-witness who could give the police an up-to-date description. He supposed he could always tie her up, but apart from giving him a brief respite, it wouldn't solve anything in the long run. Whatever clothes he stole from this house would have to be replaced again within a matter of hours.

'What time is it?' he asked tersely.

She glanced at the gold watch on her left wrist. 'Almost twelve o'clock.'

'Well, in that case, I guess I'll stay here awhile.' Waldron smiled. 'It shouldn't be too much of an ordeal for you; the *Warren Harding* sails at three.'

'And then what?' she asked in a low voice.

'I reckon that's up to you, Miss . . .?'

'Goddard, Katherine Goddard.' She bit her lip, as if immediately regretting telling him her name. 'I'm expecting my brother to return at any moment,' she added quickly.

'Is that a fact?' Waldron glanced at the Webley lying on the floor. Ten to one she was bluffing; ten to one the revolver wasn't loaded either. Retrieving the hand gun, he broke it open and found he was right. 'You must think I was born yesterday,' he said, and spun the cylinder like a roulette wheel.

'I do have a brother, Mr Waldron; his name's Steven.'

Steven Goddard, he learned as the words spilled out of her, was a junior executive at Butterfield and Swire and a pilot in the light aircraft section of the Hong Kong Volunteer Defence Corps.

'And you keep house for him?' Waldron asked, when she finally paused for breath.

'No.' She shook her head. 'No, I'm the resident nurse at the Peninsula Hotel. I live above the shop.'

'Come again?'

'I have a rent-free apartment. It goes with the job.'

'That's nice,' Waldron said vaguely.

'This just happens to be my day off. Steven gave a dinner party last night and I decided to stay over.'

The worried frown came back again and he guessed she was casting around for some other distraction to keep him in check until the Chinese houseboy returned from the market or wherever. Chances were she'd been out in Hong Kong long enough to acquire a smattering of Cantonese, sufficient at any rate to tell the houseboy to fetch the police without him knowing it. Somehow he would have to persuade her that that wouldn't be a very good idea.

'I know what you're thinking, Miss Goddard,' Waldron said quietly, 'but you're wrong. Maybe what I said about certain people wanting to see me dead sounded a little crazy to you, but it happens to be true.'

'I've only got your word for that, haven't I?'

'Yeah.' Waldron paused and wondered how he was going to convince Katherine Goddard when he didn't have a shred of evidence to show her. 'Have you ever heard of the "America First" organization?' he asked.

'Not until you mentioned it a few minutes ago.'

'They're a bunch of isolationists. How and why I became involved with them is a somewhat complicated story, but you could say it started with my father. He was killed in France in 1918 when I was two years old, and my mother had this fixation that he'd died young and needlessly in a European war that didn't concern America. To her way of thinking, Europe was one big cesspool we should avoid at all costs. The older I got, the more I was inclined to agree with her. I began to have second thoughts when France capitulated in June '40, but by that time I was caught up in the election campaign. The organization had decided to put its weight behind Wendell Wilkie. He was no isolationist, but Joe Lamont, the Vice Chairman of our New York caucus, saw him as the lesser of two evils compared with Roosevelt. The night Wilkie conceded victory, the atmosphere in our committee rooms on East Fifty-six Street was like a wake. There was some pretty wild talk from Joe Lamont.'

'Such as?'

'He said that unless somebody drew a bead on him, Roosevelt would lead the country into war. At first I put his bitterness down to the heat of the moment.'

'Yes, people often say things they don't mean,' Katherine murmured.

Waldron smiled, figuring she was having a sly dig at him. 'But not this time,' he said. 'A few weeks later, one of the accountants told me that he suspected the committee's funds were being siphoned off. Apparently, large payments had been made to an advertising agency for a sustained publicity campaign which wasn't even on the drawing board.'

'Really?'

It was, he thought, amazing how much scepticism she was able to convey in a single word. 'That wasn't the only irregularity. All of a sudden, and for no apparent reason, Lamont began to receive information about the President's movements as though he were a White House aide. There's a place in south-western Georgia called Warm Springs; Roosevelt established a foundation there in 1927 for victims of infantile paralysis, and he has a farm near the summit of Pine Mountain which is known locally as the Little White House. He goes there quite often with his personal secretary, Missy LeHand. Lamont had ringed the date of his next visit in pencil and then erased it.'

'How careless of him to have left the programme lying around where you could see it,' Katherine observed tartly.

'He didn't,' Waldron retaliated. 'I just happened to discover the combination to his office safe.'

From then on he had started to follow Lamont, shadowing

him wherever he went. He had seen him meet with Jacob
Shapiro in a small bar near Mamma Leone's on West Forty-
eight Street and again, a few days later, when the pair of them
had gone fishing in Sheepshead Bay one Sunday afternoon in
the Spring of '41.

'I knew of Jacob Shapiro when I was working for the DA.
He's a very bad number; people who get in his way have a habit
of ending up in the morgue. Anyway, I figured that with
Shapiro's reputation for openers, I had enough on Lamont to
take the story to the FBI.' But the agent he'd seen in the local
FBI office in downtown Manhattan had received his information with a good deal of scepticism, and had only reluctantly
passed it on to the bureau in Washington. Ten days later,
Waldron's apartment on East Seventy-third had been ran-
sacked; but when he had reported it he had met with a very low-
key response from the detectives of the 19th Precinct.

'I was beginning to think the whole business was a figment of
my imagination.' Waldron scratched the prickly-heat rash on
his throat. 'Then, on Thursday, June twelfth, a federal agent
walked into our office and served me with a subpœna to appear
before a Congressional Committee appointed to investigate the
activities of the "America First" organization. If anybody
pointed a finger at me, that guy did.'

Retribution had followed swiftly. As he walked home from
the bus stop on Third Avenue that night, a car had almost run
him down as he crossed the road to his apartment. It could have
been a coincidence, but he'd thought otherwise. Staying only
long enough to pack a bag, Waldron had got into his Ford sedan
and driven off to his sister's place in Yonkers.

'There was a black Chrysler parked on the opposite side of
the street about ten yards up the road from the house. I'd no
sooner pulled into the kerbside and switched off the ignition
than a neat round hole appeared in the windscreen inches from
my head. I didn't stop to find out what had caused it; I just got
the hell out of there.'

'And kept on until you crossed into Canada?' Katherine
asked.

'Yes, to a recruiting office in Toronto.' Six weeks basic training – then he'd been drafted to the Winnipeg Grenadiers in Jamaica. Ten weeks later, the battalion had left the West Indies for Vancouver, where the troopship *Awatea* was waiting to take them on to Hong Kong. 'Unfortunately, when we docked at Holt's wharf in Kowloon, the police were waiting for me.'

On the 26th October, the night before they sailed, he had phoned his sister in Yonkers. He should have known her phone would be tapped.

'So what do you intend to do now?'

Waldron hesitated. Perhaps he was reading too much into the question, but it seemed to him there was a note of concern in her voice that hadn't been there before. He began to wonder if she just might be prepared to help him.

'One thing's for sure,' he said, 'I'm not going back to the States to be a clay pigeon on a shooting range. J. Edgar Hoover may think his people can protect me, but I know different. I aim to make my own way back to Washington. Then I might just arrive in one piece before the Congressional Committee.'

'But right now you're broke and the Redcaps are looking for you.'

'And the Hong Kong Police Force,' said Waldron. 'Let's not forget them.'

'And you're also hungry.' Katherine smiled for the first time. 'I can hear your stomach rumbling.'

'A cup of coffee and a sandwich wouldn't come amiss.' Waldron rubbed his jaw. 'I need a shave, too.'

'The bathroom's across the hall. You can borrow one of my brother's suits from the wardrobe.' Katherine stood up and moved towards the door. 'Meantime, I'll get you some food.'

'I don't know how I can ever thank you.'

'Once you've eaten, I'll take you to my apartment in the Peninsula Hotel and you can lie low for a while.'

'Why are you doing all this for me?'

Katherine paused by the door. 'Don't ask me, Mr Waldron,'

she said wryly. 'If I really stopped to think about it, I might change my mind.'

Ramon Garcia was thirty-two years old and remarkably self-effacing for a man who had gained a double first in law and economics at the University of Hong Kong. His natural modesty had been inherited from his mother, a delicate, fine-boned Chinese woman, whereas his handsome appearance and Latin features were derived from his Portuguese father, a prosperous restaurateur and part-owner of a gambling casino in Macao. A financial and tax consultant with an impressive office in Union House overlooking the waterfront of Victoria, Ramon Garcia owed much of his success in commerce to his mother, who was distantly related to Li Ho Chung. It was a family connection which had proved extremely lucrative in more ways than one.

So far as the local business community was concerned, Garcia looked after Li Ho Chung's considerable investment portfolio; so far as Ramsay was concerned, he was a front man for the Red Spears, the most powerful Triad in the colony. Knowing this and proving it were, however, two entirely different matters. It was also a fact that Ramsay was not inclined to enquire too deeply into Garcia's affairs since, like his predecessor, Superintendent Challinor, he received a stipend from Li Ho Chung in return for turning a blind eye towards the Triad's activities.

'Two and a half million pounds.' Ramsay smiled. 'That's a lot of money even by your standards.'

'Yes, so you've said – over and over again.' Garcia dragged his eyes away from the window and the panoramic view of Kowloon across the water. 'I just wonder if you can pull it off.'

The doubting tone of voice and the accompanying frown were exactly right, but Ramsay knew it was merely a ploy to extract more information from him. Garcia was anxious to learn how he proposed to lift the bullion without anyone at the bank realizing that a robbery had taken place – and that was something he wasn't prepared to tell him at this stage of the game.

'All I need is a little help from you,' he said, temporizing.

'Two military vehicles and their drivers, plus escorts; six tons of ballast neatly packed in steel boxes, and one hundred thousand US dollars cash in advance.' Garcia rested both elbows on the desk and leaned forward, his shoulders hunched. 'That's your idea of a little help, is it?'

'I don't understand why you're hedging,' Ramsay said coldly. 'This is a once in a lifetime opportunity, and your client will receive the lion's share of the take. Six tons of gold bullion in exchange for half a million pounds' worth of diamonds; that's what I call a bargain.'

'Yes, but . . .'

'And he won't be risking his neck either.'

'As I was about to say,' Garcia observed impassively, 'there is the matter of the down payment. To my way of thinking, that represents a very considerable risk.'

'Unless you had something to show for it.'

'Like what?'

'Like two gold ingots from the vaults of the Hong Kong and Shanghai Bank in Kowloon.'

'That could make a difference.' Garcia thought about it for a few moments, then nodded. 'Where and when?' he asked.

'Kaznovetsky's restaurant opposite the Peninsula Hotel in Middle Road,' said Ramsay. 'Tomorrow night at eleven-thirty.'

'I'll be there.'

'Just make sure you bring the money with you.'

'But of course.'

'You know something?' Ramsay said slowly. 'The bank would never dream of sending their gold reserves to Australia unless they were convinced the Japs were about to invade.'

'Yes, I'm aware of that.'

'A lot of people are going to die when the shooting starts; soldiers, sailors, airmen and civilians.'

'Are you trying to tell me something?' Garcia said in a low voice.

'Only this.' Ramsay curled three fingers into the palm of his right hand, pointed the index at Garcia and cocked his thumb. 'One false move tomorrow night, and you might just be the first casualty of the war.'

FRIDAY
5th DECEMBER 1941

CHAPTER FIVE

Hammond opened his eyes to a glare of sunlight from between the gap in the curtains. Yawning, he turned over on to his left hip and stared through the mosquito net at the alarm clock on the bedside table. He was still not fully awake, and it was some moments before the position of the hands on the clock face made any sense to him; then, realizing the alarm would ring in less than five minutes, he lifted the mosquito net, reached out and pushed the button down. He glanced over his shoulder at Jill, seemingly fast asleep, her dark hair spread like a fan across the pillow, and wished he too could steal a few extra minutes in bed. It wouldn't, however, make up for three late nights in a row – and this was one morning when he really needed to have his wits about him. Reluctantly, he crawled out of bed and padded into the bathroom.

Ten minutes later, clean-shaven and freshened up under a cold shower, he returned to the bedroom to find Jill sitting hunched in a chair, her head propped between her hands, both elbows resting on her knees. Her eyes were puffy and her face pale and drawn; visible signs, he thought, of an almighty hangover from the night before.

'You look a bit off colour, darling,' he said diplomatically.

'I feel sick, David.'

'Poor you. Perhaps you ate something that disagreed with you?' Hammond found a clean white shirt in the chest of drawers and pulled it on over his head. 'As a matter of fact, I thought the lobster thermidor we had last night tasted a little high.'

'I didn't notice it. Anyway, that wouldn't explain why I was sick yesterday morning after you left for the bank.'

'I didn't know that. You never said anything about it to me.'

'Would you have cared? You're so preoccupied these days. I sometimes wonder if you're even aware of my existence.'

It was easily the most ridiculous accusation he'd ever heard. Maybe some of the trivial gossip Jill told him did tend to go in one ear and out the other, but that didn't mean he wasn't completely devoted to her. He practically worshipped the ground she walked on. From the day they'd met, his only aim in life had been to please her. The never-ending social whirl was not to his taste, yet he went along with it because it made Jill happy. He spoilt her, pandered to her every wish, just as her father had done from the day she was born.

Nothing had been too good for Jill. Cheltenham Ladies' College, a finishing school in Switzerland, and a London season that had left her father almost penniless and still failed to produce the desirable match her mother had so obviously pinned her hopes on. David's mother-in-law was certainly a formidable woman; the kind of ambitious matriarch who was determined her daughter should succeed where her husband, a quiet Lieutenant-Commander in charge of the naval dockyard, had failed. And certainly nobody could accuse her of allowing the grass to grow under her feet; within six months of joining her husband in Hong Kong, she had seen her nineteen-year-old daughter married in St John's Cathedral. Hammond smiled; maybe he wasn't exactly the well-connected type of husband she'd had in mind for her daughter, but a few discreet enquiries had evidently convinced her he would be able to provide for Jill in the manner to which she had become accustomed.

'I don't find it amusing, David.'

'What, darling?'

'The fact that I don't feel well.'

The faint smile disappeared from Hammond's mouth. 'Neither do I,' he said solicitously. 'You don't look as though you're running a temperature, but perhaps we'd better make sure.'

'Don't bother; I'm sure it's quite normal.' Jill looked up and frowned at him. 'You don't suppose I could be pregnant, do you?'

Pregnant? A baby on the way was the most pressing and valid reason Hammond could think of for packing Jill off to Australia before the balloon went up; but he also knew that if he raised that vexed subject again, it would only upset her.

'I don't know,' he said evasively. 'How long have you felt like this?'

'Only today and yesterday, but my period's a fortnight overdue and it's never been that late before.'

Certainly Jill appeared to have some of the symptoms. But how could she be pregnant when they always took precautions? Or had they? What about that Sunday afternoon five weeks ago when they'd both returned in a foul mood from a curry lunch party at the Blakeneys'? He had accused her of openly flirting with Tom Blakeney, and they'd had a blazing row driving home in the car. As soon as they got back, Jill had stormed through the house and run upstairs to their bedroom, slamming and locking the door behind her. For once he'd been determined that he wouldn't be the first to apologize and he'd kept that vow for all of two hours; then finally he'd capitulated and slowly made his way up to their room – only to find the door now unlocked and Jill lying on the bed, waiting for him. Thinking about it, he was pretty certain he hadn't bothered to take any precautions that afternoon, and he doubted very much if Jill had either. However, the anxious expression on her face told him that this was probably the very last thing she wanted to hear.

'I'm no doctor,' he said, 'But for what it's worth, I think you may have a stomach upset. It's possible you've picked up a bug of some kind.'

'Yes.' Jill nodded eagerly. 'Yes, I'm sure you're right, David.'

Hammond opened the wardrobe and removed a lightweight gaberdine suit from the hanger. 'All the same, I think it would be best to get a check-up,' he said carefully.

'Doctor Munroe?' Jill bit her lip. 'He's such a crotchety old man and I know he doesn't care for me. Still,' she added as a thought struck her, 'I don't want to miss the charity ball at the Peninsula Hotel tomorrow night.'

It seemed some of the things he told Jill also went in one ear and out the other. Tomorrow was the day he put on uniform and ceased to be a civilian. Clearly she had dismissed that unpleasant fact of life from her mind. Tom Blakeney had bought two extra tickets, and as far as Jill was concerned, that was that.

'It's for a good cause,' she told him. 'The committee are hoping to raise a hundred-and-sixty-thousand pounds towards the purchase of bombers for Britain.'

'It doesn't make any difference, Jill,' he said quietly. 'I still can't go.'

'I don't see why not. Tom's in the Volunteers, and he and Rhoda are going.'

Tom Blakeney might be able to slip away from his post on some pretext or other, but he couldn't. Come Saturday, the entire gold reserves of the Hong Kong and Shanghai Bank would be lodged in the vaults of the Kowloon Branch and he wouldn't rest easy until the bullion was safely on board the *Delphic Star*.

'Most of the staff officers from Fortress Headquarters will be there too, David.'

'I'll lay you any odds you like they won't stay to the end.'

'You're just a pessimist,' Jill said petulantly, 'like that police officer who came to see me yesterday afternoon.'

Hammond sighed. 'Don't tell me you've been caught speeding again?' he said.

'Oh, very funny.' Jill stood up and flashed him a withering glance.

'I didn't mean it like that,' he said, suitably contrite. He smiled. 'Am I forgiven?'

'I'll think about it,' she said and moved towards the bathroom.

It seemed the apology fell short of what she expected from him. Wondering how he could make it up with her without actually telling her the truth about tomorrow night, he followed her to the door and stood there, racking his brains for something to say while she ran the tap and splashed her face with cold water.

'This police officer,' he said presently. 'Exactly what did he want to see you about?'

'He was checking up on the servants.' Jill reached for a hand towel and dried her face. 'He wanted to know if we thought they were reliable.'

'Reliable?'

'Oh, for goodness' sake, David, don't you ever read the newspapers? He was talking about potential Fifth Columnists.'

'That's interesting. I wonder why we were singled out?'

'We weren't. He was visiting all the other houses in Macdonnel Road, which I thought was rather a pity.'

'Why so?'

'Because he was a very handsome Irishman.'

'Was he really?'

'And he was also very charming and attentive to me.' Jill turned about and grinned at him. 'Not like some people I know,' she said, her smile changing to a pout.

'We'll soon see about that,' Hammond said, and folded his arms around her waist.

Waldron moved to the bedroom window and looked down at the street below. Katherine Goddard's apartment in the Peninsula Hotel was on the top floor of the building, directly above the tradesmen's entrance next to the Kowloon branch of the Hong Kong and Shanghai Bank on Middle Road, and the view was somewhat restricted. It was also less than inspiring. Apart from Kaznovetsky's, which was obviously a tourist attraction, the dingy silk emporiums, souvenir and trinket shops on either side of the restaurant reminded him of the decaying tenements on Manhattan's Lower East Side. Around midnight yesterday, he had counted literally hundreds of Chinese refugees sleeping rough on the pavements; now, almost nine hours later, they had all vanished, leaving the street deserted except for two police constables and a Sikh armed with a shotgun, who was perched on a stool outside the entrance to a jeweller's shop.

As he watched, a large black sedan turned into the street from the direction of Nathan Road and pulled up outside the rear entrance to the Hong Kong and Shanghai Bank. The Chinese police constable sitting next to the chauffeur got out, opened the nearside rear door and snapped to attention, his right arm quivering to a salute. The constable was about five foot seven and slim with it; the European who emerged from the car was roughly the same height, but many pounds heavier. Most of the black Sam Browne belt around his waist was hidden by rolls of fat, and his khaki drill tunic looked as though it was about to come apart at the seams. Languidly acknowledging the constable's salute, he turned about and waited, arms akimbo, for his companion to join him on the pavement.

The second European to appear from the sedan was a good four inches taller, and although his receding dark-brown hair suggested that he was probably in his mid-forties, there wasn't an ounce of spare flesh on his muscular frame. He was wearing a light grey pinstripe and had deliberately left the double-breasted jacket unbuttoned, to conceal the tell-tale bulge of the shoulder holster under his left arm – or so Waldron reckoned.

The constable closed the rear nearside door, saluted again and got in beside the driver. Then the black sedan pulled away from the kerb and went on down the street towards Hankow Road. Above the fading drone of the car, Waldron heard the sound of muffled voices in the adjoining sitting room and turned away from the window. A few moments later, Katherine Goddard unlocked the communicating door.

'Hungry?' she asked him, smiling.

'I could eat a horse,' Waldron said, and followed her into the other room.

'That's what I told room service.' Katherine pointed to the breakfast tray on the occasional table in front of the couch. 'The orange juice and the eggs and bacon are for you; the bowl of cornflakes is for me, and we get to share the toast and marmalade.'

'And the cup and saucer?'

'Well, I could hardly order a pot of coffee for two without causing some comment.'

Waldron thought it likely that her new-found appetite was already the subject of some speculation amongst the staff. Since she had a reputation for eating scarcely enough to keep body and soul together, the large T-bone steak she had ordered for dinner last night must have set a few tongues wagging. And the fact that she was no longer taking her meals in the residents' dining room would not have gone unnoticed either.

'What about the housemaid?' he said, voicing his train of thought aloud. 'How long have we got before she arrives to clean and tidy your apartment?'

'At least three-quarters of an hour. She's never here before ten fifteen.'

'I'll have to make myself scarce then.' Waldron cut up the second slice of bacon and chewed it slowly. 'Although that's easier said than done. I mean, there are only three rooms to your apartment and they're all interconnecting. I'm too big to hide in the wardrobe and I can't squeeze under your divan bed.'

'You could go down to the lobby, find yourself a comfortable armchair and hide behind a newspaper for half an hour.'

'Half an hour? You must have a very conscientious house-maid.'

'Maybe you'd better wait there until you see me walk through the lobby. Then you'll know it's safe to return.' Katherine opened her handbag and gave him the key to her apartment. 'You'll need this,' she said.

'How are you going to manage?'

'I shall borrow a pass key from the office.'

'I don't want to get you in trouble,' he said quietly.

'Don't worry about me, I know what I'm doing.'

He wondered if she did. Aiding an escaped prisoner was a serious offence, but for some reason, Katherine Goddard appeared to regard it as a rather exciting game. The fact that the military police had been watching the Star Ferry terminal in Victoria yesterday afternoon hadn't disturbed her in the least. They'd walked past a pair of redcaps with her holding on to his arm, smiling and making small talk as though she didn't have a care in the world.

'We've been very lucky so far,' he said, 'but that could change any time.'

'You're a pessimist, Mr Waldron.'

Waldron placed his knife and fork together and pushed the empty plate aside. They were still at the 'Mr Waldron' and 'Miss Goddard' stage, despite the fact that he'd spent the night in her apartment. True, he'd slept on the couch in the sitting room, but even so, the polite formality that existed between them seemed downright ridiculous in the circumstances.

'The name's Frank,' he said firmly.

'Yes.'

'And I'm not a pessimist either.' Waldron jerked a thumb towards the window behind them. 'It's just that I get very nervous when the police are in the neighbourhood.'

'I think you're worrying unnecessarily . . . Frank,' she said, murmuring his first name. 'They always patrol this area, usually in pairs.'

'I'm talking about two very senior police officers, one dressed in civilian clothes, the other got up like a boy scout. They arrived in a large black sedan about fifteen minutes ago.'

'Yes, well, I doubt if they're looking for you.'

Damn right, Waldron thought. Whether he was considered important enough to warrant their attention was immaterial. The way he saw it, they would have been knocking on the door long before now if they had been tipped off. One thing was certain, he hadn't made the front page of the *South China Morning Post*. From the far side of the breakfast tray, the headlines leapt at him: '8th ARMY RENEWS OFFENSIVE IN WESTERN DESERT', and in smaller type below, *'Fierce tank battle at El Adem'*. Just what other news items were reported on the inside pages was, however, anybody's guess.

'Do you mind if I glance through your newspaper?' he asked.

'Please do.' Katherine passed him the *South China Morning Post* and then sauntered over to the window.

Due to the wartime shortage of newsprint, the newspaper consisted of only eight pages. Leafing through it, Waldron was relieved to find that, although he rated a small paragraph at the foot of page six, the authorities had failed to supply the editor with his photograph. On the debit side, the shipping news was less than informative. No United States merchantmen were in port and although the SS *Delphic Star* was due to arrive that afternoon, her departure date and final destination had been censored. Disappointed, he went through the newspaper again, glancing at each heading in turn. A small piece on page four about the forthcoming charity ball at the Peninsula Hotel caught his eye, and amongst the list of VIPs expected to attend, he saw the name of Harold Quarrie, foreign correspondent of the *Chicago Herald Tribune*. Although he had never met, nor even heard of Harold Quarrie until that moment, it suddenly occurred to him that the newspaperman could be the means of his survival. If he told his story to Quarrie and the *Chicago Herald Tribune* printed it, the attendant publicity might afford him the kind of protection the FBI had failed to provide.

'Your two policemen are still there, Frank,' Katherine told him quietly from the window.

'What are they doing now?'

'Nothing. They're just standing outside the bank as though they're waiting for someone to arrive.' Katherine pressed the left side of her face against the windowpane to get a better view. 'I think I recognize the one in uniform,' she said presently.

'Yeah?'

'I've seen his photograph in the newspaper. Kelloway? Or was it Kellerman? Yes, that's it; his name's Kellerman. He's the Assistant Commissioner in charge of the Kowloon Division.'

'That's interesting,' Waldron said, trying to sound as if he meant it.

'What the hell does Hammond think he's up to?' Kellerman demanded irritably. 'It's gone ten o'clock and he was supposed to arrive at nine forty-five.'

'Maybe he's stuck in a traffic jam on Nathan Road.' Ramsay gestured towards the manager's office behind them. 'We know the vehicular ferry docked at Jordan Road five minutes ago, but I could check with Pascoe again if you like?'

His tone of voice implied that he thought Kellerman was behaving like a dithering old woman, and he hoped the Assistant Commissioner would get the message and stop fussing. Pascoe was in radio contact with the armoured truck, and Ramsay had lost count of the number of times he'd been in and out of the manager's office to check on the vehicle's progress from the moment it had left the head office in Victoria.

'I don't like the set-up,' Kellerman said, ignoring the half-hearted offer.

'I don't see how we can improve it, sir.'

The 'sir' was very much an afterthought, and was deliberately intended as such. Two unmarked cars had been detailed to escort the armoured truck from the Hong Kong and Shanghai Bank on Des Voeux Road to the Star Ferry vehicular terminal half a mile away on Connaught Road Central. When the ferry had docked in Kowloon, two other unmarked cars had been waiting in Jordan Road to escort it the rest of the way to the Peninsula Hotel. He had posted Sub Inspector Pascoe and Sergeants Li Chan and Moa Hing inside the bank, covering the unloading area, and Thirsk across the street inside Ram Gopal's jewelry shop. Between the four of them, they had enough firepower to stop a small army.

Kellerman said, 'I was referring to the Sikh guarding the jeweller's shop, Chief Inspector.'

'He's always there.'

'I'm aware of that, but how much has he been told about this operation?'

'Nothing,' said Ramsay. 'He doesn't even know that Inspector Thirsk is inside the shop he's supposed to be guarding. As for Ram Gopal, he's under the impression we received information that somebody was planning to break into his shop during the night.'

'You won't be able to get away with that story two days running,' Kellerman said, and smacked the palm of his left hand with his swagger stick for emphasis.

'I was planning to conceal a marksman in a delivery van tomorrow.'

'Thirsk?'

Ramsay shook his head. 'He'll have done sixteen hours' straight duty by the time I pull him in. With only twelve officers available, I've got to juggle the roster.'

'Quite.'

Ramsay wondered if this might be an opportune moment to complain about the shortage of manpower but on reflection, decided not to push his luck. He had already planted the idea in Kellerman's head that the roster he'd approved would have to be changed before Sunday, and that was enough to be going on with. Tomorrow, certain events would persuade Kellerman that whether he liked it or not, Donovan would have to be temporarily attached to the CID.

'What have you done about that American, Frank Waldron?'

'I've circulated his description and warned the dock and harbour police to be on the look-out for him. We'll pick him up sooner or later.'

'Later would seem to be the operative word,' Kellerman said acidly.

'We could give his photograph to the newspapers. That might speed things up, especially if we offered a reward for information leading to his arrest.'

'What do they call that little brown book every soldier is issued with?'

'An AB 64,' Ramsay said promptly. 'It's a record of service and trade qualification.'

'Right. When did you see one with a photograph on the inside cover?'

'Somebody may have a snapshot of him.'

'You're not thinking straight,' Kellerman told him curtly. 'Waldron enlisted in the Canadian army to save his skin. What makes you think he'd be stupid enough to pose for a snapshot? Besides, even if the army could produce one, we've no legal right to use it or offer a reward for information leading to his arrest. Waldron hasn't committed a civil offence. Or had you overlooked that simple fact?'

Ramsay turned his head away, his face red with anger. It

never paid to underestimate Kellerman. He had a sharp, incisive brain and an acid tongue to go with it.

'You should be doing something about the refugees, too, Chief Inspector,' Kellerman said, changing the subject abruptly. 'They ought to be screened more often. God knows how many of Wong Chang Wai's sympathizers have slipped through the net. Kowloon must be stiff with Fifth Columnists by now.'

'I've put Inspector Adams on to it this morning,' Ramsay said coldly. 'He and Sergeant Lee are screening some of the refugees camping out in the Kai Tak area.'

'About time,' Kellerman muttered.

Bastard, Ramsay thought, then, following Kellerman's gaze, he saw the armoured truck turning into Middle Road.

CHAPTER SIX

Born in April 1910, Sergeant Henry Lee was Hong Kong Chinese and grew up among the boat people of Aberdeen on the south side of the island. Orphaned at the age of six, when Typhoon Annie had capsized most of the sampans in the anchorage and drowned both his parents in the process, he owed his life to a police constable who had fished him out of the angry sea, more dead than alive. Missionary educated, he had left school at the age of fourteen to become first an office boy, then a junior filing clerk with Jardine Mathesons and Company, before joining the Police Force five years later.

Lee had been the best recruit of his intake, but his subsequent advancement had been less than meteoric. Although he had sat for the written examination to sergeant as soon as he was eligible to take it and passed it with ease, he had continued to pound the beat until 1936, when he was transferred to the CID as a detective constable on Superintendent Challinor's recommendation. Two years later he made sergeant and then, in 1940, he had been moved sideways into the Special Branch, a reassignment which owed more to the fact that he was totally incorruptible than to any natural aptitude for the post.

A family man with three small children under the age of seven, Lee was noted for his friendly disposition and cheerful personality. With one notable exception, he got on well with all his colleagues, irrespective of whether they were British or Chinese. The exception was Detective Inspector Derek Adams, who had joined the force from the ranks of the Military Police. Loud-mouthed, coarse and brutal, Adams was the kind of interrogator who resorted to violence at the slightest provocation when questioning suspects. So far as Lee was concerned, the less he saw of that Englishman, the better he liked it. Today, however, was one of those infrequent but highly unpleasant occasions when he found himself working directly under Adams.

For more than five hours now, they had been driving round Kowloon from Lai Chi Kok and Shamshuipo on the northern outskirts to Kai Tak on the east side of town. 'We're looking for Fifth Columnists amongst those refugee friends of yours,' Adams had told him, but to Lee's way of thinking, they were going about it in a very haphazard manner. Of course, their task was well-nigh impossible. There were no official refugee camps, and the Cantonese people who fled to safety across the border either slept rough on the pavements, or made a ramshackle home for themselves out of matchwood and empty kerosene tins on a strip of wasteland. To cordon and search one such shanty town they would have needed the entire resources of the Kowloon Division; whereas all they had to assist them were two police constables from the uniformed branch. Furthermore, the random spot checks they were making here, there and everywhere were next to useless; with no specific information to go on, Lee thought they should have concentrated on one small area of the city, screening as many people as they could in the circumstances.

Adams shifted into third and eased his foot on the accelerator.

'What do you reckon to those shanties over there, Sergeant?' he said, breaking a long silence.

Lee glanced to his left. They were driving east on Boundary Street, heading towards Kai Tak for the second time. Just ahead and lying back from the road he could see half a dozen shanties beyond a large, derelict shed. Several corrugated-iron sheets missing from the roof told him where the refugees had found some of their building materials.

'A month ago, there were only two shanties,' he said slowly.

'That's what I thought.' Adams braked, shifted into reverse and backed up. Then, turning off the road on to a narrow, uneven dirt track, he drove towards the hovels. 'Any idea who owns that shed?' he asked casually.

'The Yam Kwong brothers. They used to run their laundry business from here before they moved to larger premises on Argyle Street.'

'And then they found they couldn't sell this place?'

'So I heard, sir.'

'How come?'

'I don't know.' Lee shrugged his shoulders. 'Perhaps it's too far out of town?'

Adams thought Ramsay couldn't have chosen a better site. The disused laundry was about three miles from the Kowloon branch of the Hong Kong and Shanghai Bank, and he could see at a glance that it was large enough to conceal the two bullion trucks. The refugees would have to be moved on, but that was only a minor problem.

'You could be right.' Adams pulled up and switched off the ignition. 'All right, Sergeant,' he said tersely, 'I'm going to take a look inside that shed. Meantime, you and the two constables can rout out those refugees. I want the whole bloody lot standing in line; the old, the young, the sick, the lame and the lazy. There will be no exceptions made for anybody. Understand?'

'Yes, sir.' Lee opened the door and got out of the Chevrolet sedan. Beckoning the two constables to follow him, he set off towards the motley collection of hovels.

A child playing in the dirt saw them coming and ran inside the nearest shanty, wailing; moments later, the small commune came to life and people began to appear in the open doorways. Their faces were impassive, but as Lee drew nearer he could tell they were apprehensive. He smiled, and in a friendly voice assured them that they had no reason to fear the police, that he merely wanted to make their acquaintance. Then, singling out a frail old man from amongst the crowd of faces, he enquired after his health and asked to be introduced to his family.

The informal approach won them over. No longer apprehensive, the refugees gathered round him, smiling and chattering excitedly amongst themselves. Gradually, Lee got them into some kind of order and started to take down their names in his notebook. With the forty-six men, women and children standing patiently in line, he was still talking to the frail old man and family when Adams tapped him on the shoulder. Turning about, Lee saw that he was holding a small, battery-powered transmitter.

'Guess where I found this, Sergeant?' Adams said, grim-faced.

'In the shed?'

'Right. It was wrapped in a piece of cloth and hidden in one of the soak-aways.'

The shed was a good fifty yards from the nearest hovel, far enough removed to ensure that nobody could hear the operator tap out a message on the morse key. On the other hand, Lee seemed to remember seeing the transmitter somewhere before; it was very similar to one the police border post at Lo Wu had found a few weeks back, when they'd stopped and searched a crowd of refugees crossing the railway bridge over the Sham Chun river. It was also a fact that most of the Fifth Columnists recruited by the Japanese came from Formosa, and this particular group of refugees was definitely Cantonese.

'You'd better ask them what they know about it, Sergeant.'

Lee nodded and turned about to face the refugees again. One

glance was enough to convince him there was really no need to translate the question into their tongue. Although none of them understood a word of English, it was pretty obvious from their frightened expressions that they knew why the big Taipan was angry with them.

'Well?' he demanded. 'What have you got to say for yourselves?'

A pitiful collection of men, women and children, barefoot, half-starved and dressed in ragged clothes; Lee doubted if there was a single Fifth Columnist amongst them, but their silence was deafening.

'Talkative lot, aren't they, Sergeant?'

'They're very nervous, sir.'

'They'll be scared stiff before I've finished with them.'

Lee sighed. By the time Adams had finished with the refugees, Wong Chang Wai, the puppet leader the Japanese had installed in occupied China, would have forty-six more supporters.

'Better draw your revolver and keep them covered, Sergeant. I don't want any trouble from this rabble while I'm searching their stinking hovels.'

It seemed to Lee that Adams was deliberately going out of his way to invite trouble – that he actually *wanted* the refugees to start a riot. In which case, it was more than possible that the Englishman had borrowed the transmitter from the property room at Police Headquarters and concealed it in the glove compartment of their Chevrolet sedan until he was ready to produce it as evidence.

From the direction of one of the ramshackle huts, an earthenware jug sailed through the air, hit the hard-baked ground and smashed to pieces. An indeterminate number of threadbare blankets and a few eating utensils followed it. A young woman at the far end of the line started wailing, and the frail old man advanced towards him, trembling with anger. Somehow Lee managed to pacify him, but the needless destruction continued until every shanty had been gutted. Then, slowly and methodically, Adams began to search every man woman and child, handling them roughly as though they were inanimate objects. Ashamed to be a part of it, Lee turned his back on the ugly scene.

A high-pitched scream rose above the general babble of noise, and he spun round again in time to see Adams pawing the naked breasts of a young girl. The youth standing next to her reached out, grabbed the Englishman's arm and tried to pull him away. Releasing the girl, Adams drove his right fist into the boy's stomach and then punched him in the face. Blood spurting from his shattered nose, the boy clutched his stomach, sank down on to his knees and rolled over. As the line began to surge forward to attack him, Adams stepped back, drew a Colt .45 automatic from his shoulder holster and fired a warning shot above their heads. He didn't have to say anything: the gun in his hand was sufficiently eloquent. Nobody doubted that he wouldn't hesitate to use it in earnest. Cowed and sullen, the crowd moved back into line. Ten minutes later, Adams completed the body search.

His voice truculent, Lee said, 'Apart from the transmitter, what else did you find, sir?'

'Nothing.' Adams looked him over, his eyes bleak. 'But then we don't need any more evidence, do we, Sergeant?'

'I don't see that we can charge anybody,' Lee said obstinately.

'Neither do I.'

'So what are we going to do? Arrest every man, woman and child and take them in for further questioning?'

Adams shook his head. 'That wouldn't be very practical, Sergeant. We'll simply put a torch to these hovels and move them on.'

'You don't have the power to do that.'

'You're wrong, Sergeant. Under the emergency security regulations, I can do anything I damn well like. With Kai Tak airfield just a mile down the road, you've got to be out of your tiny mind if you think I'm going to allow these people to stay here. Now, why don't you tell them to collect their personal belongings and get the hell out of it?'

'Is that an order?'

'You bet your fucking life it is,' Adams said harshly.

Lee supposed he could always lodge an official complaint through the proper channels. Ramsay would be obliged to pass it on to the Assistant Commissioner. But what good would it do? At the end of the day, it was highly unlikely that Kellerman would do anything about it. In his experience, senior officers tended to stick together, and he could see no reason why Kellerman should side with a Chinese detective sergeant against an English inspector.

His face impassive, he told the refugees to clear out and then stood there, his eyes pricking as they began to file away, carrying their pathetic belongings with them. They were only two hundred yards off when the first hut burst into flames.

Given any say in the matter, Donovan would have chosen a less conspicuous rendezvous than the Police Headquarters on Nathan Road, but he assumed Ramsay knew what he was doing. Leaving his car in the yard, he walked through the sandbagged entrance and on down the corridor to the first door on the right beyond the muster room. Glancing left and right to make sure nobody was watching, he knocked twice, opened the door and stepped inside the office.

Ramsay looked up from the file he was reading and greeted Donovan with a faint smile. 'I'd almost given you up for lost,' he said in a low voice. 'What kept you?'

'I'm no longer my own boss, am I?' Donovan pulled up a chair and sat down, facing Ramsay across the desk. 'I don't know what Kellerman told the station officer at Shamshuipo, but he's had me buzzing round like a blue-arsed fly ever since I reported for duty first thing this morning. Eight solid hours without a break.'

'You have my deepest sympathy.'

'Thanks,' Donovan sad dryly.

'Don't mention it.' Ramsay lit a cigarette and leaned back in his chair. 'Now tell me what you've learned about Mrs Hammond.'

'You're taking a risk, aren't you? What if somebody walks in on us?'

'They'll knock first.'

'You hope.'

'Whatever you may think, it's safer than ringing you at home,' Ramsay said evenly. 'Kellerman's still after your hide.'

'Tell me something new.'

'Your phone could be tapped.'

Donovan gaped at him. 'That does make a difference,' he said slowly.

'I thought it might.' Ramsay paused, then said, 'About Mrs Hammond?'

'She's in her early twenties, tall, slender, dark-haired and very shapely.' Donovan used both hands to outline her contours. 'The kind of young woman who becomes the centre of attention the moment she walks into a room. She's also very aware of her sexual attraction and she's used to getting her own way. I'd say she could twist any man round her little finger if she wanted to.'

'Including her husband?'

It was a pertinent question, one Donovan found difficult to answer on the strength of a very brief acquaintance. He had seen Jill Hammond supposedly about a security matter concerning her servants and they'd talked for roughly half an hour. There had been a certain aloofness in her manner to begin with, and he'd felt almost as though he was being interviewed for a minor position in her household; but a little flattery and the old Irish charm had produced a rapid thaw. She had flirted with him in a way that suggested she might be interested, but he'd known all along that it was only a game. When it came down to it, Jill Hammond knew which side her bread was buttered.

'She was wearing a lot of expensive jewelry,' Donovan said thoughtfully. 'A large solitaire diamond engagement ring, a half hoop of the biggest sapphires I've ever seen and a diamond and gold brooch that would have cost me a year's pay.'

'What does that go to prove?'

'Well, it seems to me that Hammond's got her up there on a

pedestal, that there isn't anything he wouldn't do to please her.'

'That's my impression too.' Ramsay stretched out his legs and hooked one arm over the chair back. 'So what do you reckon about the domestic set-up?'

'Their house sits well back from the road in a secluded position surrounded by a tall hedge. None of the neighbours can see much of the drive beyond the gate. They have five servants; two houseboys, a cook, a gardener and a washer-woman. Only the cook and the number one houseboy live in and the other servants have Sunday off, except when the Hammonds are entertaining.'

'They won't be entertaining this Sunday.'

'Right. Trouble is, you can get up to twenty years for kidnapping.'

'If you're caught,' said Ramsay.

Donovan went through his pockets, dug out a packet of Gold Flake and lit a cigarette. 'I thought we were going into the gold business?'

'The two go hand in hand, Bill; you've known that from the start. We can't make six tons of bullion vanish into thin air while Hammond's breathing down our necks.'

Hammond was the one man who could bitch everything up. That he was shrewd, quick-thinking and resourceful was only part of the problem; once the bullion had been transferred, Hammond intended to move into the Kowloon branch and stay there day and night until the gold was safely on board the *Delphic Star*.

'That's why we've got to remove him from the scene,' Ramsay continued. 'Furthermore, it has to be done in such a way that nothing could seem more natural.'

'That's pie in the sky, George.'

'You think so?' Ramsay smiled. 'Kidnapping his wife is just the first step along the road. The whole secret is gradually to increase the psychological pressure on Hammond, till we reach the point where his own chairman decides it's in the bank's interest to replace him with another man.'

'I'm impressed.' Donovan stared at the glowing ember of his

cigarette. 'I'd be even more impressed if you could tell me how the hell you propose to grab Jill Hammond.'

'With a bogus phone call on Sunday morning.' Ramsay glanced at his wristwatch, then closed the file he'd been reading earlier on and tossed it into the out-tray. 'Any other questions, Bill?'

'Offhand, I'd say about a hundred.'

'Then they'll have to wait. It's time I looked in on the bank again.'

Donovan stood up and leaned across the desk to stub out his cigarette in the ashtray. The file in the out-tray bore a Special Branch reference number and although the letters were upside down, he could see that it referred to Larissa Kaznovetsky.

'Where did you say you were going, George?' he asked slyly.

'The bank.' Ramsay smiled. 'Of course, I might just call in at Kaznovetsky's on the way.'

CHAPTER SEVEN

The Cossack doorman at Kaznovetsky's wore a voluminous pair of black trousers tucked into calf-length riding boots, a white peasant-style blouse and a fur hat. A tall Swede, whose blond hair had been dyed black so as to appear authentically Russian, he was known as Viktor to the patrons. There had been three previous Viktors that Ramsay knew of, and not one of them had been able to speak a word of Russian. There were other fakes too. Although the main salon on the ground floor was furnished in the ornate style favoured by the Romanoffs, all the waiters were Chinese, and apart from Borsch, broiled Shashlik and sturgeon baked in pastry, the *à la carte* menu was typical of any Paris bistro. The only genuine Russian was Larissa Kaznovetsky, who ran the establishment from an office above the secluded dining rooms on the second floor, and she had left her native Petrograd in October 1917 at the age of fifteen.

The Kaznovetskys were a much-travelled family. Leaving Petrograd the day after Lenin's Red Guards had seized the Winter Palace and toppled Prime Minister Kerensky and the provisional government from power, they had moved to Omsk, where Larissa's father had subsequently joined the 'White' government set up by Admiral Kolchak. Unlike many of the Tsarist officers serving the Admiral, Major-General Nikolai Alekseevich Kaznovetsky had recognized the growing strength of the Red Army and had been far-sighted enough to secure a transfer to Vladivostok in November 1919, some three months before the Bolsheviks captured and executed Kolchak. The family had stayed in Vladivostok for a little under three years; then, learning that the Japanese occupation forces were about to be withdrawn from the port, Kaznovetsky had decided to move on again, this time to Shanghai.

Just where Kaznovetsky had found the necessary capital to open a casino in Shanghai was not entirely clear, but in the Special Branch file on the family there were various reports from different sources to suggest that he had not come by it legally. Whatever the truth of those allegations, Kaznovetsky had shown considerable business acumen over the next fifteen years, acquiring an hotel, two restaurants and a sizeable fortune along the way.

However, personal happiness had largely eluded him. On the 22nd August 1924, his second daughter, Raya, had been born mentally defective, a body blow that had been compounded twelve years later to the very day, when his wife had died in mysterious circumstances. 'Suicide while the balance of her mind was disturbed', was the coroner's verdict. But Ramsay knew different. Nine months after the surviving members of the family had arrived in Hong Kong from Shanghai, there had been another mysterious death when Larissa Kaznovetsky's fiancé, Ulrich Mannerheim, had drowned in Gin Drinkers Bay one Sunday afternoon early in May 1937.

Nikolai Kaznovetsky had taken Larissa, Raya and Ulrich Mannerheim for a picnic in his motor launch. They had consumed two bottles of wine with their lunch and the temperature at noon had been 91 degrees in the shade with 92 per cent humidity. The heat, coupled with the amount of wine he'd drunk, had proved too much for Mannerheim and he'd fainted, striking his head against the gunwhale as he fell overboard. At least, that was the story Ramsay had put together at Challinor's request, and the jury at the coroner's inquest had gone along with it – despite the pathologist's report that only a minute quantity of alcohol had been found in the deceased's stomach.

The cover-up had not gone unrewarded. It had earned Ramsay promotion to Chief Inspector, a small monthly stipend from Kaznovetsky and frequent access to Larissa's bed. The latter was a bonus, one that arose from mutual attraction and Larissa's insatiable sexual appetite rather than any sense of gratitude on her part. There were other lovers of course, but Ramsay was the only one who could walk into her office any time he liked.

'Your good health,' Ramsay said, and raised his glass of brandy to Larissa.

'And yours, George,' she replied softly.

'How's your father keeping these days?'

'As well as can be expected.'

Ramsay nodded. Nikolai Kaznovetsky had suffered a severe heart attack back in January, which had impaired his speech and left him paralyzed all down one side. He was now confined to a wheelchair, his every need ministered to by a full-time nurse, a virtual prisoner in his colonial-style house high up on Victoria Peak.

'And Raya?' It was always worth reminding Larissa that he knew all about her seventeen-year-old sister, shut away in a private mental hospital near Pak Sha Wan on the east coast of the island.

'I'm afraid she's heavily sedated most of the time.'

Ramsay wasn't surprised. The staff had good reason to be wary of Raya, the pert, dark-haired, insane little nymph who'd blown her mother's brains out with a .32 calibre revolver and crushed Ulrich Mannerheim's skull with a monkey wrench. 'I'm sorry to hear that,' he said. 'It can't be easy for you.'

'No, it isn't.' Larissa crossed one leg over the other. She was wearing an ivory-coloured satin cheongsam, and the slit skirt fell away to expose a shapely thigh. Although thirty-nine, she could lop ten years off her age in the confident knowledge that no other woman would query it, let alone a man. Her face was unlined and there wasn't a spare ounce of flesh around her waist. 'Still, I don't imagine you came here merely to talk about my problems, George?'

'How well you know me.' Ramsay smiled. 'As a matter of fact, I was hoping you'd agree to do me a small favour.'

'What kind of favour?'

'I've arranged to meet Ramon Garcia here tonight at eleven-thirty.'

'Oh, yes?' Her voice was neutral, but there was a faint, knowing smile on her lips.

'We have some business to discuss – I'd like to use this office.'

'I think that can be arranged, George.'

'Good.' Ramsay drank the rest of his brandy and placed the empty glass on Larissa's desk. 'I'd also be very grateful if you'd meet Garcia in the salon and show him up to your office.'

'It's *that* sort of deal, is it?'

'Yes.' Ramsay helped himself to another brandy from the cut-glass decanter. 'Will you do it?' he asked brusquely.

'Of course I will. When have I ever refused you anything?'

'I can't remember.' Ramsay cleared his throat. 'Maybe I can repay the favour, Larissa.'

'How?'

'Well, the army's convinced the Japs will attack us any day now, and somehow I think both the Yanks and our friends down in Singapore are going to be much too busy looking out for themselves to help us.'

'There's always Chiang Kai-shek, George,' Larissa said.

'I doubt if the Generalissimo will launch an effective counter-attack against the Japanese. For one thing, his troops aren't up to it, and for another, he's far too busy keeping an eye on Chou En-lai and the Communist 8th Army.'

'How very unfortunate for you, George.'

'Why me?'

'Well, you're British, aren't you? So naturally the Japs will intern you.' Larissa poured herself another glass of brandy. 'I on the other hand, am a Russian, and I don't believe Tojo will be mad enough to attack the Soviet Union. Nor will Stalin declare war on Japan, not when the Germans are less than twenty miles from Moscow.'

'You've overlooked one thing,' Ramsay told her quietly. 'It so happens that Special Branch has a very detailed file on you and your family, which the NKVD would find most interesting. Especially the extract concerning Admiral Kolchak.'

'That's ancient history, George.'

'The Soviets have long memories, and they never did recover that gold Kolchak was supposed to have. Some people think the Admiral sent it back to Vladivostok in two baggage wagons attached to the train you and your father were travelling on. These same people reckon your father helped himself to a few bars and then buried the rest where neither the Japs nor the Bolsheviks would find it.'

'That's the most ridiculous story I've ever heard,' Larissa said calmly.

'The NKVD might see it differently.'

'Perhaps.' Larissa smiled at him over the rim of her glass. 'But then I'm not likely to visit Moscow again, am I, George?'

'You may not have much choice. You see, I think the Japanese may want to curry a little favour with the Soviet Union, and they might just hand over the Kaznovetskys as a token of their friendship.' Ramsay paused, then added, 'But of course they would need to lay their hands on your file before they could do that.'

'And you would ensure it was destroyed?'

'Yes.'

'For a small consideration, no doubt.' Larissa left her glass on the desk and walked over to the wall safe. 'How much do you want for the file, George?' she asked, in a voice that was arctic cold.

'It won't cost you a cent. All I want is the exclusive use of your small back room for a day or two, starting from noon on Sunday.'

Larissa turned about, a puzzled expression on her face. 'That seems a very reasonable price,' she said slowly. 'Who are you planning to entertain, George?'

'A young lady,' said Ramsay. 'But she'll be asleep most of the time.'

Captain Leslie Venables was fifty-six and looked it, with sandy hair thinning on top, a lined and weatherbeaten face and a stomach that bulged over the small table in his cabin. The *Delphic Star*, a six-thousand-ton freighter of the Indus Steamship and Navigation Company, was his last command and with only four years to go before retirement, he was profoundly thankful that his home port of Bombay was a good two thousand miles from the war zone. He had been torpedoed twice in the 1914-18 War and he very much doubted if he would survive the experience a third time.

Bombay, Calcutta, Singapore, Hong Kong, Manilla, Sydney and back to Bombay again; it was the safest trade route there was in wartime. At least, that was what Venables had thought until this last trip, when he'd called at Singapore and heard on the grapevine that the Admiralty was sending the *Repulse* and the *Prince of Wales* out to the Far East. Although neither battleship had arrived by the time he left Singapore eight days ago, there had been too many signs of increased naval activity in the anchorage for Venables to dismiss the story as just another rumour. There had been other ominous indications that the situation was deteriorating alarmingly; nearing Hong Kong, they had passed the old 'S' Class destroyer HMS *Thracian* patrolling the south-western approaches; and then, within the last two hours, they'd sighted four motor torpedo boats off Aberdeen. A lingering wishful thought that perhaps it was only a naval exercise had been dispelled by the arrival of a senior official from the Legislature and his two companions, who'd trooped up the gangplank minutes after the *Delphic Star* had docked in Kowloon.

The senior official had stayed just long enough to introduce his two companions and impress upon Venables that Major Cottis, who happened to be dressed in civilian clothes, and Mr Hammond from the Hong Kong and Shanghai Bank had the full backing of the Colonial Governor, Sir Mark Young. Subsequently, he had discovered that this meant that the two men were able to commandeer the entire upper section of Number 2 hold and re-arrange the manifest without prior reference to either the owners or the shipping agents.

'You're asking me to offload five hundred tons of jute.' Venables shook his head. 'They're not going to like that in Bombay.'

'Then they'll just have to lump it,' Hammond said tersely. 'My six tons of freight has overriding priority. It's high-risk cargo and we need the space to build a strongroom. It'll be a pretty simple affair, a sort of barbed wire cage in one corner of the hold.'

'Who do you mean by we?'

'The army,' said Cottis. 'A detachment of Royal Engineers will start work tomorrow afternoon at 1400 hours. They'll also install four bunks for the duty guard, but I'm afraid you'll have to provide accommodation for the rest of the escort.'

'What escort are we talking about, Major?' Venables said testily.

'A lieutenant and twelve men from the Royal Rifles of Canada. They'll be embarking on Sunday evening.'

Venables pushed a hand through his thinning hair. Life, it seemed, was full of surprises, most of them unpleasant and designed to make things difficult for him. The *Delphic Star* had a complement of twenty-six, of whom five were officers. The first and second mates were not exactly the best of friends as it was, and the chief engineer wouldn't take kindly to the idea of vacating his cabin so that a mere lieutenant could travel in comfort. On the other hand, 'Sparks' was the most junior as well as the most affable of his officers and there was no reason why he couldn't sleep on a camp bed in the wireless room. The crew wouldn't be very happy about doubling up, though; more than half the seamen were Lascars and moving them was bound to lead to trouble. Still, there was always a chance that the Canadians would prefer to sleep on deck; all that was needed was a little gentle persuasion.

'It's going to be a very tight squeeze, gentlemen,' Venables said ponderously. 'But I suppose we can manage to fit everybody in.'

Hammond said, 'I hate to throw another spanner in the works, Captain, but you'll also have to provide cabin accommodation for Mr Richard Jervis. He's the Bank's Finance Director.'

Venables reached into the pocket of his uniform jacket, took out his pipe and slowly filled it with tobacco from a leather pouch. As soon as one problem had been solved, another reared its ugly head. He could see that no matter what decision he made, somebody's nose was going to be put out of joint. With cabin accommodation at a premium, the second mate would simply have to double up with the chief engineer; neither of them would like it, but it was the lesser of two evils.

'You'd better warn your Mr Jervis that he might not find the food we serve quite to his taste. The *Delphic Star* isn't a luxury liner, Mr Hammond, and we don't run to haute cuisine.'

'Mr Jervis has a healthy appetite; he'll eat anything that's set before him.'

'Good.' Venables struck a match and held it over the bowl of his pipe. 'Well, if that's all, gentlemen,' he said breezily, 'perhaps you'd like to join me in a drink?'

'There are a couple of security matters we should discuss first,' Hammond said carefully.

'Such as?'

'The question of shore leave for your crew.'

'I don't see that's any business of yours,' Venables said coldly.

'Oh, but it is, Captain. If you haven't already guessed, that six tons of freight consists of gold bullion. Now, I'm not implying you'd tell anyone else, but there's bound to be a lot of speculation when the jute is offloaded tomorrow. And once those Royal Engineers start on the strongroom, it won't take the crew long to put two and two together. They may not come up with the right answer, but I can't afford to take any chances. I'm afraid they'll have to be confined to the ship with effect from 0600 hours tomorrow morning.'

'Beer and women, that's all the crew have talked about ever since they left Singapore.' Venables drew on his pipe and watched a thin plume of blue-grey smoke drift towards the ceiling. 'How the hell do you expect me to keep them on board? They'll be straining at the leash like dogs after a bitch on heat.'

'It won't be your problem. There'll be a police constable and two MPs standing at the bottom of the gangplank and nobody will be allowed on or off the ship. The MPs will have instructions to use whatever means they think necessary to enforce that order. That includes the use of firearms in the last resort.'

'You're bluffing, surely, Mr Hammond?'

'He isn't,' said Cottis. 'The MPs have got it in writing. I signed the order on behalf of the General Officer Commanding. The Commissioner of Police is issuing similar instructions to his constables.'

'I can see my crew are going to love me,' Venables said with a wry grimace.

Hammond raised an expressive eyebrow. 'By the way, there are no exemptions,' he said quietly.

'You mean the restriction applies to me as well?'

'They're even more stringent in your case. You're the only man on board who knows about the bullion.'

'So?' Venables demanded truculently.

'So there can be no discussion with your officers concerning the ship's routine for tomorrow, because they're bound to ask you a number of awkward questions and we don't want any loose talk. That means we're obliged to keep you isolated until the general restriction comes into force.'

'How are you going to do that?' Venables growled. 'Lock me in my cabin?'

'Nothing quite so drastic. We thought you might like to spend the night at my house.' Hammond smiled. 'I'll have to make an early start in the morning, but Major Cottis will pick you up at nine o'clock, straight after breakfast.'

'I wouldn't want to put you to all that trouble . . .'

'You won't be any trouble at all,' Hammond interrupted quickly. 'My wife is expecting you for dinner at eight-thirty.'

'Are you sure?'

'You don't know how much Jill is looking forward to meeting you,' Hammond said dryly.

Waldron paused near the foot of the staircase, waited for the down lift to empty and then mingled with the hotel guests who had just alighted. Turning left towards the lobby and the *rhubarb-rhubarb* noise coming from the crowded bar, he walked past the jeweller's shop in the arcade and entered one of the pay phones beyond the hairdressing salon. Conscious that the lift attendant was watching, he closed the door behind him, lifted the receiver off the hook and feeding a coin into the box, dialled 268743.

After what seemed an eternity, a brisk voice answered. Waldron said, 'I'd like to speak to Mr Harold Quarrie please.'

'Mr Quarrie?'

'Of the *Chicago Herald Tribune*. He's in room 521.'

'One moment, please.'

It was a familiar request, one he'd heard several times already that day. Tracing Quarrie to the Gloucester Hotel in Victoria had been a long and frustrating business, and Waldron had lost count of the number of telephone calls he'd made before he'd run the newspaperman to ground. The first time be phoned the hotel, Quarrie had been out. He'd met with the same result when he'd phoned at four o'clock and again at seven, and it was beginning to look as though he wasn't going to have much more luck this time.

'I'm afraid there's no answer from room 521,' the girl on the switchboard told him presently.

'I figured as much.'

'Would you like to leave a message for Mr Quarrie with Reception?'

Waldron glanced over his shoulder. Both lifts were in use and the arcade was deserted. Two, perhaps three minutes from now he might not be quite so lucky.

'Thanks all the same,' he said, 'but I think I'll call back later.'

Replacing the phone, he backed out of the booth and made his way up to Katherine Goddard's apartment on the top floor.

It started to rain shortly after eleven-thirty. By the time Ramon Garcia arrived twenty minutes later in a black Humber saloon, a gusting wind had sprung up and the fine persistent drizzle had become a heavy downpour. Clutching a briefcase in his right hand, the collar of his light-blue raincoat turned up, Garcia scrambled out of the car and glancing neither to left nor right, hurried into Kaznovetsky's restaurant. The car stayed where it was, parked close into the kerb on the wrong side of the street and facing towards Hankow Road. There were two men up front, and observing the Humber closely, Ramsay was pretty sure he could see the blurred outline of a third man in the rear. The escort didn't surprise him; Li Ho Chung didn't believe in leaving anything to chance, especially when a hundred thousand US dollars were at risk.

Ramsay pulled a cord to close the slats of the venetian blind and returned to the desk. Li Ho Chung was not the only careful man in town. Removing a Colt .45 from his shoulder holster, Ramsay pulled the slide back to chamber a round and then, leaving the safety catch off, placed the automatic in one of the filing trays on Larissa's desk where it would be within easy reach, concealed under the petty cash book. That done, he sat down and poured himself a large brandy from the cut-glass decanter. Moments later, he heard the muffled sound of footsteps on the carpeted landing outside the office, followed by a discreet tap on the door.

Larissa ushered Ramon Garcia into the room, nodded briefly to Ramsay and then withdrew. Garcia was still clutching the briefcase in his right hand, but somewhere along the way he had shed his light-blue raincoat.

'You're very punctual.' Ramsay smiled and waved him to a chair. 'Please make yourself comfortable.'

'Thank you.' Garcia sat down on a hard wooden upright and kept the briefcase on his lap, his knees and ankles pressed together like an anxious schoolgirl frightened of losing her virginity.

'Can I get you a brandy or something?' Ramsay asked politely.

'I don't drink.' Garcia cleared his throat. 'If you've no objections, I'd like to conclude our business with the minimum of delay,' he said stiffly.

'That's okay by me.' Ramsay bent down and picked up the two-foot-long oblong-shaped steel box which he'd left under the knee-hole of the desk. 'Looks like a toolbox, doesn't it?'

'I suppose it does.'

'A lot more valuable though.' Ramsay placed the heavy box on top of the desk, unclipped it and opened the lid. Reaching inside, he slid his fingers under the topmost ingot and lifted it out. 'The first of many,' he said cheerfully. 'Twenty pounds of solid gold, bearing the assay mark of the Hong Kong and Shanghai Bank.'

'I must say, I never thought you could do it.' Garcia leaned forward and stroked the ingot with his fingertips. 'May I ask how you lifted these two bars from the vaults?'

'It was a one-time effort.'

The vaults of the Kowloon branch were protected by two anti-intruder devices, a standard burglar alarm and a photo-electric beam, both of which triggered a warning bell in the information room at Police Headquarters on Nathan Road. Although in theory the system was foolproof, it had been a comparatively simple job for Ramsay, to neutralize the warning bell, merely by removing the appropriate fuse from the box in the corridor outside the information room when nobody was looking. At Ramsay's suggestion, Hammond had agreed that an armed policeman should always be stationed behind the gate leading to the vaults. Judicious manipulation of the roster had ensured that Thirsk was on duty in the right place at the right time.

'Fortunately, the Kowloon branch doesn't run to a time-lock.' Ramsay winked. 'And naturally I have to know the combination to the reinforced doors.'

'Really?' Garcia frowned. 'Why's that?'

'Because we'd look pretty silly if somebody was trying to tunnel into the vaults from the other side and we couldn't get at them.' Ramsay picked up the ingot and put it back inside the steel box. 'Of course, it's one thing to steal forty pounds of gold, but six tons of the stuff is an altogether different proposition.'

'Yes, I imagine it is.' Garcia looked down at the briefcase on his lap, seemingly reluctant to part with it. 'When are you going to tell me how you propose to do it?'

Ramsay could understand his anxiety. At current market rates, the two ingots would fetch a shade over twenty thousand US dollars. Garcia was about to hand over five times as much. Garcia also knew that if the deal went sour and the Triad was out of pocket, the fact that his Chinese wife was distantly related to Li Ho Chung wouldn't save him from ending up in the harbour with an ice pick in his brain.

'Aren't you forgetting something?' Ramsay said coldly.

'Oh, yes, the cash in advance.' Garcia placed the briefcase on the desk and pushed it towards Ramsay. 'One hundred thousand US dollars in tens, twenties and fifties. I think you'll find it's all there.'

'I'm sure it is.' Ramsay opened the briefcase and tipped the contents out on to the desk. The hundred thousand dollars would keep Adams and Thirsk happy and secure a berth for himself and Donovan on a Swedish tramp outbound from Hong Kong. Selecting a few bundles at random, he flipped through each wad in turn, as though handling a deck of cards. 'One can't be too careful, though. People have been known to place a genuine note top and bottom of blank sheets of paper.'

'My client would never do a thing like that,' Garcia said indignantly.

'Your Mr Li Ho Chung is a very thorough man; so am I.'

'That remains to be seen, doesn't it?'

Ramsay stuffed the banknotes back into the briefcase again and then placed it carefully on one side. 'You needn't worry about a thing,' he said calmly. 'The bullion will be transferred to the docks on two lorries provided by the army. The drivers and their two guards will be locally enlisted personnel and they will be told to report to the Kowloon branch of the Hong Kong and Shanghai Bank at 0300 hours on Monday morning. When the loading is complete some five hours later, the two vehicles will move off under police escort to Holt's Wharf, and that's the last anybody will see of them. You will have two identical trucks loaded with six tons of ballast ready to take their place the moment I give the word. That way, nobody will discover the bullion is missing until the crates are offloaded at Sydney.'

'It's a very audacious plan.'

'The best ones usually are,' said Ramsay.

'So where and when do I collect the genuine ingots?'

'I'll phone you at home and tell you where to meet me. As soon as I receive the rest of the agreed payment, you'll be told where to find the missing trucks and their precious cargo.'

'I don't think my client will be altogether happy with those arrangements. After all, half a million pounds' worth of diamonds is a very considerable fortune.'

'Let's not quibble over minor details,' Ramsay said irritably. 'If it will set Li Ho Chung's mind at rest, you can bring an escort with you. Furthermore, neither you nor I will leave the rendezvous until your associates are satisfied the gold is where I say it is.'

'That would seem a more satisfactory arrangement.' Garcia pressed his fingertips together to form a steeple, a mannerism that warned Ramsay he was about to raise another objection. 'There is the matter of the final payment,' he said judiciously.

'What about it?'

'My client feels it is a little excessive.'

'Li Ho Chung is getting six tons of bullion to the value of two and a half million in return for a little over five hundred and twenty thousand pounds. By the time those ingots have been melted down and debased with lead, he'll probably have upped their value by another ten to twenty per cent, depending on how greedy he is.'

'I had a feeling that would be your attitude.'

'Well, now you know.' Ramsay stood up and pushed the steel box towards Garcia. 'Mind how you go with this,' he said. 'It's heavy enough to pull your arm out of its socket.'

Waldron climbed the last flight to the top floor and then glanced left and right to make sure the corridor was deserted before making for Katherine's apartment. Unlocking the door with the key she had given him, he walked into the sitting room to find Katherine still curled up in an armchair, her nose burried deep in a book. He noticed, though, that in his absence she had made up a bed for him on the couch and changed into a blue satin nightdress and matching robe.

'Any luck?' she asked, looking up from the book.

'No. Quarrie must be painting the town several shades of red. In the end I left my name with Reception.'

'You did what?'

'I said a Mr Frank Waldron wanted to get in touch with him and would call again tomorrow. Provided he gets the message, I guarantee he won't leave the Gloucester Hotel before he hears from me.' He smiled wryly. 'Of course, I'm gambling that as a good newspaperman he'll have read today's *South China Morning Post* and spotted that small paragraph on page six.'

'And then what, Frank?'

'I guess I'll meet him somewhere.'

'And what if you find the police waiting for you?'

'There is that possibility,' he admitted.

'Unless I went to his hotel and led him to you, of course.'

'I don't think I could let you do that, Katherine.' Waldron sauntered over to the window and pulled the curtains aside. 'It's too risky.'

Across the street, a large black saloon pulled away from Kaznovetsky's restaurant and swerved across to the left-hand side in the direction of Hankow Road, provoking an angry blast from an oncoming vehicle. In that same instant, a whore in a bright green cheongsam emerged from the doorway of the gift shop adjoining the restaurant, tried to flag down the passing taxi cab and then retreated swiftly in the wake of a tidal wave from the gutter as the driver ignored her and sailed on by.

'The offer's still there, Frank,' Katherine told him quietly.

'Yes, I know – and I'm grateful.'

'If nothing else, at least think about it.'

'Right.' Waldron froze. 'That's funny,' he muttered.

'What is?'

'Remember the guy we saw standing outside the bank with Kellerman this morning?'

'Yes. What about him?'

'Well, he's been in and out of Kaznovetsky's restaurant like a yo-yo all day.'

'I don't see anything odd about that, Frank. After all, it could be his favourite restaurant.'

'Half an hour ago he went in carrying a toolbox, now he's come out with a briefcase.' Waldron turned away from the window to find Katherine standing close to him. 'Doesn't that strike you as rather peculiar?'

His voice sounded husky and the question went unanswered. Slowly, and very tentatively, he slipped an arm round her waist and kissed her lightly on the mouth. For a moment he thought Katherine was going to push him away, but then she opened her mouth and pressed her soft body against his, and he forgot all about Ramsay.

SATURDAY
6th DECEMBER 1941

CHAPTER EIGHT

Pascoe lived in Carlton Mansions, a small run-down block of flats at the wrong end of Boundary Street. It was all he could afford on a Sub Inspector's pay. The only redeeming feature of the apartment house was that it lay within reasonable walking distance of Police Headquarters on Nathan Road. An ambitious young man, Pascoe made no secret of the fact that his ultimate goal in life was to become Commissioner of Police, a candid admission that didn't exactly endear him to his colleagues. Loathed by all the European officers with the exception of Kellerman, Pascoe was only too aware that he was always first in line for any dirty job that happened to come along. If there wasn't one in the offing, then Ramsay saw to it that he did more late and early shifts than anyone else in the CID.

"Sovereign" was the lastest example. Of the twelve detectives and Special Branch officers assigned to guard the vaults of the Hong Kong and Shanghai Bank, his was the only name to appear on the early shift for the second day running. It was bad enough having to crawl out of bed at the unearthly hour of four o'clock in order to be there on time, but Ramsay had added insult to injury. Anyone would have thought he'd just raped a leading socialite in Victoria and used an official car to get there, the way Ramsay had reacted when he'd asked for transport to pick him up from the house. 'Who the hell do you think you are?' he'd roared. 'This is the police force, not a fucking taxi service.'

Pascoe drew back the curtains and looked out of the window at a thick blanket of mist swirling in the grey light of daybreak. Raincoat weather, he thought, and took his dark blue trench mac out of the wardrobe. Still buckling the belt around his waist, he walked out of his ground floor flat.

The street was as silent as a graveyard and no lights were showing in the neighbouring apartment houses. Pascoe decided there was no point in hanging about; very few cabs plied for trade in Boundary Street and the chances of finding one at that hour of the morning were about zero. Pausing just long enough to light his first cigarette of the day, he strode off towards Nathan Road.

Somewhere behind him in the mist, a car door closed with a hard, metallic clunk; then moments later, an engine fired into life.

The car moved forward, slowly gathering speed as it came towards him. More in hope than expectation, Pascoe drifted over to the kerbside and stood there staring into the grey, misty blanket, his thumb poised, ready to hitch a lift. Two small pin-points of light appeared out of the gloom and grew larger; smiling, he jerked his thumb in the direction of Nathan Road.

The smile was still there on his face when the driver pushed his foot down on the accelerator, but it vanished the moment the car mounted the kerb and came straight at him. The radiator grille smashed into his thighs and the impact flipped him up into the air. Sailing over the roof in a swallow dive, he hit the road head first, shattering his skull as though it were a delicate piece of eggshell china.

Ramsay parked the Chevrolet sedan in Nathan Road and walked round to the rear entrance of the bank. Yeuh-Shen, the Detective Inspector in charge of the graveyard watch, had rung him at home at six-thirty to report that Pascoe hadn't arrived at the Kowloon branch with the other reliefs, and for the sake of appearances he had then spent the next hour and a half telephoning Pascoe's neighbours and every hospital in town, until he had finally located the missing police officer at Queen Alexandra's on Chatham Road. Thirsk, he thought, had done a thorough job. Pascoe was now lying exactly where he wanted him, on a slab in the morgue.

Yeuh-Shen opened the door to him and stood to one side. 'No sign of Sub Inspector Pascoe, then?' he said.

'He's dead.' Ramsay stepped past him into the building. 'Some hit-and-run driver knocked him down outside his apartment house. It must have happened before the fog lifted.'

'Witnesses?' Yeuh-Shen was phlegmatic. If he had been shocked by the news of Pascoe's death, it wasn't evident from his expression or tone of voice.

Ramsay shook his head. 'The Traffic Police are still investigating; they may come up with one.'

'I wouldn't bet on it.'

'Neither would I.'

'So what happens now?' Yeuh-Shen asked. 'We've got two officers inside the bank and a third across the street in an unmarked van, but we're still one man light. Do you want me to stay on?'

'No, that won't be necessary. I'll hold the fort until Pascoe's replacement arrives. He should be here shortly.'

'Right.' Yeuh-Shen edged towards the door, then hesitated. 'You'd have thought Derek Adams would have stopped by to give Pascoe a lift. They were on the same shift and Boundary Street isn't all that far out of his way.'

'Maybe Pascoe didn't like to ask him? They weren't exactly the best of friends.'

'No, that doesn't surprise me, George.' He snapped his fingers. 'Before I forget, the Branch Manager arrived twenty minutes ago.'

'Does he want to see me?'

'No, I just thought you'd like to know.'

'Thanks.'

Ramsay took Yeuh-Shen by the arm and gently ushered him out into the street. Closing and locking the door behind him, he then walked through the passageway into the main hall to find Adams behind the counter, a pump-action shotgun within easy reach. Less than six hours ago he had received an advance payment of twenty-five thousand US dollars, but no one would ever have guessed that from the sour expression on his face.

'What's eating you, Derek?' he asked.

Adams moved nearer the grille and kept his voice down. 'I'm

having problems with Sergeant Lee; he's pretty sore about the way I handled those refugees yesterday.'

'He'll get over it,' said Ramsay.

'I hope you're right, George, but I've a nasty feeling he may ask for an interview with Kellerman.'

'We can't have that.'

'Damn right we can't,' Adams muttered. 'You wouldn't like to have a word with him, would you?'

'Do you think it'd do any good?'

'It can't do any harm.' Adams jerked a thumb towards the passageway. 'You'll find him down below in the vaults.'

Ramsay nodded and turned about. Just how he was going to smooth things over was far from clear. Lee wasn't the kind of man who could be easily dissuaded from doing what he thought was right; beneath his usually placid exterior there lurked a will of iron. Somewhat reluctantly, Ramsay went on down the short flight of steps to the vaults.

Detective Sergeant Lee was seated on a high chair behind the gate, a Thompson .45 sub machine gun with a fifty-round drum across his lap. Hearing Ramsay's footsteps, he stood up, slipped the web sling over his right shoulder and curling his fingers round the pistol grip, pointed the barrel downward at the floor.

'Morning, Henry.' Ramsay glanced at the sub machine gun and smiled. Lee was a mere five foot four and the Cutts compensator on the muzzle was only a few inches from the floor. 'You look as though you've got a third leg.'

'A crutch would be a more apt description, sir.'

'You're probably right.' Ramsay produced a packet of Churchmans, passed a cigarette through the bars to Lee and then leaned forward to take a light from the detective's Zippo. 'How did the screening operation go yesterday?' he asked casually.

Lee avoided Ramsay's gaze and looked down at his feet. 'I'm sure Inspector Adams submitted a full written report,' he said in a subdued voice.

'I dare say he did; trouble is, I haven't had time to read it yet. That's why I'm asking you.'

'Inspector Adams is upstairs, sir,' Lee said woodenly.

'I'd still like to hear it from you, Henry. You're the real expert, the only man in Special Branch who can tell a Formosan infiltrator from a Cantonese refugee.'

Lee thought about it, then raised his eyes to look Ramsay in the face. 'Inspector Adams found a portable wireless transmitter in that disused laundry belonging to the Yam Kwong brothers on Boundary Street.'

'And?'

'Well, I don't believe the refugees who were living nearby knew anything about it.'

Ramsay flicked his cigarette, spilling ash on to the floor. Lee was a very private man, patient and uncomplaining, but he was hard to move when he did take a stance; persuading him to open up was about as easy as getting blood out of a stone.

'Did you tell him that, Henry?' he asked quietly.

'I didn't think it would do any good. Inspector Adams was in no mood to listen to me.'

'He was angry?' Ramsay suggested.

'Very angry. It seemed to me that he'd already made up his mind that the refugees were potential Fifth Columnists and was determined to teach them a lesson. He and the two police constables tore their shanties apart and then searched every man, woman and child.'

'Did they find anything?'

'No.' Lee stared at his cigarette, a pensive expression on his face. 'I did ask Inspector Adams if we were going to take the refugees in for further questioning, but he said we should just put a torch to their hovels and move them on. Even though we were empowered to do that under the emergency security regulations, I still think it was wrong to burn them out of house and home.'

The rights and wrongs were of no interest to Ramsay. The two army vehicles carrying the gold bullion had to vanish into thin air, and now that the refugees had been dispersed, the disused laundry would make an ideal hiding-place.

'I'm thinking of asking for a transfer,' Lee said abruptly.

'Why?' Ramsay thought his voice sounded a long way off.

'Because I don't want to have anything more to do with Inspector Adams, sir. I don't care for his methods.'

'Did he manhandle some of the refugees?'

'I'd rather not say.'

'Are you telling me you don't want to make an official complaint about a senior officer?'

'I'm asking for a transfer,' Lee repeated stubbornly.

A transfer was out of the question. Lee's request would have to go through Kellerman, and the Assistant Commissioner was bound to want to know why he wanted to leave the Special Branch.

'I don't want to lose you, Henry.' Ramsay dropped his cigarette on to the concrete floor and ground it under his heel. 'Maybe I can fix it so that you never have to work with Inspector Adams again.'

'Is that possible?'

'I think so. Have you heard the news about Sub Inspector Pascoe?'

'No, sir.'

'He was knocked down and killed by a hit-and-run driver early this morning.'

'That's terrible.' Unlike Yeuh-Shen, who hadn't batted an eyelid, Lee seemed genuinely upset by the news.

'I think he may have been murdered.'

The Traffic Department were treating it as a routine accident, just as he'd hoped they would, and in a way it was ironic that he should be casting doubt on their assumption. But with a little embroidery, Pascoe's death would provide a useful diversion to keep Lee occupied. Taking his time, Ramsay began to outline a plausible theory to account for Pascoe's death, drawing a connection between the fatal accident and operation "Sovereign".

'Pascoe was a loner,' Ramsay went on, 'a man who kept himself to himself. Nobody knew what he did, where he went or what company he kept when he was off duty.'

'He was very ambitious.' Lee felt the cigarette burn down

between his fingers and hastily dropped the stub on to the floor.

'You're right, Henry; he was ambitious, and he only had his foot on the bottom rung of the ladder. It could be that he looked elsewhere for a different kind of advancement.'

'Do you think he was on the take?'

'The possibility had crossed my mind,' Ramsay said smoothly. 'If I'm right, he may have talked about the bullion transfer and then got cold feet and threatened to blow the whistle when the people who were bankrolling him asked for more information. That would have given them a very strong motive for silencing him.'

'I suppose so.' Lee frowned. 'Of course I didn't know Sub Inspector Pascoe all that well, but he always struck me as an honest kind of a man. Somehow I can't see him taking a bribe.'

'Until this morning I would have agreed with you, but with six tons of gold bullion at risk, we've got to look at Pascoe in a different light. To be specific, I want to know if maybe one of the Triads had him on their payroll.'

'I see,' Lee said in a neutral voice.

'That's why it's a job for you, Henry. Where the secret societies are concerned, you're a walking encyclopedia.'

'When do I start?'

'As soon as you come off shift; earlier if I can find a relief.' Ramsay pushed his cuff back and looked at his wrist-watch. 'Time I went back upstairs,' he said. 'The Assistant Commissioner will be arriving any minute now and it wouldn't do to keep him waiting.'

In the event, ten o'clock came and went with no sign of Kellerman. Forty minutes later, Hammond arrived in the armoured truck with the second and final load of bullion.

Garcia stood by the window, both hands clasped behind his back. Despite the partial mobilization of the Hong Kong Volunteers, it was hard to believe the Japanese really were about to invade; the Star Ferry was still shuttling back and forth between Kowloon and Victoria, the number of cargo vessels berthed at Holt's wharf had not diminished and a Pan Am flying boat rode at anchor off Kai Tak. Although all the information he'd received in the past twelve hours pointed in one direction only, Garcia still nursed a faint hope that the war clouds would vanish from the horizon, just as the early morning fog had suddenly lifted to herald another fine day.

Garcia returned to his desk and sat down. If by a miracle the threat of war did recede, the Hong Kong and Shanghai Bank might well think twice about sending their gold reserves out of the colony. Without a doubt, that would be a bitter disappointment for Li Ho Chung, but he personally would breathe a damn sight easier. There were now half a million pounds' worth of diamonds in his safe, and too many things could go wrong – especially when dealing with a man like Ramsay. With his contacts, Ramsay would have little difficulty in finding a burglar who was prepared to break into the Chubb safe for a small consideration.

The office intercom crackled, breaking the silence, and then Garcia heard the thin, reedy voice of his secretary Rosemary Da Costa.

'Mr Garcia, there are two Chinese gentlemen in my office who say they have an appointment to see you. They won't give me their names.'

'It's all right,' said Garcia, 'I'm expecting them.'

'There's nothing in my diary for twelve-thirty.'

'I'm afraid that's my fault, I forgot to tell you.' Garcia paused; then, adopting a more authoritative voice, he said, 'You may as well go on home, Miss Da Costa. I shan't need you again before Monday.'

Moments later, two hard-faced men walked into the room and identified themselves as the two nightwatchmen Li Ho Chung had assigned to guard the office safe over the weekend.

At exactly two-thirty, Katherine Goddard strolled into the lobby of the Gloucester Hotel and sat down in one of the vacant chairs near the reception desk, choosing a position where she would be easily seen. Looking cool and elegant in a navy-blue silk two-piece with a white carnation pinned to the lapel of the jacket, she drew furtive but admiring glances from both the bellboy and the desk clerk. Others also took notice; the pilot and crew of a Pan Am clipper drinking at a nearby table eyed her speculatively. But right on time, a tall, loose-limbed man with greying hair strolled purposefully towards her.

'Miss Goddard?' he said, halting in front of her.

'Yes.' Katherine looked up at him. 'Are you Mr Quarrie?'

'Indeed I am.' Quarrie smiled and waited for her to get up before shaking hands. 'I'm not usually this lucky with a blind date,' he murmured.

Katherine laughed. 'There's no answer to that,' she said.

'No, I guess there isn't.' Quarrie placed a hand under Katherine's elbow and gently steered her towards the door. 'I'll tell you one thing; I envy Waldron. He's a very lucky guy.'

'And you have a very smooth line, Mr Quarrie.'

'Well, I'm a newspaperman,' he said, as if that explained everything.

Suddenly, Katherine stopped in the arcade outside the hotel and turned to face him. 'I've only got your word for that,' she said quietly.

'Do you want to see my press card?'

'Is your photograph on it, Mr Quarrie?'

'No.'

'Then I'd sooner you showed me your passport.'

Quarrie reached inside his jacket, brought out his passport and flipped it open at the appropriate page. 'I'm afraid it's not a very good likeness.'

'They rarely are,' said Katherine, 'but I can see it's you, and that makes it all right.'

'It does?'

'Well, at least I'm satisfied you're not a policeman.'

Katherine walked out into Des Voeux Road and turned right, Quarrie at her side. They strolled on slowly past Prince's Building and the Hong Kong and Shanghai Bank, the crowds jostling them on the pavement, the street a cacophony of snarling trucks, blaring horns and the metallic squeal of tram-cars passing in either direction en route for Kennedy Town,

Happy Valley and North Point. Rickshaws weaved in and out of the traffic with a careless abandon that verged on the suicidal.

'How do you know the police aren't following us?' Quarrie asked with a lopsided grin.

'I don't,' Katherine said tersely.

Frank hadn't liked the idea one bit, but she had talked him round and in the end he had figured out a way to minimize the risks. But no plan was foolproof, and if things did go wrong, she stood to lose more than just her job at the Peninsula Hotel.

'You don't have to worry about the police,' Quarrie told her presently. 'I've never broken a confidence in my life.'

'Good, I'm glad to hear it.'

Katherine waited for a break in the traffic, then crossed over the road and turned left at the next intersection. The Supreme Court was on their left, an enclosed cricket field to the right and straight ahead down by the waterfront, Quarrie recognized the imposing façade of the Hong Kong Club, the most exclusive bastion of privilege in the Far East. By now they had walked into an oasis of calm, leaving the noise and bustle of Des Voeux Road behind them.

Katherine stopped and turned to face Quarrie again. 'This is where I leave you,' she said calmly.

'What is this, some kind of joke? I thought we were going to meet up with Waldron?'

'You are.' Katherine pointed to a bench seat on the far side of the cricket ground beyond the Club. 'If you'd like to go over there and sit down, Frank will join you in a few minutes from now.'

'Clever.'

'What is?'

'This stake-out,' said Quarrie. 'I don't pretend to know where Waldron is at this precise moment, but I'd bet a month's pay he's got his beady eyes fixed on us. And he won't try to contact me until he's satisfied I'm alone. Right?'

'You're very quick on the uptake, Mr Quarrie.'

'It comes of experience,' he said modestly, and reached out for her hand. 'Will I see you again?'

'I doubt it,' Katherine said gently.

'That's what I thought.' Quarrie smiled. 'I've said it before, I'll say it again – Waldron's a helluva lucky guy.'

Slowly and more than a little reluctantly, he finally released Katherine's hand and stood there gazing after her as she walked on down Jackson Road to the waterfront, a tall, very attractive young woman in a navy silk two-piece that emphasized every contour.

CHAPTER NINE

The night had closed in rapidly, as it always did. One moment there had been a brilliant sunset, the cloud base shot through with shades of pink, scarlet and orange; the next, there was total darkness, as though somebody had suddenly switched off the lights. Now, as he sat in the Assistant Commissioner's office under the slowly circulating electric fan, Ramsay could see the reflection of the flickering multicoloured neon signs in Nathan Road high up on the wall behind Kellerman's back.

It was past seven o'clock and Kellerman was still in uniform, his khaki drill jacket dark with sweat above and below the Sam Browne belt around his waist and under both armpits. He had spent the entire day attending one meeting after another, starting with an early morning conference at Police Headquarters in Victoria, then moving on to one with the army at Fortress Headquarters, which in turn was followed by an informal late afternoon session at Government House. He was tired, sticky and hungry, and more than a little irritated that he'd only just heard the news about Pascoe. The fact that Ramsay had been unable to reach him all day only increased his frustration.

'What about Pascoe's next of kin?' Kellerman demanded. 'Have they been informed?'

'I sent his parents a cable expressing our deepest sympathy.'

'Good. When did you say the coroner was holding the inquest?'

'Ten o'clock on Monday,' said Ramsay. 'I can't be there, but it should be a mere formality.'

'Let's hope so.' Kellerman took out a handkerchief and wiped his face. 'What arrangements have you made for the funeral?'

'None that can't be unscrambled. I haven't spoken to the Dean yet, but I imagine the Commissioner would like the funeral service to be held in St John's Cathedral?'

'He most certainly will.'

Ramsay nodded. 'I thought Tuesday afternoon around four o'clock would be suitable. I've warned the uniform branch that they'll be required to provide a firing party. Naturally the pall-bearers will be found by the CID.'

'We'll need a bugler to sound the last post,' said Kellerman.

'I assumed Superintendent Bramwell would detail one.'

Bramwell was in charge of the uniform branch. In the course of one of his fleeting visits to Police Headquarters, Ramsay had passed him in the corridor and exchanged a few brief words. Pascoe's name had cropped up during their short conversation, and Ramsay had said he supposed the uniform branch would do their usual stuff at the funeral. That was the full extent of the arrangements he'd made; the rest was just so much bullshit to impress Kellerman.

'We can ill afford to lose men like Pascoe. He was a very promising young officer.'

Ramsay fingered his top lip, hiding a derisive smile. The Assistant Commissioner was absolutely right; he could ill afford to lose his blue-eyed boy. Pascoe's untimely death would make Kellerman's task of purging the CID infinitely more difficult to accomplish.

'I presume everything went off all right at the bank today?' Kellerman said, abruptly changing the subject.

'Well, Hammond said he was very impressed with our

efficiency. I gather he's going to write a letter to the Commissioner expressing his appreciation.'

'It's nice to receive a pat on the back for a change,' Kellerman said.

'It could be his congratulations are a little premature. I've heard whispers that one of the Triads has heard about the bullion transfer.'

'Which one?'

'The Red Spears,' said Ramsay. 'Of course, there may not be anything to it, but we can't afford to take any chances. That's why I put Sergeant Lee on to it; he knows more about the secret societies than any other man on the Force.'

'That'll leave you rather short-handed, won't it?'

'I've managed to fill the gap temporarily, but I'll need two replacements standing by for tomorrow.'

'See Bramwell,' Kellerman said. 'Tell him I said you were to have the pick of his people.'

'Donovan could be made available,' Ramsay said tentatively. 'From what I hear, he's pretty much of a spare number at the Shamshuipo police station.'

'For all I care, he can be sitting on his backside twiddling his thumbs. Donovan stays where he is, and that's final.'

'Whatever his faults, he's a good man to have by your side in a tight corner. You can rely on him – which is more than you can say for some. I could name you a dozen officers who would conveniently disappear at the first whiff of real trouble.'

'That's a gross slander, and you know it.' Kellerman glared at him, his eyes narrowing to pinpoints. 'Still, I suppose it's natural you should have such faith in him. After all, you and Donovan have always been very close.'

'That doesn't alter the fact that he has three commendations for bravery.'

'You can forget Inspector Donovan.' Kellerman brought the flat of his hand down on the desk for emphasis. 'Do I make myself clear?' he grated.

'Not entirely,' Ramsay said calmly. 'A few moments ago you told me I could have the pick of Bramwell's lot, only to veto my first choice in the very next breath. That's not exactly helpful, is it?'

'You'd better watch your step, Chief Inspector.'

. . . Or else you'll find yourself on an adverse report; Ramsay knew that was the inference behind the warning, and it wasn't an idle threat either. Kellerman had initiated a spate of adverse reports in his bid to purge the CID of its more corrupt officers. A few days ago, he would have backed down and apologized, but the major share of half a million pounds' worth of diamonds was the difference between then and now.

'I must have top-notch people with me on this job.' Ramsay paused, then said, 'I don't think Mr Hammond would be very happy if he got the impression the bank was being palmed off with second-raters.'

It wouldn't stop there and they both knew it. A word from Hammond and the Chairman of the Hong Kong and Shanghai Banking Corporation would be on to Government House and the Assistant Commissioner would find himself out on a limb.

'This tip-off you've had – how reliable is it?'

Ramsay sensed he was about to run up the white flag. All Kellerman wanted was an excuse to save his face; the question was simply a means to that end.

'The informant has always been pretty sound in the past,' he said blandly.

'Well, in that case, I suppose you'd better have Donovan.'

It was grudgingly done, but Ramsay thanked him politely, and Kellerman muttered something about merely doing his job. He even managed a faint smile which lasted all of ten seconds, the time it took him to reach the door.

Hiding his elation, Ramsay went on downstairs, telephoned the Shamshuipo police station from his office and arranged to meet Donovan in the Chungking Restaurant on Yu Chau Street in an hour's time.

Waldron broke off another piece from the bar of Cadbury's Dairy Milk and ate it slowly. There would be no cosy dinner for two like last night and the chocolate was supposed to keep him going until breakfast; but ever since he was a kid, he'd been unable to resist candy, and there were now only a couple of squares left. He eyed the remaining pieces, vowed he wouldn't touch them until he felt really hungry; then immediately stretched out a hand.

'Someone's got a sweet tooth,' Katherine said from the doorway of the bedroom.

'Yeah, I know,' he said. 'I'm too weak-willed to resist temptation, that's my trouble.' He turned in her direction, his jaw dropping as his eyes took in the green, strapless, three-quarter-length evening dress she was wearing.

'How do I look?' she asked, smiling hesitantly.

'Like a million dollars.' Waldron cleared his throat, conscious that his voice had sounded like a croaking bullfrog. 'Everybody's going to be looking at you.'

'Flattery will get you everywhere, Frank.'

'So they tell me.' But not tonight, he thought. Tonight, Katherine had a long-standing engagement with some friend of her brother Steven. 'What time is your date picking you up?' he said, voicing his train of thought aloud.

'He's not my date; I'm just making up a foursome.' Katherine sat down in an armchair and crossed one slim leg over the other. 'And he isn't calling for me, either. I told Steven I'd meet them downstairs in the bar.'

'Why all the concern?' he said. 'You're a free agent. You don't owe me any explanations.'

'Do you think Mr Quarrie will help you, Frank?' Two high spots of colour accounted for the abrupt change of conversation.

'Quarrie's a newspaperman; he knows a good story when he hears one.'

So far there had been no commitment. Quarrie had listened attentively, then asked a number of pertinent questions. Finally, he'd promised to get back to him after he had checked the facts with the paper's office in Chicago. As a parting gesture, he had pressed fifty Hong Kong dollars on him. 'Call it a loan,' Quarrie had said, as though he were some bum asking for a hand-out; even now it still left a sour taste in Waldron's mouth whenever he thought about it.

'I'm supposed to phone Quarrie again on Monday.'

'And?'

Waldron shrugged. 'I guess we'll get together and work something out. It shouldn't be too difficult to get a berth on a Dutch freighter bound for Sumatra or Java.'

'If you've got a passport and the fare.'

'The fare's no problem,' said Waldron. 'The *Herald Tribune* will stake me.'

He was whistling in the dark. Quarrie hadn't talked money, nor had he said anything about obtaining a passport for him. If he did get out of Hong Kong, chances were it would be as a stow-away.

'You'll make it, Frank, I know you will.'

'Sure.' He smiled to show he meant it, then said, 'What time are your friends expecting you?'

'Eight o'clock.' She glanced at her gold wristwatch, made a plaintive face and reluctantly got to her feet. 'I really ought to be going.'

'Yeah.'

'I hate to leave you on your own.'

'Don't give it another thought,' he said and followed her to the door. 'Just have a nice time.'

'I'd sooner spend the evening with you,' Katherine said, and kissed him lightly on the mouth.

The Chungking Restaurant in Yu Chau Street was less than a quarter of a mile from the army barracks at Shamshuipo. A small eating house dimly lit with Chinese lanterns, it was a popular haunt with the Canadians most weekday evenings, but was invariably more dead than alive on a Saturday night, when most of the troops went downtown. Tonight was no exception; apart from Donovan, who was waiting for him in a booth near the kitchen, there were only two Canadians present and Ramsay could see at a glance that they were far too busy feeling up a couple of bar girls to take any notice of him. Feeding the jukebox in the corner with coins, he punched five buttons at random and then joined Donovan.

'Been here long, Bill?' he asked.

'About ten minutes.' Donovan pointed to a bottle of San Miguel. 'I ordered a beer for you.'

'Thanks.' Ramsay felt the bottle, found that it was still ice-cold, and filled his glass slowly. Two booths away, peals of high-pitched laughter rose above 'The Best Things in Life are Free', wafting over from the jukebox.

'The girls are trying to teach those Cannucks to use chopsticks,' Donovan told him solemnly.

'Is that what all the giggling is about?'

'You only need one hand for chopsticks, George.'

'Is that a fact?' Ramsay took a draught, then topped up his glass and placed the empty bottle on one side. 'How does it feel to be back with the CID again, Bill?'

'You mean Kellerman okayed it?' Donovan stared at him. 'I don't believe it. What did you do to him?'

'Twisted his balls,' said Ramsay.

'I bet he hollered.'

'He did at first, but then I let go and he sort of quietened down.'

'First you squeeze a hundred thousand dollars out of Ramon Garcia, then you lean on Kellerman. I don't know how you do it, George.'

'Didn't anyone tell you? I'm a genius.'

The record changed on the jukebox and Vera Lynn began to sing 'I don't Want to Set the World on Fire'. Raising a hand, Ramsay signalled the waiter to bring them two more beers.

Donovan said, 'I reckon the Japs are just about to do that at any moment.'

'Do what?'

'Set the world on fire. The Royal Rifles of Canada and the Winnipeg Grenadiers have been loading their ammunition trucks all day. I hear they're moving over to the Island tomorrow, while the 2nd Royal Scots, the 5th/7th Rajputs and the 2nd/14th Punjabis occupy the Gin Drinkers Line. Two battalions going one way, while three others pass them heading in the opposite direction.' Donovan shook his head. 'Seems crazy to me.'

'It would, but then you're not a General.'

'Too bloody right I'm not.'

'And we've got more important matters to discuss.'

'Like Jill Hammond?' Donovan suggested.

'Right first time,' said Ramsay.

Hammond gazed at the telephone, his right hand playing a thumb and four-finger exercise on the desk. Half an hour ago, Tom Blakeney had phoned the Branch Manager's office to say that he, Rhoda and Jill had arrived at the Peninsula Hotel nextdoor, and when was he going to join them? Tom had been all too understanding when he'd tried to explain why it was out of the question; but when Jill had come on the line, she'd been anything but accommodating. 'The ballroom's full of men in uniform,' she'd said tartly; 'so why the hell is my husband the only officer who can't leave his post for an hour or so?' Hammond sighed; countering that argument would have been an impossible task anyway, but she'd hung up on him before he had a chance to get in so much as a word in his defence.

Jill had a point, though. Nobody on the board had suggested that he should live with the bullion, and he'd never lost a night's sleep when the gold reserves had been lodged in the vaults of the Head Office on Des Voeux Road. So why all the fuss now? Security was just as stringent at the Kowloon branch, and quite apart from the normal anti-intruder devices, there were an extra four armed police officers on the premises. Between them, they had two pump-action Winchesters and two Thompson sub machine guns; one more captain in the Hong Kong Volunteers, armed with a .455 Webley revolver, was neither here nor there.

Unbuckling the web belt around his waist, Hammond locked the pistol and holster in the office safe and walked out into the main hall. Yeuh-Shen, the inspector in charge of the night detail, was perched on a camp stool behind the counter, his head below the level of the grille.

'I'm going to take an hour off,' Hammond told him. 'If anybody needs me, I'll be in the ballroom of the Peninsula Hotel.'

Yeuh-Shen nodded, picked up his shotgun in his left hand and followed Hammond to the side entrance. Taking a key from his pocket, he bent down, unlocked and raised the steel shutter. Then, unbolting the revolving door top and bottom, he stepped back out of the way. Hammond thanked him, said he would phone through to the manager's office to let Yeuh-Shen know when to expect him back, and then passed through the revolving door into the lobby of the Peninsula Hotel.

The charity ball was in full swing, the dance floor so jam-packed with couples that it took Hammond several minutes to spot Jill amongst the milling throng. Tom Blakeney had assured him that he would look after Jill in his absence, and Hammond saw he was doing just that, holding her close, while his right hand moved up and down her spine in seductive caressing movements. Gyrating slowly, Blakeney eventually saw him and lifted his right hand in a friendly wave. Jill turned her head, flashed a brilliant smile in his direction, then pointed towards the bandstand and signalled she would join him in a minute. Edging his way round the dance floor, Hammond gravitated towards the bandstand, where he found Rhoda sitting alone at a small table, a bottle of champagne in an ice-bucket within easy reach.

Rhoda was the wrong side of forty. A former nurse, she had married Tom Blakeney in 1929, six months after she had arrived in Hong Kong to take up the appointment of theatre sister at St Thomas's Hospital. Her friends told her that she had hooked one of the Colony's most handsome and eligible bachelors, and they were right. Even in those far-off days, everybody who was anybody in the insurance world knew that Tom would eventually become the General Manager of Cathay Prudential; the one thing no one had foreseen at the time was that twelve years on and approaching fifty, Tom would still regard himself as the most eligible bachelor in town. Although, in the main, Rhoda had learned to live with his roving eye, she hated to feel neglected. It showed in the way she tapped her foot on the floor and in the sulky expression of her mouth, two outward signs that made it easy for Hammond to guess what was running through her mind.

'Having a good time then, Rhoda?' Hammond said, pulling out a chair.

'Hullo, David.' Rhoda looked up at him and smiled. 'So you managed to get away after all?'

'Only for an hour or so.'

'Still, better than nothing.' Rhoda lifted the magnum from the ice-bucket and filled a spare glass with champagne. 'Have some bubbly and help the war effort. They charged Tom eighty dollars for this bottle; the excess profit goes towards "Bombers for Britain".'

'So I guess the committee must have raised the hundred and sixty thousand pounds they were aiming for?'

'That and more,' said Rhoda. Her lip curled. 'Our Chinese friends have been particularly generous. I hear Li Ho Chung has donated forty thousand.'

'Dollars?'

'Pounds.' Rhoda helped herself to more champagne. 'No doubt he's hoping to get a knighthood out of it.'

'I can think of more deserving candidates.'

'Who couldn't? The Hong Kong Chinese are all the same; they believe in backing every likely horse in the race. Tom says some of the richer merchants have already started buying all the diamonds they can lay their hands on.'

'That's a sign of the times,' Hammond said dryly.

'Yes. Well, in their shoes I would buy gold.'

'Diamonds are easier to hide from the Japanese.'

'I hadn't thought of that.' Rhoda toyed with her glass, twiddling the stem between thumb and index finger. 'Do you think I should buy some?'

'It's a little late in the day, but you might find them useful.' He thought it best not to mention that the Japanese would undoubtedly search Rhoda before they put her in an internment camp. Some things were best left unsaid.

'I bet Li Ho Chung and his kind have already cleaned up the market.'

'Really?' Hammond lit two cigarettes and gave one to Rhoda. 'When did the panic buying start, then?' he asked casually.

'Yesterday – or was it Thursday?' Rhoda frowned. 'You'd better ask Tom, he's the expert.'

'Ask me what?'

Hammond felt a hand on his shoulder and looked round. Jill brushed his cheek with her lips, breathed a 'Hello, darling' in his ear and then sat down beside him, all sweetness and light now that she had got her own way.

'Ask me what?' Blakeney repeated.

'Rhoda was telling me there's a sudden boom in diamond buying and I asked her when it had started.'

'I heard about it last night; my contacts tell me the rush started early on Friday morning.' Blakeney slid into a chair between Rhoda and Jill. 'You can't blame the Chinese, David – they're only following your example.'

'My example?'

'The Hong Kong and Shanghai Bank.' Blakeney leaned forward and lowered his voice. 'The big boys all know you're sending the gold reserves out of the Colony.'

'So that's what all the fuss has been about,' Jill said brightly.

Her tone of voice was a warning to Hammond: unless he killed the speculation there and then, she was liable to go on and mention Captain Leslie Venables, the unwanted dinner guest he'd foisted on her at such short notice.

'That's ridiculous, Tom,' he snapped.

'Oh, come on, David, I've been around too long for you to try and pull the wool over my eyes.'

Hammond supposed it was inevitable that word of the transfer should have leaked out. Too many of the bank's employees had been involved in the operation, and although they had all been screened beforehand, no vetting system was infallible. Someone had either been guilty of careless talk, or else the speculators had had inside information.

'You don't have to worry, David. The people in the know will keep it to themselves. It's as much in their interest as yours to prevent a run on the bank.'

'I hope you're right, Tom,' he said.

'Are you two men going to talk shop all evening?' Rhoda said impatiently.

'No,' said Hammond, 'I'm about to take the floor with my wife.'

Quarrie looked at the ice cubes melting in his empty glass, then glanced at Malcolm Vines, the gossip columnist of the *South China Morning Post*. 'Same again?' he asked.

'Might as well,' said Vines.

Quarrie signalled to the barman for two Scotch on the rocks, then turned sideways on the high stool to watch the dance floor. 'This is some shindig,' he murmured.

'The social gathering of the year, Harold.'

Quarrie was prepared to believe him. There were times when he got the impression that Vines spent every spare minute of the day immersed in the pages of *Debrett, Burke's Peerage* and *Who's Who*. A snob, and one of the most boring men he'd ever had the misfortune to meet, Quarrie only tolerated him because he was a source of useful background information. In his experience, it often paid to know who was hopping into bed with who else's wife.

Vines said, 'There are some faces that are conspicuous by their absence, though. Li Ho Chung for one.'

'Is that a fact?' Li Ho Chung was of little interest to Quarrie at that particular moment. Amongst the couples on the floor, he had suddenly spotted Katherine Goddard dancing with a second lieutenant in the Hong Kong Volunteers. 'Do you know who that girl is, Malcolm?' he said, pointing her out.

'A nobody,' Vines said contemptuously. 'I forget her name, but she's the resident nurse at the Peninsula Hotel.'

A nobody? That's all you know, Quarrie thought. He had a hunch that wherever Katherine Goddard was, Frank Waldron would not be far away.

'Now there's what I call a really attractive woman,' said Vines.

'Where?'

'Jill Hammond, that dark-haired girl over there in the slinky black dress.'

'Very nice,' Quarrie said appreciatively. 'You must introduce me sometime.'

'Feeling randy, are you, Harold?' Vines smiled and shook his head. 'You'd better look elsewhere. You won't get very far with Jill Hammond.'

'A regular tease, is she?'

'You could say that. Tom Blakeney certainly had a fine old time fondling her bottom until her husband arrived, and then she became all prim and proper.'

'Wise girl,' said Quarrie.

'Oh, she knows which side her bread is buttered all right. And David Hammond certainly isn't the kind of man I'd care to tangle with.'

Quarrie nodded. 'You and I appear to be the only two civilians here,' he said, changing the subject.

'There must be something wrong with your eyesight, Harold. I can see dozens.'

'Yeah? Well, it seems to me that the entire army, navy and air force are attending this jamboree.' Quarrie looked back over his shoulder, saw that the barman was hovering expectantly and peeled off a ten dollar note. 'I'd have thought they had better things to do – digging trenches, for one.'

'Well, you know what we British are like,' Vines said pompously. 'We pride ourselves on keeping a stiff upper lip – Drake calmly finishing his game of bowls on Plymouth Hoe before destroying the Armada, the Duchess of Richmond's Ball on the eve of Waterloo – all that sort of thing.'

'Somehow, Malcolm, I don't think this is going to be another Waterloo.'

'Neither do I,' said Vines. 'The Japs aren't going to invade us – they've got their hands full with Chiang Kai-shek.'

Vines couldn't have been more wrong. Thirty miles to the

north, Colonel Doi Teihichi was briefing the battalion commanders of the 228th Imperial Japanese Infantry Regiment. Their
objective was the Shingmun Redoubt, the key defensive position of the Gin Drinkers Line, and the marked maps they had
been issued with showed the exact location of every pillbox.

SUNDAY
7th DECEMBER 1941

CHAPTER TEN

Waldron swung his feet off the couch and sat up, rubbing a crick in his neck. His eyes still bleary with sleep, he peered at the electric clock high up on the opposite wall and was surprised to see that it was only eight-thirty. The glare from the sun between a chink in the drawn curtains and the stuffy atmosphere inside the room had made him think it was later than that.

His gaze fell on the whisky bottle and the ashtray brimming with cigarette stubs on the coffee table, two visible reminders that the Tin Hat Ball last night had ended somewhat prematurely, and on a despondent note. Shortly before midnight, the President of the American Steamship Line had appeared on the balcony above the dance floor and appealed for silence. Then, through a megaphone, he'd announced that all merchant seamen whose ships were in harbour were to report for duty at once, and there had been a sudden exodus. Katherine had told him this when she'd returned to the apartment, tense and preoccupied. 'You look as though you need a pick-me-up,' he'd suggested, and Katherine had produced a bottle of Haig and two glasses from a cupboard in the sideboard. They had drunk three, maybe four whiskies each, smoked God knows how many cigarettes and talked a lot. He supposed they must have gotten a little maudlin in the process, and then one thing had led to another and they had made love. It was as simple as that – or was it? They had known each other for less than three days, and no two people could have come together under less auspicious circumstances; but there had been a mutual attraction right from the start. It wasn't something he could explain, but these things did happen; two strangers would meet and there would be a certain chemistry between them and they would know straight off that they would always get on together. And that was the trouble; 'always' meant at all times, meant a state of continuity. And there was unlikely to be much continuity in their lives.

Waldron got up, walked over to the window and drew back the curtains. The street was deserted, the shops on the opposite side of the road shuttered and barred. For all the panic last night, it was just another peaceful Sunday morning. He wondered how much longer it would last.

His face clean-shaven and smelling of eau de cologne, Ramsay left the barber's shop on Nathan Road, walked fifty yards on down the street towards the Star Ferry and then turned into Gingle's restaurant. A large fat man who was never without his malacca cane, Gingle was somewhere in his mid-fifties. Known only by his surname, he had served in the United States Navy during the 1914-18 War and had at some time in the past been connected with the fight game, though in exactly what capacity had never been clear to Ramsay. The informal photographs of Gene Tunney, Jack Dempsey and a very youthful-looking Joe Louis displayed behind the long bar suggested that he had owned a gym in downtown New York, but on the one occasion Ramsay had asked him, Gingle had neither confirmed nor denied it. Just why he had chosen to open a restaurant in Hong Kong was something of a mystery, but whatever the reason, he'd made a name for himself, serving good food at reasonable prices and staying open at all hours of the day and night. Gingle's also happened to be the only restaurant in Kowloon that served breakfast on a Sunday.

Choosing a table in the window, Ramsay consulted the menu. Usually for him, breakfast consisted of a cup of coffee and two slices of toast, but he had been up since five that morning and there was no telling when he would eat again. Beckoning to a waiter, he ordered a sirloin steak with two fried eggs sunny side up and then lit his first cigarette of the day.

Although everything had gone like clockwork so far, the real test would come when he telephoned Jill Hammond at ten-thirty. He had told Donovan exactly what he proposed to say to her, but while the story had sounded plausible enough to both their ears, it was difficult to predict how she would respond when she heard that her husband had suddenly been taken to hospital. Supposing she reacted like some women he knew and rang a close friend? That was the kind of last-minute snag he could do without. The only solution to that problem was to keep Jill Hammond on the phone until Donovan arrived at the house.

Perfect timing, ruthless execution and an element of luck; that was all they needed to pull it off. Of these three essential requirements, Ramsay knew he could rely on Donovan to be utterly ruthless. For all his easy-going manner, the renegade Irishman was ice-cold, exactly the kind of man the Intelligence officers at Dublin Castle had been looking for when they decided to take a leaf out of Michael Collins' book and form their own murder gang to combat the IRA. Perfect timing was something else; you could work out how long the job would take and allow for a margin of error, but there was always the unexpected – the servant who appeared at just the wrong moment, or the friend who dropped by uninvited. The element of luck was something nobody could predict; it was either running your way or it wasn't.

The waiter approached his table with a tray and placed his breakfast order in front of him. Stubbing the cigarette out in the ashtray, Ramsay picked up his knife and fork and began to attack the steak and eggs. There was, he thought, no point in dwelling on matters that were beyond his control. Better to review the moves he'd already executed and see if he had overlooked anything. The bank? No potential hitches there that he could see. The shift had changed at 0600 hours and he had contrived to get Hammond out of the office long enough for Adams to unscrew the mouthpiece of his telephone and discon-nect the two wires inside. With the chief cashier's phone jiggered in the same fashion, there was no way Hammond could contact his wife unless he used one of the pay phones in the Peninsula Hotel. If he was so inclined, Adams would use every pretext to prevent him doing so before ten-thirty. After that, it didn't matter a damn what time he tried to phone his wife, because she wouldn't be there to answer the call.

He wasn't worried about Kellerman. The Assistant Commissioner could drop in on the Kowloon branch any time between now and 2200 hours and he wouldn't find anything to complain about. But it could be a different story when the final shift came on duty; then, Kellerman might wonder how it was that Thirsk, Donovan and Adams were on watch together, and he'd need to be ready with a plausible explanation.

No immediate problems, then. Time to finish his breakfast in peace, drive back to his flat in Chatham Road and pack a few things into a suitcase before calling Jill Hammond.

'How's the steak?' asked a deep nasal voice.

Ramsay looked up and found Gingle standing by his shoulder. 'It's very tasty,' he said.

'Good.' Gingle took out a handkerchief and mopped his face. 'Feels like it's going to be a warm day.'

'The signs are all there.'

'And a busy one for the army, too,' Gingle continued.

Ramsay followed his gaze and looked out of the window in time to see a single-decker bus drive past the restaurant heading towards the Star Ferry terminal. It was jam-packed with Canadians.

'That's the third busload of troops I've seen in as many minutes,' Gingle said.

'Really? I hadn't noticed.' Ramsay finished the steak, placed the knife and fork together and poured himself a cup of coffee.

'I can see I'm going to lose a lot of customers.'

'War is hell, Gingle, or so they tell me.'

'You think those little yellow bastards across the border are about to pay us a visit?'

'It's on the cards,' said Ramsay.

Sergeant Lee dismounted from his bicycle fifty yards short of Carlton Mansions and padlocked the chain to the crank. He had been released from the bank detail at two o'clock on Saturday afternoon and except for a hurried meal with his family, had spent the rest of the day and most of the night running down every informant who had passed him worthwhile information in the last six months. It had been a total waste of time and effort. No matter what Ramsay might think so far as the Triads were concerned, none of the men he had spoken to had ever heard of Sub Inspector Pascoe. Only the fear of finding himself teamed up with Adams again had persuaded Lee to pursue his inquiries; and it would be premature to submit a written report, he decided, before visiting the scene of the fatal hit-and-run accident in Boundary Street.

Apart from black tyre marks which showed where the car had mounted the kerb, there wasn't much to see. Visibility had been down to under forty feet at the time, and a friend in the Traffic Department had told him that Pascoe's injuries indicated that the vehicle had been doing between twenty-five and thirty miles an hour when it had struck him. No witnesses had come forward, and although the investigating officers had interviewed every resident in the neighbourhood, it appeared nobody had either seen or heard the accident. The car had almost certainly been damaged by the impact, and as a matter of routine, they had visited every garage in Kowloon and warned the owners to report any vehicle sent in for repair that looked as though it had been involved in a traffic accident. But it was a long shot, and Lee reckoned the police would be extremely lucky if that line of inquiry produced any tangible results.

He walked on a few paces and then turned about to examine the tyre marks from a different angle. The mist had been a thick grey blanket, and nobody who was sober would do more than ten to fifteen miles an hour in such adverse conditions. On the other hand, assuming he was drunk, Lee thought it remarkable that the driver had regained control of the car so rapidly after mounting the pavement. The skid marks suggested that he had stamped on the brakes the moment he saw Pascoe; but it could be that he'd put his foot down on the accelerator and the rear wheels had spun on the moist surface before finding a purchase. Murder or manslaughter?

Lee reached inside his jacket, took out his notebook and

checked the list of names the investigating officers had questioned. Top of the list was Pascoe's house servant, but she had
been unable to help the police because she lived out and the
accident had occurred before she came into work. He wondered
if the woman would show up today. Not that it mattered all that
much; if she was there, he would wave his warrant card under
her nose; if she wasn't, he had the means to let himself into
Pascoe's apartment. Lee bent down and removed the cycle clips
from his trousers; then, stuffing them into his jacket pocket, he
walked on down the road and strolled into Carlton Mansions.

Checking the list of residents displayed on the board inside
the hallway, he saw that Pascoe had occupied flat number 2 on
the ground floor, which was on the right beyond the staircase. A
cautious man, he rang the bell several times, and when satisfied
there was no one in the apartment, took out a bunch of skeleton
keys from his pocket, found one that fitted the yale lock and
opened the door.

The flat consisted of a kitchen, a lounge-diner and a medium-
sized bedroom with a bathroom *en suite*. Most of the furniture
had been provided by the landlord, and Pascoe appeared to
have added very little to the basic necessities. There were two
suits, a pair of cavalry twill trousers and a sports jacket hanging
up in the wardrobe, none of which looked particularly expensive, and the shirts in the chest of drawers certainly weren't
hand made. There were few potential hiding-places in the
bedroom; the fitted carpet had been laid with underfelt over a
concrete floor, and the mattress on the divan bed had not been
tampered with. He checked all the drawers and looked under
and behind every item of furniture, but nothing had been taped
to any of the flat surfaces. Determined not to overlook anything, he lifted the two suitcases down from on top of the
wardrobe and then measured them to see if either one had been
fitted with a false bottom.

One down, two to go, Lee thought as he moved into the
lounge-diner. He checked the pictures on the wall, examined
the dining room table and chairs, and stripped the hessian from
the three-piece suite so that he could look inside the sofa and

armchairs. Then, using a penknife, he loosened one of the oak blocks on the floor and lifted it up, only to find that the strips had been laid on concrete. Still not satisfied, he walked up and down the room, testing every square foot with his weight to see if there was a cavity underneath. He opened the writing desk, found a wad of Pascoe's bank statements in one of the pigeon-holes and scanning them very quickly, noted that the average credit balance at the end of each month was under twenty Hong Kong dollars.

A search of the kitchen proved equally fruitless. After rooting around inside the broom cupboard, looking under the sink, behind the electric cooker and pulling the refrigerator out from the wall, Lee came to the conclusion that if Pascoe was on a Triad payroll, he was inordinately clever at concealing it. Angry with himself for having doubted the man's honesty, he left the apartment and walked out into the street.

A thin figure wearing a black pyjama suit emerged from the alleyway between the apartments on the opposite side of the road and started walking towards Kai Tak. Lee thought he looked vaguely familiar. But what was a coolie doing in this neighbourhood on a Sunday? Then suddenly the penny dropped and remembering where he had seen him before, he started across the road. The youth heard him coming, turned his head, and seeing who it was, took off at the double.

It was an uneven contest. Lee was in the peak of physical condition and had won the hundred and two-twenty-yard sprints at the annual police athletics meeting for the past three years, while the youth was half-starved and riddled with TB. Overhauling him rapidly, Lee stretched out a hand, grabbed hold of his collar and pulled him up. The youth swung round, lashed out with his arms and legs and spat in his face; then, gasping for breath, he doubled up in a paroxysm of coughing, the fight gone out of him. Lee seized his wrists and held them in a vice-like grip while he waited for him to recover his breath.

'Take it easy,' he said, 'I'm not going to hurt you.'

The youth didn't believe him, and with some cause. His nose was still mis-shapen and swollen where Adams had hit him.

'What's your name?' Lee asked quietly.

'Shih Sai-loong.'

The hazel eyes regarded him warily, but at least they were making some progress. 'That's better.' Lee smiled. 'You don't have to be frightened of me. I'm not like the big man, the one who hit you.'

'Then why are you holding me?'

'I don't really know.' Lee released his wrists and stepped back a pace. 'You haven't done anything wrong, have you?'

'Of course not. I'm not a thief.'

'So why did you run away when you saw me?'

'Because I knew you were a policeman.' Sai-loong bit his lip and looked down at the pavement. 'And I thought you were angry with me for coming back here.'

'If you believed that, you should have stayed away.'

'I was hungry and I was looking for something to eat.'

'Around here?' Lee said incredulously.

'There's plenty of food in the dustbins.'

'I should have thought of that.' Lee scowled. The English were notoriously wasteful, and it angered him that someone like Shih Sai-loong, a refugee from the Japanese, should be treated no better than a stray dog. 'How long have you been living like this?' he asked.

'Who knows? One day is like another.'

'Not always. Yesterday morning was different; there was a thick early morning mist and a man was killed not far from here.'

'I know.'

'You saw the accident?' Lee said quickly.

'I saw a car,' Sai-loong said reluctantly. 'It came slowly, its eyes gleaming.'

The car had been going towards Kai Tak and had stopped near the alleyway where Sai-loong was sleeping. A man had got out and walked across the road; moments later he had returned and driven off down the road, out of sight but not out of earshot. Somewhere in the mist, he had turned round and parked the car on the other side of the road.

'I heard him get out again and close the door very quietly. Later there were footsteps going that way.' Sai-loong pointed over Lee's shoulder towards Nathan Road.

'And?' Lee prompted.

'Well, then the car drove past me going very fast and there was a loud bang.'

'What did you do?'

'I ran away.'

Lee nodded; it was the answer he'd expected. Shih Sai-loong wasn't stupid; he knew that what he'd witnessed hadn't been an accident and he wanted no part of it.

'You must have seen the driver?' he said.

'Yes.' Shih Sai-loong gazed into the far distance as though in a trance.

'So what was he like?' Lee demanded impatiently.

'Tall with big shoulders and a long face, like all the white men have.'

Suddenly, everything was far too complicated; suddenly, Lee felt out of his depth and found himself wishing that Pascoe had simply been knocked down and killed by a drunken driver.

Ramsay left the suitcase and overnight bag in the hall and went into the lounge. Opening the sideboard, he took out a bottle of Haig, fixed himself a large whisky and soda, and then sat down in an armchair near the telephone. Although it was a little early in the day to be drinking, he needed something to help him relax and unwind. He told himself that everything was going smoothly, that Donovan would have caught the vehicular ferry on time and was now approaching Macdonnel Road, but it didn't ease the nervous tension. His experiences in the last war had taught him that no matter how good a plan might seem in theory, there was a tendency for it to come unstuck soon after it was translated into action.

Any number of things could go wrong. Who could guarantee that the self-drive Ford V8 sedan that Donovan was supposed to have hired from Shau-chi would not develop a mechanical fault between Kowloon and Macdonnel Road? What if Donovan were to be involved in a minor traffic accident and some police constable asked to see the vehicle documents and found they didn't match up with the licence plates? The list of possibilities was endless and didn't bear thinking about.

Ramsay glanced at his wristwatch, gulped down the rest of his whisky and set the glass down on the occasional table. Then, lifting the receiver off the hook, he dialled 135462 and waited. The number rang out for a good two minutes before a cool, well-modulated voice answered.

'Mrs Hammond?' Ramsay asked politely.

'Yes. Who's that?'

'My name's Kellerman,' Ramsay said. 'I'm the Assistant Commissioner of Police in charge of the Kowloon division.'

'Oh yes?'

Her voice told him that she was puzzled and not a little apprehensive. 'There's no need to be alarmed, Mrs Hammond, but your husband has had a slight accident.' Ramsay heard a sharp intake of breath and hastened to reassure her. 'Believe me, it's nothing serious. It's just that he was on his way down to the vaults when he slipped and banged his head on one of the concrete steps. Although he wasn't knocked unconscious, we thought it best not to take any chances, so one of my officers drove him to Kowloon General Hospital to have his skull X-rayed.'

'I see.' Jill Hammond cleared her throat, then said, 'Where is David now, Mr Kellerman?'

Ramsay smiled; she had remembered the name just as he'd hoped she would. 'He's still at the hospital. The X-rays were negative and the doctor tells me there are no signs of concussion, but your husband did fall rather awkwardly and I'm afraid he fractured his left wrist.'

'How badly?'

'I think they said it was a greenstick fracture, but it seems your husband had breakfast at eight-thirty this morning, which means they've got to wait four hours before giving him an anaesthetic.'

'Otherwise he'd be sick.'

'Exactly,' said Ramsay. 'Unfortunately, the doctors are unable to convince Mr Hammond that it's in his interests to wait, and he's adamant that he must return to the bank.'

'That sounds like David all right.'

'Yes, well, I thought that perhaps you might be able to talk some sense into him, Mrs Hammond.'

'I can try.'

'Good.' Ramsay clenched the phone with a sweaty hand. Donovan should have been there by now, and he was running out of ideas to keep her on the phone. 'I hope you won't think I've been too presumptuous,' he said, 'but I've arranged for Inspector Donaldson to collect you.'

'Inspector Donaldson?'

'Yes. I believe you met him the other day?'

'Oh, you mean the charming Irishman?'

'Quite.' Ramsay thought her description of Donovan fitted him to a T. Obviously he'd made a very favourable impression on her.

'When can I expect your Inspector Donaldson?'

'He should be with you any minute now.'

'How right you are, Mr Kellerman. I think I can hear a car in the drive now.' The phone went down with a clatter; a few seconds later, Jill Hammond picked it up again, thanked him for being so thoughtful, said a hurried goodbye and hung up.

'Perfect timing,' Ramsay said, replacing his phone with a sigh of relief.

After collecting his suitcase and overnight bag from the hall, he let himself out of the flat. Two minutes later, he backed the Chevrolet out of the driveway and went on down to the bank.

Donovan got out of the Ford sedan, walked round to the back and unlocked the trunk. Raising the lid a few inches, he reached inside, took out the cotton pad that had been soaked with ether and cupped it in the palm of his right hand. Everything was looking good; the car was invisible from the road, and the tall hedge screened the driveway from the neighbouring houses. Without a backward glance, he walked boldly into the porch and rang the bell. In that same instant, he heard the *clip-clop* of high heels in the hall and guessed that Jill Hammond had just finished talking to Ramsay. Then the door opened and she greeted him with a fleeting, nervous smile.

Donovan said, 'Hello, Mrs Hammond. I expect you know why I'm here?'

'Yes.' She nodded, closed the door behind her and moved towards the car. 'Mr Kellerman telephoned me a few minutes ago.'

'Then he'll have told you there's nothing to worry about,' Donovan said cheerfully.

'I'll believe that when I see David,' she said in a subdued voice.

'Well, take my word for it, your husband's doing just fine. He's the healthiest-looking invalid I ever saw.'

Donovan reached past her and opened the nearside door of the Ford sedan with his left hand. He stepped back, opening the door to its fullest extent; then, as she moved forward and ducked her head below the sill, he grabbed her from behind in a bear hug and clapped the pad over her nose and mouth. The face mask had been soaked with enough ether to put out an orang-outang, and after the first sharp intake of breath, she sagged at the knees and went out like a light.

Lifting Jill Hammond in his arms as though carrying his bride over the threshold, Donovan walked round to the back, opened the trunk with a knee and dumped her limp body inside. That done, he slammed the lid down and got in behind the wheel. Cranking the engine into life, he shifted into first gear and drove out into Macdonnel Road.

Although the cook and number one houseboy lived in, they hadn't seen him, which Donovan thought was just as well for them. Had either one of them put in an appearance, there would have been two less Chinamen on the island. Whistling cheerfully to himself, he turned into Garden Road and went down the hill to Victoria.

CHAPTER ELEVEN

Ramsay parked the Chevrolet in Hankow Road, grabbed his overnight bag from the passenger seat, locked all four doors and then walked through the arcade into the Peninsula Hotel. The lobby was practically deserted; three members of the staff were pasting strips of brown paper over the windowpanes to strengthen the glass against blast in case the Japanese decided to bomb Kowloon, and one of the elderly permanent residents was seated in an armchair, busy knitting what appeared to be an outsized cardigan. None of them paid the slightest attention to Ramsay as he strolled towards the side entrance of the bank.

Adams knew to the exact minute when to expect him back. As he drew near the revolving door, Ramsay saw that the steel shutter on the inside had been raised in anticipation of his return and smiled approvingly. Adams grinned back at him through the glass and then drew the bolts top and bottom of the door, allowing him to pass through into the main hall of the bank.

'How's everything?' Ramsay asked casually.

'We've got a small problem with the telephones. Both of them are on the blink.'

'Oh?' Ramsay contrived to sound perplexed and raised his voice for the benefit of the Chinese detective constable guarding the main entrance. 'When did you discover this?'

'Mr Hammond told me he'd tried to phone his wife and couldn't get through.' Adams pointed towards the lobby. 'He left the bank about five minutes ago, said he was going to use one of the booths in the hotel to call the exchange.'

Ramsay nodded. Most likely, Hammond would try to phone his wife again after reporting the fault. What happened then largely depended on what he learned from the servants, assuming the houseboy answered the telephone.

Telling Adams to stay by the side door, Ramsay walked over

to the counter, opened the gate and went into the chief cashier's office. Aware that every second counted, he closed the door behind him, dumped his overnight bag on the desk and lifted the phone off the cradle. A purring noise told him that Adams had already restored it to working order. So far so good, he thought, but they weren't out of the woods yet. Unzipping the overnight bag, Ramsay took out a small screwdriver, slipped it into his pocket and walked out of the office.

'I thought you told me the phones were out of order?' he said in a loud voice.

Adams turned away from the revolving door, saw that the detective constable had looked up from the newspaper he was reading, and took his cue from Ramsay. 'They were a few minutes ago.' He shrugged his shoulders. 'Maybe the telephone company discovered the fault for themselves and rectified it?'

'You're probably right,' Ramsay said. 'All the same, I think I'd better check the other phone to make sure.'

It wasn't necessary to prolong the charade; the detective constable had lost interest in their conversation and had gone back to his newspaper.

Entering the manager's office, Ramsay left the door slightly ajar and then went to work on the telephone. His hands steady as a rock, he unscrewed the mouthpiece, shook out the diaphragm, inserted the two leads under the retaining screws and tightened them down with the screwdriver. That done, he re-assembled the mouthpiece, depressed the bell buttons on the cradle and replaced the receiver. Seconds later, the sound of English voices in the hall told him that Hammond was back and he walked boldly out of the office to greet him with a cheerful 'Hello, David.'

Hammond said, ''Lo George. How long have you been here?'

'About five minutes.' Ramsay smiled. 'Inspector Adams tells me both telephones have been on the blink.'

'Yes, I've just reported the fault to the telephone company. They're sending an engineer over to have a look at them.'

'He'll be wasting his time, David; they're back in working order.'

'That's strange. A few minutes ago, the switchboard operator told me that she'd tried both numbers and they were definitely out of order.'

'The switchboard's obviously at sixes and sevens this morning. I suppose that's no surprise, all things considered.' Ramsay opened the gate in the counter for Hammond and stepped aside to allow him to pass through. 'I mean, the whole garrison is on the move – the switchboard must be jammed with calls.'

'That's one possible explanation,' Hammond said.

'And inefficiency's another. I reckon you'd need an adding machine to compute just how many crossed lines and wrong numbers people have been getting this morning.'

'Are you speaking from personal experience?'

'I phoned Shamshuipo police station a while back and got the China Light and Power Company.'

'On a Sunday?' Hammond raised a sceptical eyebrow.

'Well, I admit it's a bit unusual to find the management working, but as I say, there's a flap on.' Ramsay snapped his fingers. 'Which reminds me – one of us had better call the phone company and tell them we don't need their lineman.'

'Yes, I suppose so.'

'I'll do it if you like,' Ramsay said.

'It's very kind of you, George, but I don't see why you should be put to that trouble.'

'It's no trouble, David. Besides, I've got nothing better to do at the moment.'

Hammond was vaguely surprised that Ramsay was so eager to please him, but then George had gone out of his way to establish a close and cordial working relationship almost from the very moment they had been introduced to one another. Hammond thanked him and went into the manager's office. Closing the door behind him, he walked over to the desk and sat down. There was, he thought, little point in phoning the house again; Chan Chak, the number one houseboy, had told him that Missy Hammond wasn't at home and no, he didn't know where she had gone. All he knew was that the telephone had rung and then Missy had left the house and he had heard her drive off in a car. Hammond had phoned the Blakeneys after that, but there had been no answer; it was possible they'd invited Jill to go to church with them. The Blakeneys weren't regular church-goers, but they did attend Matins every now and again, usually if they were going on to a drinks party after the service.

Hammond glanced at his wristwatch. Eleven-fifteen; if the Blakeneys had gone to church, it would be a waste of time calling them again before twelve. All the same, he was worried about Jill. Lifting the phone off the hook, he rang the Blakeneys again. The number rang out for what seemed an eternity, then Rhoda came on the line.

Hammond said, 'Hullo, Rhoda, it's me, David.'

'Well, hullo,' Rhoda said, 'this is a pleasant surprise.' She sounded as though she was genuinely pleased to hear from him. 'Was it you who rang earlier on, David?'

'Yes. I thought you and Tom might have gone to church.'

'I was in the garden. You rang off before I could get to the phone.'

'I might have guessed there'd be some simple explanation.' Hammond paused. Reluctant to ask Rhoda if she knew where Jill was, he backed off and sought a more indirect approach. 'Is Tom there?' he asked casually.

'I'm afraid he's gone down to the air raid post on Queens Road. I gather all the wardens in the district are required to attend a briefing or some such nonsense.'

Nonsense was the right word. If Tom was attending a briefing, it was the first he'd heard about it. More likely, he'd taken Jill out to his beach house in Big Wave Bay on the east coast and was busy screwing her.

'Can I take a message, David?'

Hammond bit his lip. 'No,' he said, 'it's not that important. Tell you what, though – perhaps you'd ask Tom to call me at the bank when he gets back?'

Rhoda said she would do that small thing, wished him a cheery goodbye and hung up. Hammond put the phone down and then sat there, sick at heart, staring blankly into space.

When was it Jill had told him she thought she was pregnant?

Thursday? Or was it only the day before yesterday? What the hell did it matter anyway? Chances were it wouldn't be his child she was carrying . . . Then he pulled himself up short, ashamed of his suspicions; Jill had never given him cause to doubt her. Maybe Tom was in the habit of fondling her whenever he got the chance, but that didn't necessarily mean Jill enjoyed it. Or did she? She hadn't attempted to move Tom's hands away from her buttocks when he saw them dancing close together last night. There was, however, one sure way of putting a stop to the affair before any real damage was done; all it would take was a word in Rhoda's ear and Tom would run a mile.

Hammond reached for the phone again, then paused, his eyes suddenly drawn to the mouthpiece: it was askew. Odd that he hadn't noticed it until now. He lifted the receiver off the cradle to examine the mouthpiece more closely and saw that it was on cross-threaded. He supposed Ramsay must have unscrewed it when he checked the phone – except that George hadn't said anything about inspecting the instrument.

A sudden thought occurred to him and leaving the phone off the hook, he looked up the China Light and Power Company in the directory and then dialled 319555. A few moments later, a voice with a Welsh accent said, 'China Light and Power.'

Hammond said, 'I'm sorry, we seem to have a crossed line. I dialled 319550.'

'Really?' The Welshman clucked his tongue. 'Well, this is 319555.'

'I don't know what's wrong with the phones this morning,' Hammond said, doing his best to sound vexed. 'This is the fourth wrong number I've had in the past hour.'

'I've not had any problems with this line,' the Welshman said. 'Perhaps there's something the matter with the dial on your instrument. Sometimes they stick.'

Hammond said he hadn't thought of that, thanked him for the tip, apologized again and hung up. He leaned back in the chair, clasped both hands behind his neck and frowned up at the ceiling. He tried to reason out why Ramsay had lied to him, but his thoughts kept coming back to Jill.

Donovan pushed himself up out of the chair and walked over to the bed where Jill Hammond lay spreadeagled, her wrists and ankles lashed to the old-fashioned brass rails. She was still unconscious, breathing shallowly through the nose, and he wondered if she was in a coma. One thing was certain, Jill Hammond was going to be a very sick young woman when she did come round. Turning her head over on one side, Donovan removed the gag to prevent her inhaling her own vomit.

He went over to the window and looked down at the Ford V8 sedan parked in the courtyard of Kaznovetsky's restaurant. 'Perfect timing, ruthless execution and an element of luck'; those were Ramsay's words and the reason for their success. Any number of things could have gone wrong, but he'd had a clear run all the way from Macdonnel Road; no traffic jams in Victoria, no waiting for the vehicular ferry to Kowloon and no army convoys to delay him between Jordan Road and Kaznovetsky's. From then on, it was a piece of cake. He had backed the Ford sedan into the courtyard and checked with Larissa Kaznovetsky to make sure none of the staff were on duty in the kitchen; then he had lifted Jill Hammond out of the car trunk and carried her up to this small back room on the top floor.

Donovan heard the sound of light footsteps on the landing and turned away from the window. He knew Larissa was working in the office down the corridor, but the footsteps sounded as though they were coming towards the bedroom from the direction of the staircase, and they were a lot too stealthy for his liking. He slipped his right hand inside his jacket and curled his fingers round the butt of the .38 short-barrelled Colt revolver in the shoulder holster. Then the door opened inwards and Ramsay walked into the room.

Donovan said, 'You shouldn't go creeping around like that, George. You don't know how close you were to getting yourself shot.'

Ramsay ignored him, went over to the bed and stood there looking down at Jill Hammond. 'How much ether did you put on that pad, for Christ's sake?' he said quietly.

'Enough to put her to sleep for quite a while.'

'Or to put her out for good?'

Donovan shrugged. 'What are you beefing about, George? We'll have to kill her sooner or later. She knows too much.'

About you, Ramsay thought. Donovan was the only man at risk, the one potential weak link in the chain. 'Lesson number one,' he said. 'You don't discard the merchandise until it's served its purpose.'

'That's a very cryptic remark, George. What's it supposed to mean?'

'It means that right now Hammond doesn't know where his wife is, and he's beginning to sweat a little. Before I've finished, I intend to have him bathed in it. Unfortunately, he doesn't panic easily and he may turn out to be obstinate; if that's the case, we may just have to put Jill Hammond on the phone to make him jump through the hoop.'

'Even so, we can't risk turning her loose at the end of it,' Donovan said flatly.

'I know that, Bill.'

'So how are we going to dispose of her?'

'Don't worry, I've got it all figured out.' Ramsay lit a cigarette and blew a smoke ring towards the ceiling. 'Remember Chung Hom Kok?'

For a moment, Donovan was at a loss to see what Ramsay was getting at; then everything clicked and the innuendo became crystal-clear. Chung Hom Kok had been a small-time gangster, specializing in armed robbery. One Friday in September 1937, he had busted into a factory at Tsun Wan, seven miles north of Kowloon, and tried to steal the payroll. As Donovan remembered it, the cashier had refused to hand over the money and Hom Kok had shot him dead, but a Chinese girl in the outer office had sounded the alarm. Before he could make a getaway, two constables from the nearby police station had responded to the alarm and Chung Hom Kok had found himself bottled up inside the factory yard. Unwilling to give himself up, he had run back into the office and seized the girl as a hostage. Less than an hour later, Ramsay had arrived on the scene to lead the assault on the building. In the resultant shoot-out, Chung Hom Kok had been killed and the girl wounded in the leg.

Donovan laughed. 'You know something, George? I have a feeling Jill Hammond won't be quite as lucky as that Chinese girl.'

'You can bet on it,' said Ramsay.

'But we'll need a couple of dead kidnappers to make it look right.'

'Sure we will. Garcia's going to supply them. Naturally, I shan't tell him we're going to use them for target practice.' Ramsay saw the doubtful expression on Donovan's face and knew what he was thinking. 'You don't believe I can talk him into it, do you?' he said.

'Garcia won't buy it in a million years.'

Ramsay walked over to the window and looked down into the courtyard. 'Who did you hire the Ford sedan from, Bill?'

'Shau-chi's garage, like you told me to. And I switched the number plates.'

'Well then, do I have to spell it out for you?'

Donovan shook his head. Shau-chi was just a front man for the Red Spears Triad, and it didn't take much imagination to see how Ramsay would use the V8 sedan to tie Li Ho Chung in with the kidnapping of Jill Hammod, should Garcia seem uncooperative.

'You really have got it all figured out, haven't you, George?' he said admiringly.

'We'll be in trouble if I haven't.'

'Yes, well, you'll need to keep an eye on Larissa Kaznovetsky. Somehow I get the impression you're no longer quite as popular with her, George.'

Ramsay stubbed out his cigarette on the windowsill. 'Maybe you're right. I'd better have a word with Larissa and see what's on her mind.'

'You do that,' Donovan said, and pointed towards the office at the far end of the landing.

The account books were open on the desk, but Larissa Kaz-novetsky didn't seem particularly interested in them. She had a glass in one hand, a small cigar in the other and a faraway look in her eyes.

'What are you drinking?' Ramsay asked her quietly.

'Brandy.' Her speech was slurred, and he noticed the decan-ter was almost empty. 'You want to join me, George?'

'Why not?' Ramsay prised the glass from her grasp.

'Hey, that's my drink,' Larissa protested.

'So? You've had one too many already.' He was used to seeing Larissa drunk, had been ever since she had been forced to put her mad little sister into a private mental hospital. The periodic benders were usually prompted by a secret fear that insanity ran in the family – but not on this occasion. 'I hear you've got a bone to pick with me?' he said casually.

The explosion came ten seconds later, a long, venomous tirade which lasted all of five minutes. Much of it was incohe-rent and sprinkled with obscenities in both English and Rus-sian, but when Larissa finally got round to it, the ultimatum was absolutely clear.

'. . . Either you get that woman out of here right this minute, or I'll pick up the phone and talk to your superiors.' Her eyes narrowed to pinpoints of spite. 'I mean it, George,' she snap-ped. 'Make no mistake about that.'

'What makes you think Kellerman doesn't have a hand in this?' Ramsay said calmly.

Larissa stared at him, mouth open, her throat working as though she was about to retch.

'Of course, you could always go over Kellerman's head,' he went on. 'But it wouldn't do you any good. If I go down, I'll take you with me. By the time I'm arrested, that Special Branch file on your family will be on its way to the Japanese Consulate.'

'You're bluffing,' she said hoarsely.

'You won't think so when the Japs put you on a slow boat to Vladivostok. I doubt the NKVD will bother to question your crazy little sister; they'll just shoot Raya through the back of her neck and blow what's left of her brains out. Then they'll go to work on your father – and it won't matter a damn how many times you tell them you don't know where Admiral Kolchak hid their precious gold, because they won't believe you.'

The nervous tic under her right eye showed Ramsay that she was terrified. He knew he had Larissa in the palm of his hand, knew also that it was time to dangle a carrot in front of her.

'The girl in the back room won't be a problem. She'll be gone long before daybreak tomorrow, and we'll keep her blindfolded until she's released.'

'Unharmed?'

'Why should we kill her? She doesn't know anything.' Ramsay finished off the brandy and placed the empty glass on the desk. 'The file's yours, Larissa, if you just sit tight and do nothing.'

'When do I get it, George?'

'I plan to collect it after the shift changes at two o'clock. You can have a look at it later this afternoon. But it stays in my possession until we release the girl – understood?'

'Yes.' Her voice was a harsh croak.

'Good.' Ramsay smiled. 'Mind if I use your phone?'

'What for?'

'You need a couple of extra waiters tonight and I know where to get them.' Ramsay stood up, leaned across the desk and gently squeezed her breast. 'Don't look so worried,' he said. 'They won't be serving your customers.'

Then he lifted the phone and called Garcia at home.

Quarrie had taken an active dislike to Spencer Jarrold before he had even met the career diplomat face to face in the Vice Consul's office. His manner had been arrogant and condescending, as though he were dealing with some illiterate 'wet-back' from Mexico who'd just swum the Rio Grande and entered the United States illegally. Quarrie had been a newspaperman for more than thirty years, during which time he had interviewed every movie star who'd ever visited Chicago, and with the exception of Warren Harding, had talked to every American President from Woodrow Wilson to Franklin Delano

Roosevelt. In all his dealings with the famous and not-so-famous, both at home and abroad, Quarrie could not recall one instance when he had not been treated with courtesy and consideration. Until he encountered Spencer Jarrold.

The invitation to call in at the Consulate in Garden Road opposite the Peak tramway station had sounded like a summons, and one he wasn't at liberty to refuse. 'I can't discuss this matter with you over the telephone,' Jarrold had told him primly. It was just the kind of snotty answer that was guaranteed to put his back up.

It wasn't as though Quarrie had been in a particularly good mood to start with; thanks to Malcolm Vines, he had woken up that morning with an almighty hangover and was still trying to sleep it off when Jarrold had phoned the Gloucester Hotel.

First impressions were usually inaccurate, especially when the mental image of the stranger had been formed on the basis of a short telephone conversation. But for once, this wasn't the case. Jarrold turned out to be exactly as Quarrie had pictured him, a prissy young man in his late twenties, around five foot six with close-cropped black hair, a long thin nose and even thinner lips. He also wore rimless glasses and had a handshake that was limp and decidedly unfriendly.

Jarrold didn't thank him for coming; instead, he came straight to the point. 'I understand you're acquainted with a Mr Frank Waldron,' he said in his clipped Ivy League accent.

'Frank Waldron?' Quarrie scratched his forehead as though trying to place the name. 'I'm afraid the name doesn't ring a bell with me.'

'It should. You telephoned the night desk of the *Chicago Herald Tribune* about him at half past four yesterday afternoon.'

Quarrie pulled a face. Jarrold had him cold and there was no point in denying it. 'I guess somebody must have been listening in.'

'Cable and Wireless,' Jarrold said tersely. 'The British have been monitoring all trans-Pacific calls since the beginning of the month.'

'Seems to me the Limeys have got a goddamned nerve.'

Quarrie thought it would do no harm to sound indignant. Jarrold had him over a barrel, and right now offence was the best means of defence he could think of. 'What right have they got to spy on me? Haven't they heard of the freedom of the Press?'

'They've got every right to listen in, the Far East situation being what it is.'

'For Chrissakes, I called Chicago, not Tokyo.'

'There are Japanese nationals living in the United States,' Jarrold said. 'And you're evading the issue.'

'I am?' Quarrie said innocently.

'Waldron escaped from military custody on Wednesday night. In the process, he assaulted a Corporal Dobson and a Private Frazer of the Winnipeg Grenadiers, causing them actual bodily harm. At least, that's how the British describe it.'

'Is that so?'

'He's also wanted by the Hong Kong police, as I suspect you well know.'

Quarrie avoided Jarrold's gaze and stared instead at the tramcar slowly climbing the funicular railway to Victoria Peak, which he could see through the window. He knew Jarrold was about to pitch him a fast ball and he needed time to decide how to play it.

'Aiding and abetting a fugitive is a very serious offence, Mr Quarrie. That's why I want you to tell me where Waldron is hiding.'

'I can't.'

'Can't or won't?' Jarrold purred silkily.

'I haven't the faintest idea where Waldron is hiding. He's the one who says where and when we're to meet.'

'You'll have to do better than that. I've got a complete transcript of your conversation with Chicago, and it's very clear you know exactly where to find him.'

'Even if I did,' Quarrie said angrily, 'I'm not about to break the habit of a lifetime and become an informer.'

'You could find yourself *persona non grata* if you persist in being uncooperative,' Jarrold warned.

'What does that mean in plain English?'

'It means you could be deported from Hong Kong.' Jarrold pressed his thin lips together in what passed for a smile. 'I might add there's a Pan Am clipper leaving for San Francisco on Monday.'

Quarrie mulled it over. Without actually saying so, Jarrold had made it very clear that if the British did decide to deport him, there would be no official protest from the American Consulate. If he resisted, he might as well forget the war in South China he was supposed to report. But that was only a minor consideration; the Japanese consular office in Hong Kong were still sitting on his request to visit the Canton province; the way things were going, he doubted if they would grant him an entry permit. It was also a moot point whether or not the *Chicago Herald Tribune* would back his stance; there was a Congressional committee in Washington anxious to question Waldron, and that might just colour the attitude of some people he could name. Knowing the proprietor of the *Chicago Herald Tribune*, Quarrie thought there was an even chance he would be fired on the spot.

'Waldron didn't tell you about those two Canadian soldiers, did he?' Jarrold said significantly.

'I didn't even know he was in the army.' The fact was that Waldron hadn't kept anything back, but Jarrold was offering him a let-out and right now it suited his purpose to go along with the suggestion.

'Good. At least we've agreed that's the story we'll give the British authorities.'

Quarrie smiled ruefully. Jarrold was a lot sharper than he'd thought. 'Do you think they'll swallow it?' he said, temporizing.

'There will be a diplomatic row if they don't.'

'I guess I'm off the hook, then.' Quarrie stood up and walked over to the door. 'I don't know where to find Waldron, but you could always ask Katherine Goddard.'

'Who's she?'

'The resident nurse at the Peninsula Hotel.'

'Thank you,' said Jarrold.

'You're welcome,' Quarrie said, and closed the door behind him.

Quarrie reckoned it would take him a good fifteen minutes to reach the Gloucester Hotel, and that was far too long. If he was going to beat Jarrold to the punch and warn Katherine Goddard in time, he'd have to phone her from one of the public call boxes at the Peak tramway station across the road.

CHAPTER TWELVE

Waldron folded the newspaper in half and tossed it on to the coffee table. The Japs could cross the frontier at any moment, but no one would ever have known that from reading the columns of the *Sunday China Mail*. The way they told it, the war was confined to Russia, the Western Desert and the North Atlantic and was not likely to spread elsewhere. Apparently, as far as the editor was concerned, the only local news worthy of reporting was yesterday's race meeting at Happy Valley, where the band of the Royal Scots had entertained the spectators; the rugby match at the Cricket Club against the Middlesex Regiment, and the Tin Hat Ball at the Peninsula Hotel, during which some of the guests had been forced to leave regrettably early. There were, it seemed, no war clouds on the horizon; yet downstairs in the lobby, the staff were busily pasting strips of brown paper criss-cross fashion on the windowpanes, and Katherine had told him that the Canadians were moving out to their battle positions on the island. Vaguely disgruntled, he walked over to the window and stood there puffing on a cigarette.

'Restless, Frank?' Katherine asked.

'Just a little. I guess I've got a guilty conscience.'

'What about?'

'Me being here.' He shrugged his shoulders. 'I know this may sound crazy to you, but I feel like a deserter. I keep telling myself that I was discharged from the Canadian army, but it still doesn't do any good. Right now, the guys I served with are somewhere over on the island, digging in; that's where I ought to be, too – with a rifle in my hands and in uniform. Suddenly, this whole business of the 'America First' organization seems petty and irrelevant. I begin to wonder why I'm so concerned to save my own neck. Why shouldn't I join the other clay pigeons in the shooting gallery? I mean, I'm not special.'

'I know someone who's fishing for compliments,' Katherine told him dryly.

'Who me?' Waldron smiled. 'I'm just naturally modest.'

'Words fail me,' she began; then a shrill summons from the telephone interrupted her and with an apologetic shrug, she went into the bedroom to answer the call.

Probably one of the hotel guests, he thought. As resident nurse, Katherine was at everybody's beck and call, most times dispensing remedies for minor ailments – stomach upsets or the odd case of sunburn. A sharp ping told him that Katherine had hung up, and he wondered who had wanted her this time, and for what.

'That was Mr Quarrie on the phone.'

'Yeah? What did he want?'

The answer came fast and in a series of disjointed sentences. Quarrie's conversation with the *Chicago Herald Tribune* had been monitored by Cable and Wireless, and he had just spent a very unpleasant half hour with the American Vice Consul, who was about to get in touch with the Commissioner of Police. According to Quarrie's reckoning, Waldron had ten, perhaps fifteen minutes in which to make himself scarce.

'Doesn't give me much time, does it?' Waldron stubbed out his cigarette in the ashtray. 'Not that I really care. To tell you the truth, I'm tired of running.'

He would have to run though; he owed it to Katherine. It

didn't matter where the police picked him up, provided it was a long way from the Peninsula Hotel.

'How are you off for cash, Frank?' she asked.

'Quarrie gave me fifty Hong Kong dollars.' Waldron dipped into his pocket and brought out a few crumpled notes and a handful of loose change. 'I still have most of that left.'

'It's more than enough for a room at the Roxy Hotel.'

'Whereabouts is that?'

'In Peking Road, almost directly behind Kaznovetsky's restaurant. It's not a particularly nice hotel – in fact it's known locally as The Poxy.'

'Then I think I'll give it a miss.'

'Don't let its reputation put you off,' she warned.

'It doesn't. It's just that the Roxy is too close to this place for comfort. I think I should go farther afield.'

'No, that won't do at all, Frank. I've got to know where I can find you after I've met Mr Quarrie.'

'The hell with Quarrie,' Waldron said, scowling. 'You're not going to see that guy again. He can't be trusted.'

Katherine let it pass and went into the bedroom. Moments later she returned with a washbag containing the shaving tackle he'd purchased. 'It wouldn't do for the police to find this,' she said calmly.

'Right.' Waldron removed his jacket, stuffed the washbag into one of the pockets, then folded the coat shoulder to shoulder and draped it over his arm to conceal the tell-tale bulge. 'How's that?' he asked.

'Perfect,' Katherine said, steering him towards the door. 'Now, you book yourself into the Roxy and I'll meet you there as soon as I can.'

'I still think it's a lousy idea.'

'Please, Frank, there's no time to argue about it,' Katherine said coaxingly. 'Just do as I ask. All right?'

'Sure.' Waldron leaned forward and kissed her on the mouth. 'Are you going to be okay?'

'Don't worry about me, I can take care of myself.'

Katherine opened the door, looked both ways, then beckoned to him. Waldron kissed her again, stepped outside and walked down the corridor towards the staircase. Both lifts were in use and except for two housemaids on the second floor who were too busy with the linen cupboard to spare him more than a passing glance, he made it to the vestibule without incident. All the shops in the arcade were closed, and the bell boy was deep in conversation with the desk clerk and had his back towards him. Willing himself not to break into a run, Waldron strolled out into the street and turned right.

One look at the Roxy in Peking Road was enough to convince him that the hotel deserved its nickname and shady reputation. The net curtains in the windows downstairs were blackened with grime, the green paint on the ledges had peeled away to expose bare wood, and two of the letters were missing from the neon sign above the entrance.

The lobby was just as bad. The walls were an indeterminate colour and evidently had not been distempered in years; strips of insect-encrusted fly-paper hung from the ceiling, and the coconut matting on the concrete floor was scuffed and worn, as was the emaciated desk clerk behind the bamboo counter.

Waldron said, 'I'd like a room at the front.'

The desk clerk looked him up and down, then opened the hotel register and handed him a pen. As he signed in, Waldron noticed that according to the list of names, Winston Churchill, Genghis Khan and King George the Sixth were all currently staying at the Roxy.

'You want jig-a-jig?'

Waldron looked up. 'Come again?' he said.

'Jig-a-jig.' The desk clerk jerked a thumb at the two Chinese girls hovering near the staircase. One wore a black pyjama suit, the other a bright orange cheongsam and high-heeled sandals; both of them had festering acne.

'I'm not looking for a good time,' Waldron told him grimly.

It seemed the girls were part of the service. With or without them, the room still cost thirty dollars a night. Peeling off three notes, he collected the key and went on upstairs to the first landing. The girl in the black pyjama suit followed hopefully as far as the bedroom door before she gave him up as a dead loss.

Spencer Jarrold paid off the cab in Holywood Road and walked through the heavily sandbagged entrance of the Central Police Station. Inside, the muster room was busier than Grand Central in the rush hour, but the general air of chaos didn't surprise Jarrold. Following his interview with Harold Quarrie, he had spent a fruitless hour trying to contact the Chief Secretary of the Legislature. It had taken three phone calls to the Colonial Secretariat to discover that he was conferring with Sir Mark Young at Government House, and no one seemed to know when or if the Chief Secretary was expected to return. Jarrold had then rung Government House, only to be told by a haughty British official that the top-level conference was still in progress and that it was quite impossible for the Chief Secretary to come to the phone.

Angered by the rebuff, Jarrold had called the Consul General at home to inform him that the British were being singularly uncooperative and that as far as he was concerned, they could whistle for the information they had requested. Officials of the US State Department were not errand boys for the Hong Kong Police. There were recognized procedures for dealing with diplomatic situations such as this, and he intended to observe them to the letter and go through all the proper channels. Unhappily, the Consul General had taken a different viewpoint, brusquely informing him that the British were expecting the Japs to invade the colony at any moment, that in the circumstances, protocol had gone by the board and would he therefore kindly get the lead out of his pants and go see the Commissioner of Police.

Jarrold glanced round the chaotic muster room, looking for somebody in authority he could deal with. At a rough count, he reckoned there were at least half a dozen young English women rushing here, there and everywhere, lugging typewriters, tables and chairs from one office to another. Between laughing and joking amongst themselves, they somehow found time to issue a stream of contradictory instructions to a couple of harassed engineers from the Post Office, who were vainly trying to install additional telephones. The desk was manned by a fat, moon-faced sergeant who looked decidedly Mongolian, but he was jabbering away to three Chinese civilians and was not inclined to take any notice of him.

Rapidly losing patience, Jarrold wandered off down one of the corridors and was almost immediately intercepted by a burly police inspector, who demanded to know who he was and where the hell he was going. Jarrold produced his passport and in a voice that was ice-cold with fury, proceeded to enlighten the Inspector in no uncertain terms. Somewhat chastened by his outburst, the Inspector said he wasn't sure whether the Commissioner had returned from Government House yet, but he would have a word with his PA and meanwhile, perhaps Mr Jarrold would like to make himself comfortable in the waiting room?

Jarrold was under the mistaken impression that he wouldn't have long to wait; forty minutes and several cups of tea later, he knew different. At one-thirty, just as he was about to call it a day, the Commissioner of Police finally returned from the conference and Jarrold was shown upstairs to his office.

Hammond glanced at his wristwatch and swore. Almost two hours had elapsed since Tom Blakeney had phoned him shortly after midday, and he still hadn't managed to trace Jill. Somebody had called her at ten-thirty and Tom Blakeney had returned home to Rhoda at five minutes past twelve. If Jill had gone off with Blakeney, it was extremely unlikely that he had taken her out to his beach house. Big Wave Bay was a good eight miles from Victoria, and with only ninety minutes to play with, it would have been a waste of precious time driving out there and back. On the other hand, Blakeney's office was only a few minutes from Macdonnel Road, and Jill could have stayed on in town to give them some sort of alibi . . .

The thought sickened him, and he despised himself for doubting her. Whatever her faults, he was sure she would never stoop to such a lousy trick. Somebody *other* than Tom Blakeney must have picked her up from the house. But who? He had already telephoned the casualty clearing station at Happy Valley where Jill was supposed to report for duty when the hospital was mobilized, but the matron hadn't seen her, nor had any of the other auxiliary nurses he'd spoken to. Maybe there was some girlfriend of Jill's that he'd overlooked? But scanning the list of names he had scribbled down on his millboard, it didn't seem to him that he'd omitted anyone.

'Penny for your thoughts, David.' Ramsay grinned at him from the doorway. 'Sorry if I startled you, but I did knock.'

'I'm sure you did, George.' Hammond found it difficult to be polite. Ramsay was beginning to set his teeth on edge. It wasn't anything he could put his finger on, but he was having the same effect on him as a piece of chalk grating on a blackboard.

'Yes. Well, I thought I'd let you know the shifts have just changed over. Talbot's the man in charge now. I don't think you've met him before; he wasn't on duty yesterday.'

The roster didn't make a great deal of sense to Hammond, nor did it seem entirely fair. Some people appeared to have it easy, whereas Inspector Yeuh-Shen had already been on duty twice to his knowledge.

'I'm about to slide off for a bite to eat,' Ramsay went on. 'How about you?'

'I'm not particularly hungry at the moment, George,' Hammond said.

'You must have the appetite of a sparrow – I haven't seen you eat a thing all morning.' Ramsay eyed him thoughtfully. 'Is there something on your mind, David?'

'I've been thinking about Jill.'

'Yes?'

Hammond frowned. Was his imagination working overtime, or had Ramsay deliberately steered their conversation in a certain direction?

'I don't know whether I told you this before,' he said slowly, 'but Jill's a nurse, and I can't help wondering what'll happen to her if the Japs occupy Hong Kong.'

A brief flicker of the eyes told Hammond that this wasn't quite the answer Ramsay had been expecting. For a brief moment, he had looked confused.

'I can see it must be pretty worrying for you,' Ramsay said, recovering. 'It's times like these when I'm glad I'm a bachelor.'

'I still reckon I'm a very lucky man,' Hammond told him quietly.

'Of course you are. It was rather a thoughtless remark – I'm sorry.' Ramsay backed off, smiling. 'Time I was going,' he said with false bonhomie.

'Don't let me keep you, George.'

'Right. I'll see you in about an hour from now.'

Hammond nodded and then turned his back on Ramsay. Their conversation had re-awakened a dormant but unfounded suspicion that Ramsay was in some way connected with Jill's disappearance. It was that business with the telephones that had sparked it off – that, and the stupid lie Ramsay had cooked up about getting the China Light and Power Company when he'd rung Shamshuipo Police Station. At the time, Hammond had decided the theory was too absurd to be taken seriously. Now, suddenly, he wasn't sure it was so far-fetched after all.

Ramsay had shown a great deal of interest in the anti-intruder devices when they'd first visited the vaults of the Kowloon branch after the briefing on Wednesday afternoon, and he'd also questioned him pretty thoroughly about the whole set-up. Moreover, he had made a number of practical suggestions that had subsequently been implemented. The more Hammond thought about it, the more he convinced himself that six tons of gold bullion was a very strong motive for kidnapping the wife of the bank's chief security officer.

Hammond glanced at the phone. There had been no ransom demand as yet, and it was no use going to Kellerman until he had some hard evidence to support his theory. Right now, Ramsay was simply playing cat and mouse with him. But he could always take a leaf out of his book and apply a little reverse pressure. For openers, he could check out the bullion. He didn't expect to find anything wrong at this stage, but word would get back to Ramsay that he had been poking around in the vaults and that might just make him begin to sweat. He would give Talbot another five minutes to settle in and then he would make a snap inspection. Smiling grimly to himself, Hammond lit a cigarette and leaned back in his chair.

Lee picked at his food, stirring the prawns and rice with his chopsticks like a child, hoping they would disappear of their own accord. His poor appetite was in no way attributable to the two bottles of beer he'd had before returning home for lunch, though it was obvious from the disapproving expression on Choi-Hung's face that his wife thought otherwise. In English, Choi-Hung meant Rainbow, and normally the name was apt; Lee just hoped it wouldn't be too long before her sunny disposition reasserted itself.

'You're setting a bad example to the children, husband,' Choi-Hung said, voicing her thoughts aloud in Cantonese.

Lee glanced at the empty bowls in front of Matthew, Mark and Luke, and smiled. 'It would seem my sons were too hungry to pay much attention to their father. Anyway, you gave me far too much to eat.'

'No more than usual, husband.'

Lee sighed. There were times when he wished his wife would unbend a little and stop referring to him as 'husband', but Rainbow was not westernized as he was, and she clung to the old ways. He had tried to teach her English when they were first married, but after six months of patient and unrewarding tuition, he had been forced to recognize that, intelligent though she was, his wife had no intention of learning the language.

'Perhaps the prawns and rice are not to your liking?'

'There's nothing wrong with your cooking.' Lee pushed the bowl aside. 'I'm just not hungry, that's all.'

'You look worried, husband.'

Lee saw little point in denying it. The Pascoe affair was very much on his mind, but he didn't want to discuss the various implications with Choi-Hung – at least, not in front of the children. Collecting the bowls together, he took them out into the kitchen, scraped the remains into a waste-bucket under the sink, and then stacked the dishes in the washing-up bowl.

'Is it the Nipponese who make you frown so much?' Choi-Hung said, following him into the kitchen.

'There's nothing I can do about them. They are like a typhoon, violent and unpredictable. But one can learn to live with that.'

'It is something else then.'

It was the kind of emphatic statement that demanded an explanation. So he told her about Sub Inspector Pascoe and why Ramsay thought there might be more to the hit-and-run accident than first met the eye. In halting phrases, he described the clandestine meetings with his informers on Saturday night, and how none of them had ever heard of Pascoe.

'I should have told Ramsay that Pascoe was not working for the Triads and left it at that.'

'But you didn't,' Choi-Hung said.

'No. I decided to visit the scene of the accident and see for myself what had happened.' Lee smiled fleetingly. 'I prefer working on my own, and I suppose I was looking for any excuse to spin things out.'

There was no need for him to elaborate; Choi-Hung already knew how he felt about Adams and what had happened to the refugees living near Kai Tak.

'Anyway, that's why I cycled over to Boundary Street this morning.'

'And now you wish you hadn't.'

Choi-Hung's father had been a highly respected soothsayer, and though he was reluctant to admit it, there were occasions when Lee was half-convinced that she had inherited some of his remarkable powers. Anxious for her advice, he told her how he had met Sai-loong and exactly what he had learned from him.

'Clearly, it wasn't an accident,' Choi-Hung said calmly.

'It wasn't a Triad killing either. Sub Inspector Pascoe was murdered by one of his colleagues; at least, that is what I believe.'

'A white man?'

Lee said, 'I can't think of a single reason why Inspector Yeuh-Shen or any other Chinese police officer should want to kill the Englishman.'

'Then you should keep this matter to yourself, husband. It is their quarrel, not yours.'

'I can't do that.'

He glanced sideways at his wife, but her impassive face gave nothing away. The long silence dragged on, each passing second seeming more like ten. He stared at the tap, counting the drips as they splashed into the sink and formed a growing pool of water around the dishes in the bowl; the washer obviously needed to be replaced, but he couldn't be bothered with it now.

'Do you trust this man Lamsay?' Choi-Hung said finally.

Lee suppressed a smile. Ramsay's name was difficult to pronounce and his wife never could get her tongue round the letter 'r', which was probably one of the reasons why she had resisted all his efforts to teach her English.

'I think so,' he said gravely.

'In that case, you should tell him what you know and seek his advice.'

Lee thought Choi-Hung had chosen her words with care. There was a world of difference between what he knew and what he believed. She was right: he should stick to the facts and let Ramsay draw his own conclusions.

Slipping an arm around her shoulders, he hugged her close and kissed her on the cheek. 'You are very wise,' he said fondly, 'and I'm going to do as you suggest.'

'When?'

'There's no time like the present. I'll go to Police Headquarters in Nathan Road. If he isn't in his office, I'll phone him from there.'

Giving Choi-Hung another hug, he told her he wouldn't be long and then let himself out of their tiny ground-floor apartment in Shamshuipo.

Ramsay set the combination lock to the opening number and turned the dial four times in a clockwise direction before moving it on to 45, the second number in a sequence of three. Reversing the dial twice, he moved it forward again until the figure 67 was in line with the zero mark, then yanked the safe open. Reaching inside, he removed the two Swedish passports which he'd doctored, and closed the safe.

The passports belonged to Sven Uddenberg and Gundar Mattson, both of whom were merchant seamen. Uddenberg was thirty-seven and hailed from Lyskil on the west coast of Sweden; Mattson was two years older than his companion and had been born in Stockholm. The photographs inside the front covers showed a thoughtful-looking Ramsay and a somewhat grim-faced Donovan. The official embossed stamps over both photographs were not as good as Ramsay could have wished, but he reckoned they would pass muster. Tucking the passports into the inside pocket of his jacket, he left his office and went nextdoor.

The Special Branch dossiers were kept in a filing cabinet to which he had a key. Unlocking it, Ramsay opened the second drawer down and removed the Kaznovetsky file. Some three inches thick, it included duplicate copies of all the items of information the Shanghai police had gathered on the family before they moved to Hong Kong, as well as the later stuff Challinor had compiled before he died. Ramsay was familiar with the contents; after skimming through the file and dog-earing the more important folios, he, tucked it under his arm and returned to his office. He was just beginning to feel an euphoric conviction that everything was going perfectly, when he saw Sergeant Lee waiting for him in the corridor.

'Hello, Henry,' he said, forcing a smile. 'What are you doing here on a Sunday afternoon?'

'I was about to phone you, sir.' Lee paused and took a deep breath. 'About Sub Inspector Pascoe,' he added.

It would be, Ramsay thought; and ten to one the little slant-eyed bastard had come up with something. 'You'd better step inside the office,' he said, and opened the door.

His notion that Lee was bad news was confirmed the moment the sergeant told him that he'd visited the scene of the accident.

The fact that some bloody Chink refugee had seen Thirsk get out of the car to check his bearings in the fog gave him an even nastier jolt. But worst of all was the knowledge that Lee knew the killer was a member of the detective squad. The way he tiptoed round the subject, merely describing the European and leaving Ramsay to draw his own conclusions, was proof of that.

'You've done a good job, Henry,' he said, forcing some enthusiasm into his voice. 'It's a very clever piece of detective work.'

'Thank you, sir.'

'Question is, where do we go from here?' Somehow Ramsay managed another smile. 'I assume you took a statement from this character Sai-loong?'

Lee shook his head. 'We'd never get him into the witness box.'

Ramsay drummed his fingers on the desk. At least there was nothing in writing, then; but on the other hand, the fact that Lee had not taken a statement from Sai-loong was further proof that he knew the squad was involved in Pascoe's death.

'We'll have to trace that car, Henry,' he said presently.

Lee said, 'The Traffic Department have already put two of their officers on to that, sir. I understand they've visited all the garages in Kowloon.'

'Yes. That's standard procedure.' It was also standard proce-dure to inform Traffic that the hit-and-run accident was now a murder inquiry. 'Who else knows about this witness?' Ramsay demanded. 'I mean, have you informed Traffic?'

'Not yet, sir.'

'All right, Henry, you'd better leave that to me.' Ramsay frowned. He could sit on the information, but for how long? And what the hell was he going to do with Lee in the meantime? A sharp tap on the door interrupted his train of thought and he looked up, scowling. 'Who's that?' he shouted angrily.

'Me, George.' Bramwell, the Superintendent in charge of the uniform branch, stuck his head round the door. 'Can you spare a minute?'

'Of course I·can, Lewis.' Ramsay stood up, mindful that

although they enjoyed equal status as department heads, Bramwell outranked him. 'What's on your mind?'

'Waldron,' said Bramwell. 'Remember him?'

'The American who escaped from military custody on Wednesday night, right?'

'That's the man.' Bramwell closed the door behind him and leaned against it. 'We've just been told that he's hiding out in the Peninsula Hotel, and I'm a bit short-handed at the moment. I was wondering if you could help me out?'

Less than a minute ago he had been racking his brains for some way to keep Lee occupied. Now, like manna from heaven, Bramwell had dropped the solution into his lap. All the same, he thought, it wouldn't do to appear too eager. 'For how long?' he asked.

'An hour or two.' Bramwell hesitated, then said, 'Of course, it may be that Waldron has skipped. The information was a little slow in getting through to us.'

'In which case, you'll need my sergeant for a good deal longer than that?'

'There is that possibility,' Bramwell admitted reluctantly.

'All right,' said Ramsay, 'I'll tell you what I'll do. You can have Sergeant Lee here for the rest of the day, but if you haven't nabbed Waldron by then, I want him back with me. Okay?'

'Thanks, George. I won't forget this in a hurry.'

'Neither will I,' Ramsay said dryly.

CHAPTER THIRTEEN

The bell rang, loud and insistent, a summons Katherine Goddard had been expecting ever since Quarrie had phoned her. She had expected the police to be on the doorstep within minutes of Frank's hasty departure shortly before midday, but here it was, past three o'clock, and they'd only just arrived.

Taking her time, Katherine walked over to the door and opened it. A preconceived notion that the caller would be a burly police officer in uniform was momentarily dispelled when she was confronted with a dark-haired, middle-aged man in a gaberdine suit, who looked like a businessman and was barely a couple of inches taller than herself.

'Miss Goddard?' the stranger enquired politely.

'Yes.' Katherine swallowed, then said, 'Do I know you? I don't recall us having met before.'

'My name's Bramwell, Superintendent Bramwell.' A warrant card was held up in front of her eyes to support the claim. 'I think you can guess why I'm here.'

'Not offhand, no.' Katherine gazed at him, wide-eyed and innocent. 'Unless it's about my driving licence, which I believe is out of date. But then you'd hardly concern yourself with such a trivial matter, would you?'

'I'm referring to Frank Waldron, Miss Goddard.' The smile was still there on his mouth, although decidedly more strained. 'I'm told he's a friend of yours.'

'Actually, I don't know him all that well, but we do have a mutual acquaintance.' Katherine frowned as if genuinely puzzled as to why Bramwell had called on her. 'What's your interest in Mr Waldron, Superintendent?' she asked. 'I mean, I find it hard to believe that he can be in any sort of trouble with the police.'

'Then I have news for you,' Bramwell said grimly. 'He's wanted by the FBI.'

'Really?'

'You'd better believe it, Miss Goddard. Now, if you don't mind, I'd like to see him.'

'I'm afraid you're too late,' Katherine said demurely. 'He left some time ago.'

'I've only your word for that.'

'Are you saying you want to search my apartment?' Her tone of voice and raised eyebrows implied that she found the idea preposterous.

'I've got a warrant,' Bramwell said, reaching inside his jacket. 'Do you want to see it?'

'No, that won't be necessary. I'm quite sure you wouldn't do anything illegal.' Katherine opened the door wider and stepped to one side. 'I suppose you'd better come in,' she said, 'but I'm afraid you'll be wasting your time.'

'That's my prerogative, Miss Goddard.'

Grim-faced, Bramwell glanced round the lounge, then went into the adjoining bedroom. From the doorway, Katherine watched him open the wardrobe and bit back a flippant remark when he lifted the bedspread and looked under the bed. While she waited patiently, he checked out the bathroom. The heavy-handed way he jerked the shower curtain along the rail told her that Bramwell was in no mood for frivolous patter.

'I see Waldron remembered to take his shaving tackle with him,' he said presently.

Katherine clenched both hands, digging the nails into the palms in an effort to keep her temper. 'What exactly are you implying?' she asked.

'Oh come on, Miss Goddard, you must think I was born yesterday. Waldron has been staying with you ever since he escaped from military custody.'

'I don't think we can be talking about the same man,' Katherine said icily. 'Mr Waldron is an American citizen and as far as I'm aware, he's never served in the British Army.'

'Waldron joined the Winnipeg Grenadiers under an assumed name in order to avoid appearing before a Congressional committee. He was discharged for fraudulent enlistment when the FBI finally caught up with him.'

'That's the first I've heard of it.'

'I thought you might say that,' Bramwell said, his voice derisive. 'Next thing I know, you'll be telling me you haven't the faintest idea where I can find him.'

'Are you always so ill-mannered, Superintendent?' Bramwell meant to intimidate her and she thought attack was the best means of defence.

'I don't like your attitude either, Miss Goddard. If you'd

prefer, we can always continue this conversation down at the police station.'

'Oh no we won't.' Katherine shook her head vehemently. 'I'm not going to be bullied. I'm not going to say another word to you until I've consulted my solicitor.'

'There's no need to fly off the handle,' Bramwell said. 'It wasn't my intention to harass you.'

'No? Well, that's not the impression you gave me. It seems to me you've been making all kinds of insinuations. You tell me that Mr Waldron has escaped from military custody and then calmly infer that I was already aware of this before I met him. Perhaps you'd explain how I was supposed to know that?'

'There was a piece about it in the *South China Morning Post* on Friday.'

'Oh?' Katherine bit her lip, conscious that she might have over-played her hand and allowed Bramwell to score off her. 'I must have missed it,' she added lamely. 'I don't get much time for reading the newspapers.'

'Well, it was only a couple of lines at the foot of the page.'

She wondered why Bramwell had suddenly changed his attitude. Was he offering her a let-out? If so, his motives were immaterial; the important thing was to grasp the olive branch while it was still within reach.

'It's funny how wrong you can be about people,' she murmured.

'Well, I can understand how you feel. I'm told Waldron's a pretty smooth character.' Bramwell fingered his pencil-thin moustache. 'If you'd met some of the conmen I've had to deal with, you'd know what I mean.'

'He certainly fooled me,' Katherine said wryly. 'I suppose I should be grateful that he didn't try to borrow any money from me. Though come to think of it, he did drop a number of hints.'

'What makes you say that, Miss Goddard? Did Waldron give you a hard-luck story?'

'Not exactly.' She hesitated, uncertain how to answer what was plainly a loaded question. If she gave him too fulsome an explanation, she could end up digging a pit for herself. Bramwell was quick on the uptake and clever enough to spot the tiniest flaw in her answer. 'Mr Waldron was rather vague,' she continued, 'but I did gather that he'd been landed with a bad debt. It was something to do with a cheque he'd received from a fellow American staying at the Repulse Bay. I believe he said it had bounced.'

'The Repulse Bay Hotel? Is that where he's gone?'

'It's possible.' She smiled helplessly. 'I'm sorry I can't be more definite, but he wasn't very forthcoming about his future plans.'

'Waldron's flat broke. He doesn't have a passport and there's no way he can leave Hong Kong unless he can touch somebody for a loan.' Bramwell studied her thoughtfully. 'Look, if Waldron draws a blank at the Repulse Bay, he may try to get in touch with you again. If he does, I want you to phone me straight away.'

'Yes, of course.'

'You can reach me on 387444.' Bramwell wrote the number down in a small notebook, then ripped off the top page and gave it to her. 'You'd better have this as a reminder,' he said.

'Thank you. I'll keep it in my handbag.'

'Good.' Bramwell followed her into the lounge. 'I'm sorry we got off on the wrong foot, Miss Goddard.'

'I think that was largely my fault.' Katherine flashed him a quick smile as she walked purposefully towards the door. 'My brother's always telling me I'm too quick to take offence.'

'Brothers are like that,' Bramwell said philosophically. 'I should know; I've got three.'

'What, here in Hong Kong?' The last thing she wanted was a potted history of his family, but it seemed impolite not to say anything.

'No. One's with the army in Egypt and the other two are still at home in a reserved occupation, thank God.'

For one awful moment it looked as though Bramwell was going to linger on; but then he suddenly shook hands and said goodbye. Thankfully she closed the door behind him and heaved a deep sigh of relief.

Katherine glanced at the slip of paper she was still holding and crumpled it into a ball. That was one number she had no intention of using, and Bramwell probably knew it too. There was, she thought, a distinct possibility that the phone number was simply a ruse to lull her into a false sense of security – that Bramwell was hoping she would eventually lead him to Frank. In that case, it was reasonable to assume the police were monitoring the hotel switchboard – and that meant she'd have to call Quarrie from a pay booth. But not just yet; Bramwell was not the only one who could afford to play a waiting game.

Hammond listened to the low murmur of voices in the main hall and smiled grimly to himself. Ramsay had returned to the bank some five minutes ago and from the various snatches of conversation he'd overheard, it was evident that Talbot had wasted little time in telling him that he'd been down to the vaults. The snap check had proved negative, but that was no more than Hammond had expected. The gold bullion was packed into a hundred-and-sixty-eight steel boxes and it would have taken him all day to examine each one in detail. Ramsay was intelligent enough to know that; but if Hammond's hunch was correct, he might still wonder what had prompted the inspection. With any luck, it would create an air of uncertainty in his mind, one he intended to exploit, until either he was proved wrong, or Ramsay cracked under the strain and showed his hand. Opening the door quietly, Hammond stepped out of the office.

'Hello, George,' he said gravely. 'Have you heard the news?'

Ramsay flinched, then turned about to face him. 'What news?' he asked.

'I've just been talking to Ralph Cottis at Fortress Headquarters. He tells me the situation is looking pretty grim. According to our observation posts on the frontier, the Japs are moving bridging equipment up to the river near Lo Wu.'

Hammond could tell from the way Talbot was frowning that he was puzzled; he hadn't heard the phone ring during the time that Ramsay had been away, and hadn't heard Hammond speak to anyone. Of course, he was right: there had been no telephone conversation with Fortress Headquarters; the military build-up was pure invention on Hammond's part.

'I don't like the sound of that,' Ramsay said.

'Neither do I.' Hammond jerked a thumb towards the office. 'If you can spare the time, I'd like to have a word with you in private.'

'Sure.' Ramsay lifted the flap, opened the gate in the counter and followed Hammond into the manager's office. 'I can guess how you must be feeling, David,' he said, closing the door behind him.

'Can you?'

'Of course. Like I said this morning, this is one time when I'm glad I'm still a bachelor.'

'I hope Jill will come through this ordeal,' Hammond said pointedly.

'I'm sure she will.'

'But could you guarantee that, George?'

'I only wish I could.' Ramsay licked his lips. 'Unfortunately, everything's in the lap of the gods.'

Hammond lit a cigarette. The conversation wasn't going quite the way he had intended; but for a moment there, he thought Ramsay had sounded a little rattled. 'Not everything, George,' he said enigmatically.

'I'm not with you.'

'I'm referring to the gold. Now that the Royal Engineers have completed the strongroom, there's no reason why we shouldn't transfer the bullion to the *Delphic Star*.'

'What, now? In broad daylight?'

'Anything wrong with that?'

'Not from my point of view,' Ramsay said. 'But I thought you wanted to avoid a panic run on the bank? At least, that's what you told me at the briefiing on Wednesday afternoon.'

'A lot's happened since then, George. Come tomorrow, the bank may not be open for business.'

'Well, in that case, it won't matter if we do create a panic; people can't draw their money out if every branch in town is closed.'

Ramsay was calm, too calm. He had taken the sudden change of plan in his stride, whereas only a few minutes ago Hammond thought he had caught him off guard. Whatever else he might be, Ramsay was certainly resilient and it would take a great deal of pressure to make him crack.

'Listen, I need your advice, George,' Hammond said, feeling his way.

'What about?'

'Well, suppose we brought the deadline forward to 2100 hours tonight. Could the police cope with the revised schedule?'

'The CID could, but I'm not so sure about the uniform branch. When I saw Bramwell earlier this afternoon, he said that a lot of his people had gone missing. I gather the Sikhs have practically deserted en masse.'

Hammond wondered how much truth there was to the story. He could always check it with Kellerman when a suitable opportunity arose, but if the Assistant Commissioner denied it, it still wouldn't necessarily prove anything one way or the other. Knowing Kellerman, he'd be unlikely to admit that a number of his men had deserted, whatever the truth of the matter.

'All the same, I think we can overcome that problem.' Ramsay reached across the desk and picked up Hammond's millboard. 'Mind if I borrow this for a moment?' he asked.

'Seems you already have,' Hammond said dryly.

'Act first, ask later.' Ramsay shrugged. 'That's always been one of my failings, I'm afraid.' He stared at the list of names Hammond had scribbled down on the pad, his eyebrows drawn together in a frown as he tried to decipher the handwriting. 'Who are all these people?' he asked, looking up again.

'Oh, just friends of ours,' Hammond said quickly. 'Jill had a dinner party planned for tomorrow evening, but last night at the Tin Hat Ball we decided to call it off. I spent most of the morning phoning everyone to let them know.'

'So you don't need this list any more?'

'No, you might as well tear it up.'

Ramsay detached the top sheet from the millboard, screwed the paper into a ball and taking aim, chucked it into the wastebin. Then, moving round to Hammond's side of the desk, he began to rough out a sketchmap of the area with his fountain pen.

'Nathan Road, Hankow Road,' he said, and drew two vertical lines on the pad. 'Then from north to south, we have Peking, Middle and Salisbury Roads.' Three horizontal lines bisected the vertical uprights.

Other symbols rapidly followed to denote the Kowloon branch of the Hong Kong and Shanghai Bank, the Star Ferry terminal, the railway station south of Salisbury Road and the dockside. As a final touch, Ramsay added a couple of flashing beacons, placing one at each end of Middle Road.

'What are they supposed to represent?' Hammond asked him.

'Diversion signs,' Ramsay said. 'It's going to take us between four and five hours to load the bullion on to the trucks, but we can remove them and re-open the road to traffic just as soon as it gets dark. I know it's not an ideal solution, but we don't want to draw too much attention to ourselves, like having complaints from people wanting to dine at Kaznovetsky's restaurant.'

'You'll need to have some men on traffic duty while those diversion signs are in position, George.'

Ramsay nodded. 'So long as Kellerman is prepared to accept a temporary reduction in the number of foot patrols, Bramwell should be able to produce four police constables without too much difficulty. Excluding the bank detail, that means I'll have eight men available to cover the route from here to the docks. Of course, I'm assuming that your people will be responsible for loading the bullion on to the trucks?'

Hammond stubbed out his cigarette in the ashtray. 'That's always been understood,' he said coldly.

'Just checking. Maybe I got the wrong impression, but I thought it was your intention to complete the transfer in record time. That's why I wanted to know if you'd need any extra help from me.' Ramsay shot him a sideways glance. 'How will the change of plan affect your people?'

'They'll be able to cope.'

'Good. What about the army?'

'I haven't spoken to them yet. It's not the kind of thing you can discuss over the telephone. You never know who might be listening in, and we can't risk a leak.'

'So what are you going to do?' Ramsay asked.

'I don't have any choice. Like it or not, I'll have to make a fleeting visit to Fortress Headquarters.'

'When?'

Hammond had no intention of going anywhere near Fortress Headquarters, but the one-word question convinced him that Ramsay believed otherwise.

'Well, now that you're here,' he said, 'I can leave straight away.' He gazed at his adversary, saw the way Ramsay's jaw had dropped and knew that at last he had shaken him. 'You don't mind if I leave you in charge, do you, George?'

'How long will you be gone?' Ramsay asked, sounding as though he had suddenly developed a sore throat.

'About an hour.' Hammond stood up and walked over to the door before delivering the parting shot. 'But don't hold your breath, George,' he said, 'it could be longer.'

He went out into the main hall, asked Talbot to unlock the revolving door and then hurried through the lobby of the Peninsula Hotel. The tea house in Hankow Road would make an ideal vantage point; from there he would have an excellent view of the rear entrance of the bank.

Ramsay retrieved the crumpled piece of paper from the waste-bin and smoothed it out on the desk. Running a finger down the list of names Hammond had scribbled on the page, he stopped at the set of initials that had puzzled him earlier on: 'CCS', then a short dash followed by the letters 'HV'. A pairing-off of two single people? Or did it refer to something else, like a place or some sort of establishment? Suddenly he snapped his fingers. The answer had come to him; the initials stood for the Casualty Clearing Station at Happy Valley. And that meant Hammond had lied to him. There was no dinner party planned for Monday evening – there never had been; Hammond knew his wife was missing and the cunning bastard had been ringing everyone he could think of who might be able to tell him where she was.

So why had he been so secretive about it? Ramsay glanced at the telephone and immediately felt his stomach lurch. There was mistake number one, staring him in the face. In his haste to reassemble the mouthpiece, he had crossed the threads and the damn thing was lopsided. But had Hammond noticed it? Well, of course he bloody had; why else would he have behaved so strangely just now? All that talk about revising the schedule was just so much crap. Hammond knew it was extremely unlikely the army could provide the necessary transport at short notice, when they were buzzing around like blue-arsed flies dropping men and ammunition off at strongpoints all over the mainland as well as on the island. It was also doubtful if the captain of the *Delphic Star* would be able to comply with a revised sailing time; after all, getting a ship underway was a little more complicated than pressing the starter button on a motor car.

Ramsay moved round the desk and sat down, willing himself to stay calm and think things through. Hammond wasn't on the way to Fortress Headquarters; that was just a blind to hoodwink him. He was out there, somewhere near the bank, watching and waiting for him to make a mistake. If Hammond suspected that he was responsible in some way for his wife's disappearance, that meant he would need to be doubly careful from now on. But it was vital he brought Hammond under control again, and there was only one way to do that. Lifting the phone off the cradle, he dialled Kaznovetsky's and told Larissa to put Donovan on the line.

There was a brief pause, and then Donovan picked up the receiver and said, 'Something tells me we're in trouble.'

Ramsay scowled. It was a reasonable enough deduction; he had stopped off at the restaurant to wave the Special Branch file at Larissa before reporting back to the bank, and Donovan knew he wouldn't be calling him now unless something serious had cropped up in the meantime.

'We're going to need Jill Hammond,' he snapped.

'She's still not fully conscious,' Donovan said.

'Then you'd better wake her up,' Ramsay said grimly. 'She's got to talk to her husband.'

'When?'

'As soon as I give the word. That could be an hour from now or just over, depending on when Hammond returns.'

'Well, I hope we don't have to wait too long, George.' Donovan cleared his throat. 'I ought to get rid of the Ford sedan, and I can't do that and play nursemaid at the same time.'

'You think I don't know that? You'll just have to stay put until I can relieve you.'

'Isn't Hammond going to think it a little odd if you disappear the moment he returns?'

'Don't worry, Bill, I'll come up with something. I always have so far.'

Ramsay put the phone down and helped himself to a cigarette from the packet lying on the desk. Hammond had given him a few nasty moments, but it would take more than a little setback like this to throw him out of his stride.

The desk clerk nudged Lee in the ribs and he looked up in time to catch a glimpse of a tall, slender girl walking through the arcade towards the main entrance.

'That's Miss Goddard,' the desk clerk informed him in a low voice.

Lee nodded. He'd had to wait for close on an hour and a half for this moment, but it seemed Bramwell's hunch had paid off at last. Now the rest was up to him. Shoulder-length dark hair with an auburn tinge, a stone-coloured two-piece costume and matching handbag; Lee impressed the details of her appearance on his mind, knowing that from now on he would see only her back. He remembered the words of advice Challinor had given him the day he'd joined the CID: 'not too close, not too far behind'. After he'd finished counting slowly up to twenty, he strolled out after her into Hankow Road.

He saw that his quarry had turned left and wondered if she was going to flag down a passing cab when she reached the T-junction ahead. For an anxious moment he was tempted to close the gap between them, but then, to his relief, Katherine Goddard turned right on Salisbury Road and headed towards the Star Ferry terminal. Lee hung back, allowed her to draw ahead and then tagged on behind a Cantonese family, mother, father, two sons and a daughter, heading in the same direction. The odds that she would single him out from amongst all the other pedestrians on the broad avenue were about zero; so far as most Europeans were concerned, all Chinamen looked alike. But all the same, he didn't believe in taking any chances.

A ferry boat was waiting at the pier by the time they reached the terminal, but Katherine Goddard made no attempt to catch it. Instead, she turned away from the turnstiles and made for one of the phone booths at the far end of the shed. Reacting swiftly, Lee turned his back on her, walked over to a street vendor who was selling soft drinks from a handcart and bought himself a bottle of Fanta orange and a bag of peanuts.

The minutes ticked away slowly. A train pulled into Kowloon station across the way from where he was standing and presently a crowd of passengers emerged from the building and streamed towards the ferry terminal. Last-minute refugees, Lee thought as he eyed their possessions; farmers and their families from the New Territories fleeing the countryside to the comparative safety of Victoria before the Japanese invaded. Surrounded by the milling throng, he turned about and saw that Katherine Goddard had left the phone booth to join the queue forming at the booking office as another ferry boat approached the pier. He waited until it had docked, then joined the crowd, now some forty to fifty deep behind her.

Only a handful of passengers disembarked at Kowloon, and within a matter of seconds the crowd began to surge aboard. Dropping the empty Fanta bottle into a litter bin, Lee slapped a ten cent coin into the outstretched hand of the booking clerk and passed through the turnstile. Lost amongst the sea of Chinese faces, he followed her into the bows and found a space for himself on a bench directly across the gangway from where she was sitting.

Throughout the brief trip across the harbour, Lee chatted to the elderly peasant woman on his left and never once glanced in her direction. When the boat docked at Blake Pier over in Victoria, he waited until Katherine Goddard was about to disembark before he left his seat. Once ashore, he closed the distance between them as she went on up Pedder Street and across Des Voeux Road. The first nasty surprise occurred when she strolled into the Gloucester arcade and spent some time gazing into various shop windows before continuing on her way. The second upset happened a few minutes later on Queens Road Central, when she suddenly wheeled into the King's Theatre.

Lee waited outside on the pavement until she had left the foyer before he approached the girl in the box office. Showing her his warrant card, he learned that somebody had left a ticket for Katherine Goddard at the box office, and that it would cost him three dollars fifty to join her in the circle. Rummaging through his pockets, he dug out two crumpled one-dollar notes and found that together with a handful of loose change, he had just enough cash on him for a ticket.

Collecting it, he raced upstairs and gave it to a short, dumpy usherette, who led him to a seat five rows back from the balcony on the left-hand side of the centre aisle. After three minutes, in which his eyes accustomed themselves to the prevailing gloom, he was able to spot Katherine Goddard amongst the audience.

According to the APB he'd seen, Waldron was five eleven, had light-brown hair, was twenty-six years old and weighed one hundred-and-seventy-three pounds. Although he couldn't see his face, the man sitting next to Katherine Goddard bore absolutely no resemblance to that description.

Puzzled, Lee looked round to check the location of the various emergency exits, then settled back in his seat, one eye on Katherine Goddard, the other on William Powell, Myrna Loy and a dog called Asta, who were trying to solve a murder that had baffled the entire police force of New York.

It was a small room with grubby walls, a hard single bed, a chipped wardrobe and a rickety straight-backed chair. The mirror above the wash basin was cracked, the lampshade was thick with dust and there were cigarette burns along the whole length of the windowsill. During the past five hours, Waldron had added several more while he watched and waited for Katherine Goddard to appear in Peking Road.

As he sat there in the window observing the street, a large Ford sedan emerged from the courtyard behind Kaznovetsky's restaurant and turned right towards Nathan Road. Framed in the window of the small back room overlooking the courtyard and watching the car nose its way into the road, he could see the head and shoulders of a burly European. Even at a distance of sixty feet, Waldron had little difficulty in recognizing the unknown police officer he'd first seen standing with Kellerman outside the rear entrance of the Hong Kong and Shanghai Bank on Friday morning.

CHAPTER FOURTEEN

On the screen, William Powell, looking debonair in a silk dressing gown, and Asta, standing on her hind legs, were both peering into a refrigerator, while a bemused but very attractive Myrna Loy seemed genuinely puzzled as to why her husband and the dog should find the empty shelves so interesting. Across the centre aisle and two rows down from Lee, Katherine Goddard and her companion began to move towards the side exit.

With a murmured apology to the middle-aged British couple on his right, Lee edged past them into the centre aisle and then made his way down to the foyer. The side exit led into D'Aguilar Street, a narrow thoroughfare between King's Theatre and the Hing Wai building; provided Katherine Goddard and her companion turned right outside the cinema, Lee knew that he would be able to shadow them when they came out into Queens Road Central.

A nagging suspicion that they had fooled him and were now heading in the other direction was dispelled when he spotted them on the opposite pavement. Waiting until they had turned the corner into Pedder Street, he left the theatre and strode after them. He assumed Katherine Goddard was making for Blake's Pier; but he was less sure about the tall, loose-limbed stranger at her side. Lee guessed that she had phoned him from the Star Ferry terminal in Kowloon and had then dallied long enough in the Gloucester Arcade to ensure that he arrived at the King's Theatre before she did. It was impossible to guess just whose idea that had been, but clearly either Katherine Goddard or the stranger had considered the possibility that they might be under surveillance. If that was the case, then their present lack of concern suggested that they had compared notes while they were in the theatre and decided their suspicions were groundless.

Lee followed them down Pedder Street and across Des Voeux Road. As they neared the Gloucester Hotel, the couple gradually slowed to a halt; then Katherine Goddard and the middle-aged stranger turned to face each other and exchanged a few brief words. Presently they shook hands and parted company, Katherine Goddard continuing on down the road towards the ferry, while her companion strolled into the hotel. They had spent less than an hour together – but long enough, Lee reckoned, for her to have made certain arrangements on Waldron's behalf. According to Bramwell, the American had no money; remembering her grateful smile and the amicable way they'd said goodbye, Lee had a hunch that that particular problem had now been resolved.

There were less than a score of people waiting for the ferry to Kowloon at Blake's Pier – which suggested that the refugees from the New Territories he'd seen earlier were not alone in thinking that the island was somehow a safe haven. Tagging on to a Chinese family, Lee did his best to merge chameleon-like into the small crowd until the boat docked. When eventually it did and they were allowed on board, he chose to sit in the stern, well away from Katherine Goddard.

He wondered how much longer he would have to play cat and mouse with her, wondered too if Choi-Hung would be alarmed by his prolonged absence. He had told her he would be gone for only a short while, but now it was late in the afternoon and the way things were going, it seemed unlikely he would be home before nightfall. There was only one small consolation; Choi-Hung had been a policeman's wife long enough to know that there was no certainty about hours of duty.

Another crowd of unofficial evacuees was waiting at the terminal when the ferry boat pulled into Kowloon, and they were in no mood to hang about on the quayside until the passengers had disembarked. One of the last to leave, Lee elbowed his way ashore and set off after Katherine Goddard once more. Like a faithful dog, he followed her up Salisbury Road into Hankow Road and on past the Peninsula Hotel to the Roxy in Peking Road. The moment she entered the run-down hotel, he knew he had found Waldron.

Lee walked into the nearest shop doorway and stood there, gazing at the bolts of silk displayed in the window until he was satisfied there was no danger of him meeting Katherine Goddard face to face in the hotel lobby. The desk clerk and a couple of blowsy-looking whores were still enjoying a private joke at her expense when he strolled through the entrance, and it gave him a great deal of pleasure to be able to produce his warrant card and wipe the smiles from their faces.

Lee said, 'An English woman came in here a few minutes ago. I want to know where she's gone.'

The desk clerk eyed him sullenly, then pointed to the staircase. 'First floor,' he said. 'Room 105.'

'Thanks.' Lee reached across the desk for the telephone. 'You don't mind if I make an official call, do you?'

'It's out of order.'

'Don't give me that old story.'

'Go ahead and try it if you don't believe me.' The desk clerk winked derisively at the two bar girls, who cackled gleefully.

'Something the matter with your eye?' Lee asked him quietly.

'No, nothing.'

Lee grabbed his wrist and jerked him forward. 'There will be if I have any more lip from you,' he said.

Still holding on to the desk clerk's wrist, he lifted the receiver off the cradle, found the line was dead and put the phone down again. There was no way he could alert Bramwell now unless he used one of the pay phones at the Peninsula, and that was out of the question. Apart from the slight difference of opinion they'd just had, the Vice Squad were always raiding the Roxy Hotel, which was enough to guarantee that the desk clerk would tip Waldron off as soon as he turned his back on him.

'What was that room number again?' he asked.

'105.'

Lee released the desk clerk and checked the hotel register. Waldron had signed in as Franklin Delano Roosevelt.

'Give me a pass key,' he said, snapping his fingers.

Muttering a few expletives under his breath, the desk clerk opened a drawer under the counter and handed him a large key attached to an even larger metal tag. 'This is the only one I've got,' he grumbled.

'Good.' Lee palmed the key and moved towards the staircase.

'And I want it back,' the desk clerk called after him.

'What makes you think I'd want a souvenir from this dump?' Lee said acidly.

Both whores hooted with laughter and nudged each other in the ribs. They were still cackling and hissing when he reached the top of the staircase and made his way along the gloomy corridor to Room 105.

Inserting the master key in the lock, Lee pushed open the door and stepped inside. Katherine Goddard was perched on the edge of the bed facing Waldron, who was sitting back to front on an upright chair, his legs straddling the seat, his chin resting on folded arms. Both of them stared open-mouthed in his direction; then Waldron stood up and grabbed hold of the chair, as though to use it as a weapon.

'Just who the hell are you?' he snapped.

'I'm a police officer.' Lee eyed the American warily, suddenly conscious that he was only five foot four and that Waldron was a good seven inches taller and at least forty pounds heavier. A firearm would have redressed the balance, but Bramwell had told him it was just a routine surveillance job and he had left his revolver in the armoury. In the circumstances, he thought it expedient to produce his warrant card again. 'My name's Sergeant Lee,' he added, emphasizing his rank.

'That's just great.' Waldron relaxed his grip on the chair and smiled ruefully. 'I presume you're going to tell me I'm under arrest, Sergeant?'

'You most certainly are,' Lee said.

'And Miss Goddard? Is she under arrest too?'

Lee hesitated for a moment, then shook his head. Bramwell hadn't said what he proposed to do about the girl, and on the evidence available, he reckoned they'd be lucky to get a conviction if they charged her with being an accessory.

Waldron said, 'You'd better leave now, Katherine, while the going's good and before the sergeant here changes his mind.'

'You're not going to get rid of me as easily as that, Frank,' Katherine told him firmly. 'I'll go when I know where Sergeant Lee is taking you.'

'It's no secret, Miss Goddard,' Lee said politely. 'Mr Waldron will be accompanying me to Nathan Road, but I can't tell you what charges will be preferred against him until I've spoken to Superintendent Bramwell.'

'I see.' She faced him squarely, her jaw set in a determined attitude. 'Well, I think you should know that I intend to make sure Mr Waldron is legally represented.'

'I'll mention it to the Superintendent,' Lee told her.

'Good, you do that.' Katherine smiled at Waldron, waggled her fingers in a goodbye gesture and then walked out of the room, leaving Lee to close the door behind her.

'What's at Nathan Road, Sergeant?' Waldron asked him when they were alone.

'The headquarters of the Kowloon police division,' Lee said.

'Yeah? Shame it isn't Kaznovetsky's.'

'Why's that?'

'Well, that particular restaurant across the way seems to be very popular with at least one of your top men.'

'Who are we talking about?'

'How the hell should I know? He's a tall guy, well-built and in his late forties,' said Waldron. 'I first saw him talking to that Assistant Commissioner of yours outside the bank on Friday morning.'

Given the time and the place, Lee thought it could only be Ramsay. His behaviour seemed a little odd, though. Except now that he came to think about it, he remembered seeing Ramsay earlier that afternoon with the Special Branch file on the Kaznovetsky family. Nikolai Kaznovetsky was an invalid and his younger daughter was locked up in a mental asylum, but Larissa was still regarded as a security risk; it could be that Ramsay was going to serve her with a detention order. Lee edged nearer the window and peered at the restaurant across the street from the Roxy, wondering if Ramsay was still there. If he was, it would save him the bother of explaining to Larissa Kaznovetsky why he wanted to use her phone to call Bramwell.

'What have you done with the key to your room, Mr Waldron?' he asked abruptly.

'It's in my pocket.'

'Then I think you'd better give it to me.'

'Whatever you say.' Waldron pulled out the key and chucked it at Lee, who caught it deftly in his left hand. 'I hope it's not a long walk, Sergeant,' he said. 'Or do you have a car parked near the hotel?'

'I'm about to send for one,' said Lee. 'In the meantime, I'm going to lock you in this room.'

'No car, no handcuffs and no firearm.' Waldron clicked his tongue. 'Seems to me you came unprepared.'

'I wouldn't do anything stupid if I were you.' Lee moved towards the door. 'You're in enough trouble as it is.'

'You don't have to tell me that,' said Waldron.

Lee thought the American seemed resigned, but he knew

that appearances were often deceptive. He wondered if he should relieve Waldron of the money Katherine Goddard had undoubtedly given him, but on reflection, decided it wasn't a very good idea. If the American denied it, he'd be obliged to search him – and that could be a risky business.

Locking the bedroom door behind him, Lee went down to the lobby, told the desk clerk that he would be back in a few minutes and then walked briskly across the road to Kaznovetsky's.

Donovan ran the tap, filled a tooth mug with cold water and took it over to Jill Hammond.

'Here, drink this,' he said, folding her hands around the beaker. 'It'll make you feel better.'

He doubted very much if it would; her face was the colour of paste and her skin clammy to the touch. A few hours back, Jill Hammond had been one of the most attractive young women in Hong Kong, but now, hunched up on the edge of the bed, she looked a physical wreck, her glossy hair dishevelled, the front of her silk dress stained with vomit. She had come round while he was returning the Ford sedan to Shau-chi's garage, and according to Ramsay, had sicked up the entire contents of her stomach. Although he'd done his best to clean her up, the sour odour of vomit still clung to her.

'Had enough?' Donovan asked her, after she had taken a few sips of water.

'Yes, thank you.' Her voice was little more than a whisper and still very shaky.

'Good.' Donovan removed the mug from her grasp and placed it on the glass shelf above the wash basin. 'In a little while from now you're going to talk to your husband.'

'You mean you're letting me go?'

'Hardly.' Donovan laughed. 'You're going to phone him at the bank and tell him you've been kidnapped. You'll say that you haven't the faintest idea where you're being held because you've been blindfolded, but he's not to worry, everything will be all right so long as he obeys the instructions which he'll receive in due course. Now, that's not very difficult to remember, is it?'

'No.'

'Fine, now let's hear it from you.'

'Later,' she said and rocked forward, her legs pressed together, as if holding herself in. 'When I've attended to myself.'

'When you've what?'

'Oh, for God's sake, I want to go to the lavatory.'

'Why the hell couldn't you say so in the first place, you stupid little bitch?' Donovan walked over to the door and opened it; then, returning to the bed, he grabbed her by the arm and led her out of the room and along the landing to the lavatory next-door. Digging his fingernails into the fleshy part of her upper arm, he shoved Jill inside and steered her towards the pan. 'The seat's right in front of you,' he said harshly. 'Think you can manage the rest?'

'Yes.' She swallowed hard in an effort to hold back the tears. 'Now please go away, I don't want you watching me.'

'Don't touch the blindfold then,' he warned, 'otherwise you'll find yourself in trouble.' He placed her hand on the toilet roll. 'The paper's here,' he said. 'Okay?'

'Yes.'

'Good. I hope I can rely on you to be sensible.'

Donovan pulled the door to behind him and then froze like a statue: he could hear footsteps on the staircase. Larissa Kaznovetsky? No; the tread was too heavy and the pace too brisk for her. One of the Chinese waiters, perhaps? He moved forward to peer over the bannisters and felt his stomach knot as Sergeant Lee looked up at him, his face registering surprise.

'Hello, Henry,' Donovan said, recovering first. 'What are you doing here?'

'I need to use the phone in the office.' A hesitant smile appeared on Lee's face. 'One of the chefs in the kitchen told me I'd have to get Miss Kaznovetsky's permission first.'

'And have you?'

'No, sir; I'm still trying to find her.'

'This call you want to make,' Donovan said slowly, 'I presume it's official business?'

'Yes, sir.' Lee reached the top of the stairs and came towards him. 'I want to ask Superintendent Bramwell if he'll send a car round to the Roxy Hotel in Peking Road so that I can bring Waldron in.'

'Waldron?' The name sounded familiar, but Donovan couldn't quite place it.

'The American who escaped from military custody on Wednesday night. Headquarters put out an APB for him.' Lee frowned. 'I'm pretty sure all the border posts were included on the distribution list.'

'I must be getting old, Sergeant. It had completely slipped my memory.'

Donovan wondered if he should offer to pass the message on; it would be the quickest way to get the sergeant off his back and out of the restaurant. On the other hand, Bramwell was bound to ask where and when he'd bumped into Lee, and that could lead to all kinds of complications. He was still trying to make up his mind whether or not he should tell Lee to go ahead and use the phone, when the toilet flushed in the lavatory. Then, above the noise of the running water, he heard Jill Hammond open the door, saw the look of amazement on Lee's face and knew there was only one thing he could do. Reaching inside his jacket, he snatched the .38 Colt revolver from the shoulder holster, jabbed the barrel into Lee's chest and hugging the sergeant to him in order to deaden the noise, he squeezed the trigger.

Lee sagged at the knees and gazed up at him, blood seeping from the corners of his mouth. For a split-second his eyes mirrored bewilderment, then they ceased to focus. Lowering his body to the floor, Donovan spun round and punched Jill Hammond in the stomach, hard enough to wind her before she had a chance to cry out. As she doubled up and began to topple forward, he bent down, slipped his left arm around both legs and hoisted her over his shoulder like a sack of coal. Aware that every second counted, he carried Jill Hammond into the small back room, dumped her on the bed and holstered the Colt revolver he was still holding in his right hand. That done, he gagged her with a handkerchief and tied her wrists behind her back with a length of sash-cord. Then he went out on to the landing again, dragged Lee into the lavatory and, locking the door, pocketed the key.

Ramsay stared at the blotter on the chief cashier's desk. Every square inch of the pad was taken up with a mass of pencilled question marks, yet he couldn't remember drawing them. He had read somewhere that doodling was supposed to be therapeutic, but it hadn't done anything to soothe his worries. He was still keyed up, and it was all Donovan's fault. If everything had gone according to plan, Hammond should have been running around like a headless chicken long before now, but still there had been no phone call from his wife – only a long and tense silence that was becoming more and more ominous.

It didn't seem to bother Hammond though, and that was the thing that really bugged him. If David was anxious about his wife's disappearance, or disappointed at failing to catch him out while he'd been away supposedly visiting Fortress Headquarters, he certainly wasn't showing it. Perhaps he was being unjust to Donovan? What if Jill Hammond was physically unable to talk to her husband? No; that couldn't be it; she had been fully conscious when he'd left her shortly before six-fifteen.

Ramsay walked over to the window and stood there gazing at Kaznovetsky's restaurant diagonally across the street. He couldn't leave the bank again, not after the way Hammond had reacted last time. What was it he'd said? 'This place is like a weather house; as soon as I come in, you go out.' A jocular but very pointed remark that had made his blood run cold. Spelling Donovan so that he could return the Ford sedan to Shau-chi's garage had been a mistake; he should have got either Thirsk or Adams to do it. But it was too late for second thoughts now.

Ramsay looked up at the office on the top floor, silently willing Donovan to do something; then suddenly, as if in response to his prayer, the phone rang loud and shrill behind him. His mouth suddenly dry, he returned to the desk and lifted the receiver off the cradle.

'Kowloon 9136,' he said, reading the number on the disc.

Donovan said, 'If you aren't doing so already, George, you'd better sit down.'

'What's gone wrong, Bill?'

'Sergeant Lee is dead,' Donovan told him in a flat voice. 'I just shot him.'

'You did *what*?' Ramsay said incredulously.

'I had no choice, George. He came blundering in here, wanting to use the telephone and he saw Jill Hammond.'

Five hundred thousand pounds' worth of diamonds had just gone down the sink, thanks to a million-to-one encounter which nobody could have foreseen. The wrong man in the wrong place at the wrong time; an epitaph for Lee, and one Ramsay thought the Hong Kong and Shanghai Bank should inscribe on his headstone in gold letters.

'It could have been worse, George,' Donovan continued. 'At least none of the staff heard the shot. Of course, Lee did speak to one of the chefs in the kitchen, but I've already dealt with that problem.'

'How?'

'I told Larissa to send everybody home and close the restaurant. Luckily, she hadn't taken any reservations for tonight.'

'How much does Larissa know?' Ramsay asked.

'She doesn't know that Lee was here, if that's what you mean. She's suffering from one hell of a hangover; I found her fast asleep on a couch in one of the private dining rooms on the second floor.'

Ramsay wedged the phone between his neck and shoulder and lit a cigarette. Maybe the diamonds hadn't gone down the sink after all. Instead of two dead kidnappers, there would now be three; two from the Red Spears Triad, plus Sergeant Lee. An autopsy would reveal that he had died before the other two, but the pathologist would have a hard time proving that if the restaurant went up in flames and the bodies were charred beyond recognition.

'You know something, Bill?' he said. 'I think we can still pull it off.'

'Yeah? What do you propose to do about Waldron?'

'Are you telling me that Lee ran the Yank to ground?'

'That's about the size of it,' said Donovan. 'He wanted Bramwell to send a car round to the Roxy to pick him up. Lee had two keys on him belonging to the hotel; one's a pass key, the other has a tag labelled Room 105. I reckon that's where you'll find Waldron.'

It was a logical deduction, but Ramsay was quick to see that a piece of the jigsaw puzzle was still missing. According to the information Bramwell had received, Waldron was supposed to be hiding out in the Peninsula Hotel, yet Lee had traced him to the Roxy. That meant a third party was involved, somebody who had unwittingly led him to Waldron. But who? Ramsay scowled; he should have pressed Bramwell for more information, but when he had come cap in hand to the CID for help, his only thought had been that here was a heaven-sent opportunity to keep Lee occupied.

'Are you still there, George?' Donovan said impatiently. 'What are we going to do?'

'I'm still thinking,' Ramsay said.

'Well, don't take all night. Time's running on, and Garcia's people will be here soon.'

Waldron would have to go, Ramsay thought. He was the loose thread that could unravel the whole intricate piece of weaving.

'You'd better phone Thirsk and Adams,' he said. 'Tell them from me that they're to meet you at Kaznovetsky's and then give them the keys to the Roxy. Waldron has to disappear, and I mean disappear.'

'And they've got the job?' Donovan said quietly.

'Right.'

'Suppose they don't like the idea? Some folk can be a mite squeamish when the going gets rough.'

'Thirsk won't be,' Ramsay told him bluntly. 'He's already got Pascoe's blood on his hands.'

'Seems to me, George, you'll be the only one who'll come out of this affair smelling like a rose.'

The first sign of a split? If it was, he'd better do something about it, and quick. 'Don't be stupid, Bill,' Ramsay said, and chuckled. 'I'm in this thing up to my neck, and you know it.'

'I was only joking, George.'

'Of course you were. Now, suppose you do as I ask and then arrange for Jill Hammond to have a few words with her husband?'

'Give me twenty minutes,' Donovan said, 'and then the roof will fall in on top of Hammond.'

'Good.'

Ramsay put the phone down and stubbed out his cigarette. They had been through a sticky patch, but they were back on course again and he reckoned he had the situation under control. He didn't know who the third party was yet, but he would prise that information out of Bramwell when he rang him allegedly to ask when he could expect to have Lee back. Meantime, there was nothing he could do now except sit back and wait for things to happen.

Dusk was closing in, the shadows stealing across the room. Leaving the desk, Ramsay switched on the lights and drew the blackout curtains.

CHAPTER FIFTEEN

Its headlights reduced to narrow slits by masking tape, the saloon came on slowly down the street from the direction of Nathan Road and drew into the kerbside, to stop just short of the Roxy Hotel. Although he didn't recognize the make,

Waldron knew the car was a British model; it was compact and less than half the size of the average American sedan. Watching the two men get out and walk into the courtyard behind Kaznovetsky's restaurant, he wondered if they were police officers responding to a phone call from Sergeant Lee. On reflection, it seemed unlikely. For one thing, both men were obviously British, and he couldn't see them taking orders from a Chinese sergeant; for another, he wasn't important enough to warrant such VIP treatment. In fact, judging by Lee's pro- longed absence, the Hong Kong police attached no importance to him whatsoever.

Waldron drew the curtains and switched on the light. How long had the little Chinaman been gone now? Thirty minutes? No, it was more like three-quarters of an hour, if the number of cigarette stubs in the ashtray was anything to go by. No doubt about it, Kaznovetsky's was a popular haunt with some police officers; apparently it was the kind of place where they could be sure of several free drinks on the house at any time of the day or night, whether it was open or closed.

Suddenly, in the act of lighting yet another cigarette, Wal- dron froze; Kaznovetsky's was closed, he'd seen the staff leaving by the back way twenty minutes ago. Of course there was no reason why Lee shouldn't be enjoying a quiet drink with the proprietor, but what about the two men who'd just arrived? Apart from the fact that there were no waiters, people who dined at Kaznovetsky's didn't usually enter the restaurant via the kitchen. A gut feeling told him there was something very wrong, and switching off the light, he groped his way to the window and drew the curtains aside.

A black car in a dark street. It was a sinister reminder of another time in another place, less than six months back: Thursday, 12th June, the night he'd left New York in a hurry, only to find that the opposition had been one move ahead and were lying in wait for him ten yards up the road from his sister's house in Yonkers. The night a bullet hole had appeared in the windscreen of his sedan a mere inch or so above his head . . . He tried telling himself that this was Kowloon, not Yonkers, but the feeling of having trod this path before persisted. It grew even stronger when the two men emerged from the courtyard and started across the road towards the hotel.

Waldron removed the cigarette that was still clinging to his bottom lip and tossed it away. If Lee had set him up, he was a sitting duck. The door was locked, the pavement was a good fifteen feet below and he couldn't get into either of the adjoining rooms because the damned window ledge wasn't wide enough for him to stand on. He didn't fancy his chances much; the odds were two to one, and the only weapon to hand was an upright chair.

Correction; there were two weapons to hand – the door happened to open inwards. If he stood with his back to the wall, he could take the first man from behind, then shoulder-charge the door into his companion. Waldron scowled; it sounded all too easy in theory, but the men he was up against weren't idiots, and they weren't likely to charge headlong into a darkened room. He needed an angle, something so totally unexpected that it would throw them completely out of their stride. Katherine Goddard! He snapped his fingers; right from the moment Lee had let her go, she had been the ace up his sleeve. The sound of footsteps in the corridor warned him that time was running out. Crossing the room, he lay down on the bed.

A key slotted into the lock and unlatched it. The door flew open and banged against the bed; a split-second later a hand found the light switch and they moved into the room crabwise, their backs against the far wall. Then a harsh voice said 'Police', and he sat bolt upright, mouth agape, eyes wide open, a befuddled uncomprehending expression on his face, as though he'd just woken up. Mutt and Jeff, Waldron thought, sizing them up; one on the short side and pear-shaped, the other lean and tall with a face that looked as though it had been chiselled out of granite.

'Jesus,' he said. 'You guys almost gave me a heart attack busting in here like that.'

'Too bad.' The pear-shaped officer waved his automatic at

him. 'On your feet, Waldron,' he growled.

'Sure, anything you say.' Waldron swung his feet off the bed and stood up. 'You guys took your time, didn't you? My lawyer must be wondering what the hell's happened to me.'

'What lawyer?'

Waldron raised an eyebrow. 'The one my girl briefed to meet us at Nathan Road. I can't understand why Sergeant Lee didn't tell you.'

The pear-shaped officer glanced questioningly at his companion, and the moment's hesitation gave Waldron just the opportunity he had been waiting for. Grabbing hold of his lapels, he stuck out his left leg and hurled him sideways into his companion. Bowled over backwards, the tall, thin man cannoned into the wall, his head striking it with a sickening thud. Then, as if in slow motion, he slid down the wall and ended up on his buttocks, his legs temporarily pinning the pear-shaped officer to the floor.

Waldron stepped over them, slammed the door behind him and ran along the corridor. As he started down the staircase, an automatic boomed and a bullet gouged a lump of wood out of the bannisters. Jumping the last four steps, he tore through the lobby into the street and veered right in the direction of Hankow Road. He had no preconceived plan of action, and only a sketchy idea of the neighbourhood. His one aim was to find a bolt-hole where he could lie low for a while, and he ran as he'd never run before in his life.

Turning left at the T-junction, Waldron headed towards Salisbury Road. There was a faint chance he might be able to flag down a cruising taxi-cab before the two police officers caught up with him. Then, spotting a small restaurant on the right-hand side of the road which was open, he changed his mind, figuring there was safety in numbers, that they were unlikely to try anything in front of witnesses. Still breathing heavily, he ducked into the entrance, pushed the door open and walked inside.

The restaurant wasn't as crowded as he might have hoped, but amongst the handful of diners he saw one elderly couple who were obviously British. Catching the head waiter's eye, he pointed to an adjoining table in the window and moved purposefully towards it. Above the low murmur of voices, he heard a car drive slowly past the restaurant.

Slowly, Hammond put the phone down and stared into space. 'They've kept me blindfolded and I'm terrified of what they may do to me. If you love me, David, please, *please* do as they ask.' He could still hear Jill's voice, and her heart-rending plea was going to live with him for the rest of his life. He had wanted to tell her that there was nothing he wouldn't do to get her back, but they had hung up on him before he'd had a chance to say one lousy word.

'Everything will be all right so long as you obey the instructions which you will receive in due course.' Jill had left the house shortly after ten-thirty, and it was now almost eight o'clock. For Christ's sake, how much longer did they intend to keep him in the dark? So everything was going to be all right, was it? Much as he would have liked to believe that assurance, he knew it was a hollow promise. From what Chan Chok, the number one houseboy, had told him, it was obvious that Jill must have seen at least one of the kidnappers; and that meant they couldn't risk letting her go.

Hammond left the desk, opened the office safe and removed the web belt and pistol holster. The army had issued him with twelve rounds of ammunition for the .455 Webley revolver. He had been expecting to use it against the Japanese, but right now, the real enemy was sitting nextdoor in the chief cashier's office. It would be very satisfying to point the revolver at Ramsay and squeeze the trigger, but he knew that wouldn't solve anything. Ramsay wasn't the only one who was involved, and he wanted Jill back alive. Leaving the web belt and pistol holster on the desk, Hammond strode over to the door and yanked it open.

'Ramsay.' He spat the name out, his voice a whipcrack of suppressed fury that startled Talbot and the Chinese detective constable on duty in the main hall. Observing their anxious expressions, he wondered just whose side they would be on when it came to the crunch.

'What's the matter, David?' Ramsay appeared in the doorway of the chief cashier's office. 'You sound very het up. He gazed at him quizzically. 'Don't tell me the war has started at last?'

'I'm not sure about you, George, but it has for me.' Hammond steered Ramsay into his office and closed the door behind him. 'My wife has been kidnapped.'

'She's been *what?*'

Hammond thought no actor could have given a better performance. In three words, Ramsay had managed to convey complete surprise and inject a note of incredulity at one and the same time.

'How do you know she's been kidnapped? I mean, did you receive a ransom note, or what?'

'Jill spoke to me on the phone,' Hammond told him. 'All she could say was that everything would be all right so long as I toed the line and did as I was told. It seems my instructions will arrive in due course.'

'That's standard procedure. Meantime, they're going to leave you to sweat it out.'

'You're talking from experience, are you, George?'

'The eldest son of one of the richest Chinese merchants in Kowloon was abducted a few years back,' Ramsay said. 'I worked on the case with Challinor.'

'What happened?'

'The merchant decided to pay up and asked us to drop the investigation. It cost him a packet, but he got his son back safe and sound.'

'What do you call a packet, George?' Hammond asked him in a dangerously quiet voice.

'Two hundred thousand Hong Kong dollars.' Ramsay paused. Then, as if the thought had just occurred to him, he said, 'Could you put that much together if you had to?'

'And more, much more.'

'Then you must be a lot wealthier than I supposed.'

'Don't give me that rubbish,' Hammond said abrasively. 'I think you know exactly what I'm worth, right down to the last ingot.'

'Are you referring to the gold bullion?' Ramsay shook his head. 'But that's the craziest thing I ever heard!'

'Can you think of a better motive for kidnapping Jill?'

'Not offhand, no. But, if you're right about their motive, it means that they must have been tipped off about the shipment.'

'That thought had occurred to me.'

'I suppose somebody in the bank could have leaked the information,' Ramsay said, frowning.

'Or a police officer who was conversant with "Sovereign".'

'We're getting a bit personal, aren't we? Maybe I'm being over-sensitive, but somehow I get the impression you think I'm involved in some way.'

'How right you are, George.'

'I'm going to ignore that last remark, David. You're over-wrought – you don't know what you're saying.'

The injured party one moment, the experienced police officer full of understanding the next. Whatever else he might be, Ramsay was very adroit, and cool as an iceberg.

'It's only natural you should want to lash out,' he went on, 'but that's not the way to handle this situation. We've got to out-think and out-smart these people, and we need help to do that.'

'Who from?' Hammond asked huskily.

'Kellerman, amongst others.' Then, unhurriedly, Ramsay moved past him and picked up the phone.

Bramwell had lost count of the number of times his phone had rung since nightfall. It seemed to him that at least half the British expatriates living in Kowloon had called him up to report some imagined act of sabotage in their neighbourhood. The number of flashing lights that had been observed in the area of Boundary Street and Prince Edward Road alone had already reached double figures, and the way things were going, he reckoned it wouldn't be long before the system of policing the city broke down altogether. Instead of pounding their beats, most of his constables were running around in ever-widening circles trying to track down an elusive army of Fifth Columnists. The war hadn't started yet, but as far as some members of the public were concerned, there were spies everywhere, busy signalling to Jap planes that were still sitting on the ground at their forward airfields. Now, just as he thought things were beginning to quieten down, the damned phone was ringing again. Slowly and more than a little reluctantly, Bramwell answered it and gave the number of his extension.

'Is that Superintendent Bramwell?'

The caller had a Scots accent and sounded almost as irritable as he was.

'It is,' he said.

'Good. My name is Alastair Macdonald of Clarke, Doran and Macdonald. You may not have heard of us because we usually deal with conveyancing and like matters.'

'I see.' Bramwell didn't, but there had been a longish pause in the conversation and he assumed Macdonald was waiting for some sort of comment from him.

'However, Superintendent, it so happens that on this occasion I am acting on behalf of a Miss Goddard.'

'Katherine Goddard?' Bramwell said, interrupting him.

'Yes. Are you acqainted with her, Superintendent?'

'I met her this afternoon; she's the resident nurse at the Peninsula Hotel.'

'Then you won't be surprised to learn that Miss Goddard has asked me to represent an American friend of hers, a Mr Frank Waldron. I understand he was arrested at approximately six-thirty this evening and is now being held in custody at Nathan Road.'

'I'm afraid you've been misinformed,' Bramwell said politely. 'We're still looking for Waldron.'

'Really?' Well, I'm informed by Miss Goddard that she was present when your Sergeant Lee arrested him at the Roxy Hotel in Peking Road. Furthermore, she claims that Sergeant Lee told her that he was unable to say what charges would be preferred against Mr Waldron until he had spoken to you.' Macdonald paused. 'Now what am I to make of that, Superintendent?'

'It's all very puzzling,' Bramwell admitted, 'but the fact remains that your client is not in police custody.'

'Puzzling is not the word I would choose.'

Inwardly Bramwell groaned. He hadn't heard a word from Lee, despite his explicit instructions that he was to keep Katherine Goddard under surveillance and report her movements. The girl had obviously led him to Waldron, but instead of phoning for assistance, Lee had confronted them both and then, for some reason, allowed her to go.

'I am aware of the political manoeuvring that has been going on behind the scenes,' Macdonald continued, 'and it is my opinion that you are determined to hold my client incommunicado until arrangements have been made for his extradition to the United States.'

'That's absolute nonsense,' Bramwell said firmly. 'I can assure you we've nothing to hide.'

'Except Mr Waldron,' Macdonald said pithily.

Bramwell sighed. The last thing he needed was a crusading lawyer, especially one who appeared to think he could use the Waldron affair to put the police in a bad light and make a name for himself at the same time.

'Now look, sir,' he said diplomatically, 'you don't have to take my word for it. Why don't you call round to Nathan Road and see for yourself that we're not holding your client?'

'Don't worry, Superintendent, I intend to – after I've seen a High Court judge.'

'A High Court judge?' Bramwell repeated in a hollow voice.

'Yes. It may take me some time to run one to ground on a Sunday night, and I don't imagine I shall be exactly popular when I do. But then neither will you after I've said my piece and obtained a writ of Habeas Corpus.'

Bramwell heard the phone go down with a loud clunk and slowly replaced the receiver his end. Macdonald's threat to obtain a writ of Habeas Corpus didn't bother him one bit: the lawyer could arrive with a whole sackful and it wouldn't make a jot of difference, because no High Court judge could compel him to produce a body he didn't have. What did bother him was the fact that before Lee had allowed Katherine Goddard to leave the hotel, he had evidently told her that Waldron was under arrest and that he was taking him to Nathan Road; then, when he and Waldron were alone, something had happened to make him change his mind.

A bribe? Bramwell didn't think so. Although the CID had been riddled with corruption in Challinor's day, Lee had always been known as 'Honest Henry'. What if Waldron had attacked the sergeant, knocked him cold and then got clean away? The American was certainly a good forty pounds heavier and had probably been trained in unarmed combat while he was serving in the Canadian Army. But Macdonald had said that Waldron had been arrested at approximately six-thirty and that meant Lee would now have been unconscious for more than two hours. Or dead? Bramwell grunted. He was letting his imagination run away with him; chances were the sergeant had never moved from the Peninsula Hotel and was still there, keeping the desk clerk company. As for the rest, Waldron had decided to delay his extradition and to do that he needed a lawyer. And the quickest way to get one was for Katherine Goddard to say that he'd been arrested by the police. It was a comforting explanation, but was there any substance to it?

More in hope than anticipation, Bramwell rang the Peninsula Hotel, asked the switchboard to put him through to Reception and then told the desk clerk he wanted to speak to Sergeant Lee. The request led to an interminably long conversation with some unintelligible voice in the background; then finally the desk clerk told him that nobody had seen Sergeant Lee since he left the hotel shortly after four-thirty.

There were, he thought, only two lines of inquiry he could follow now. It was questionable who would provide the more reliable information, Katherine Goddard or the management of the Roxy Hotel, but after some deliberation, Bramwell decided he would try the bawdy house in Peking Road first. Grabbing his steel helmet and respirator from the hat peg behind the door, he left the office and went in search of his Chinese driver.

The night was still and dark, the moon hidden by scudding clouds. Up on the frontier at Lo Wu, a detachment of Engineers, covered by a platoon from 'C' Company of the 2nd/14th Punjabis, waited for the order to blow the two bridges over the Sham Chun river. Ten miles farther back, the Gin Drinkers Line, which stretched from Tsun Wan across to Tolo inlet and then down to Devil's Peak opposite the Lei Mun channel off the east coast of Hong Kong Island, was manned by the 2nd Royal Scots, the 5th/7th Rajputs and the remainder of the 2nd/14th Punjabis.

Kowloon was blacked out; so too was the bustling city of Victoria across the narrow strip of water. Around the shores of the island, the machine-gunners of the 1st Middlesex stood to in their dank concrete bunkers. Behind them in the dark hills of the hinterland, the men of the Winnipeg Grenadiers, the Royal Rifles of Canada and the Hong Kong Volunteer Defence Corps crouched in slit trenches hacked out of solid rock and hard-baked earth. Well beyond the maximum range of the six-inch coastal guns of Fort Stanley, four motor torpedo boats patrolled far into the South China Sea on the lookout for units of the Imperial Japanese Navy.

At Kai Tak airfield on the outskirts of Kowloon, an RAF sentry guarded two Walrus amphibians and three ancient Vickers Vildebeest torpedo bombers. But all that the sentry and the ground crew manning the two anti-aircraft machine guns could hear was the gentle lapping of the sea against the hull of the Pan Am clipper scheduled to take off for Manilla at eight o'clock the following morning.

CHAPTER SIXTEEN

Ramsay could tell that Kellerman wasn't sure what to make of the situation. It showed in the way he kept saying 'I see' every time Hammond paused for breath. Although the Assistant Commissioner had spent twenty years in the Hong Kong Police, Ramsay knew this particular case was like no other he'd investigated, and the absence of a recognizable pattern obviously puzzled him.

'What I don't understand,' Kellerman said in a plaintive voice, 'is why you haven't yet received a ransom demand.'

'It's all part of their plan to exert maximum psychological pressure.' Hammond turned his head in Ramsay's direction. 'Isn't that what you said, George?'

'It's the only logical explanation I can think of.' Ramsay trod warily. So far there had only been a number of veiled hints from Hammond, but it was vital he asserted himself before the accusing finger was pointed at him. 'As for the ransom,' he continued, 'I reckon we've got to assume these people are after the gold bullion.'

'That's a pretty large assumption,' Kellerman said.

'Well, I admit it takes a bit of swallowing but the fact is that the kidnappers contacted David at the bank – and I think that's very significant.'

'Too right,' Hammond said vehemently. 'It's proof to me that they must have had inside information.'

'Quite.' Kellerman frowned. 'Of course, it's possible your wife may have told them you were here.'

'I hadn't thought of that.'

Ramsay fingered his upper lip, hiding a smile of satisfaction. Things were going better than he'd dared to hope. With his timely observation, Kellerman had cut the ground from under Hammond's feet and become an unwitting ally.

'All the same,' continued Kellerman, 'I fail to see what these people can hope to achieve. They must know the police won't stand idly by while you open up the vault for them.'

'I believe you'll find they've already taken that into account, Commissioner,' said Hammond.

Ramsay broke in swiftly. 'David's right. Crazy as it may sound, I've a hunch they want the gold to stay where it is.'

Kellerman stared at him, his mouth open as though he'd just received a body blow that had left him winded. 'Who do you mean by "they"?' he asked finally.

'Either Wong Chang Wai's Fifth Column, or the Red Spears Triad.' Ramsay leaned against the office safe, arms folded across his chest. 'If I had to choose between them, I'd put my money on Wong Chang Wai's people. Even if Japanese Intelligence hasn't got wind of Operation "Sovereign", they're shrewd enough to guess our intentions, and it's only logical to suppose they'd try to stop the bullion transfer. On the other hand, we've heard on the grapevine that "Sovereign" is no longer a closely guarded secret so far as the Triad is concerned; it's always possible that Li Ho Chung is anxious to do the Japs a favour.'

'In return for what?' Hammond snapped.

'The elimination of his rivals and a free hand to run the Black Market, the only kind of economy which is bound to flourish under the Japanese. At least, I imagine that's how Li Ho Chung sees it. Still, it's all pretty academic, and we're wasting valuable time. Whether we're dealing with the Fifth Column or the Triad, you can bet they've got the bank under observation and are waiting to see how we react.'

'It doesn't make sense to me,' Kellerman said irritably. 'Until they make their demands known, we can't do a bloody thing.'

'That's the whole idea, don't you see? The longer they can keep us in the dark, the better it is for them. Time is on their side. If they have their way, we won't hear another word from them until the trucks arrive to pick up the bullion. I'm only guessing now, but if they can delay the transfer for three to four hours, the *Delphic Star* will miss the morning tide and they will have achieved their aim.'

'It's a very plausible theory.' Kellerman flexed his swagger cane, bending it in a bow between his meaty hands. 'But how can we put it to the test?'

'Maybe we can force the pace.' Ramsay turned to Hammond. 'I think you should phone your chairman, David, and tell him that Jill has been kidnapped. Give him the facts, then put the Assistant Commissioner on the line so that he can explain why you should be replaced.'

'Replaced? You mean, you want me out of the way, George?'

It was exactly what he wanted, and he proceeded to give them a number of cast-iron reasons why it was necessary. The opposition was using David as a lever, he explained; remove him from the scene and they would have to break their self-imposed silence. Up to now they had been calling the tune, but from now on things would be different; next time they rang up, the phone company would be standing by to trace the call.

'Like I said before, David, we've got to out-think and out-smart these people. And we do have one big advantage: we know they've tapped our phones.'

'Do we?'

'You doubt it?' Ramsay shook his head. 'Surely you remember the trouble you had this morning when you thought they were out of order? Take it from me, there was no temporary fault on the line; you couldn't dial out because they were busy tapping into the junction box.'

'We're going to feed them with false information? Is that the idea?'

'Right.'

'So why do I have to leave the bank?'

'Because if you don't, they'll think we're bluffing.'

'I don't like it,' Hammond told him. 'Suppose I go along with your suggestion and we don't hear from them again? What happens then?'

'We're not putting all our eggs in one basket, David. Naturally we'll question all your neighbours – it's more than likely one of them will be able to give us a lead. People don't simply vanish into thin air without leaving a trace.'

'You're whistling in the dark, and you know it. My place is here at the bank where they can reach me whenever they want.'

'We need your cooperation,' Ramsay said, looking grave. 'Unless we get it, you may not see your wife again. I'm sorry to be so blunt about it, but you have got to face the facts. There is no way we can help you if you insist on tying our hands behind our backs. It's as simple as that.'

'Chief Inspector Ramsay is absolutely right, Mr Hammond,' Kellerman said. 'If necessary, I'm prepared to go over your head and speak to your chairman myself.'

It was, Ramsay thought, the decisive turning-point. He had won Kellerman over. Now he was home and dry.

'I suppose Richard Jervis could take over from me,' Hammond said reluctantly. 'He's the Director of Finance.'

'Can we get hold of him easily?' Kellerman asked.

'It shouldn't be difficult. Jervis embarked on the *Delphic Star* earlier this evening. He's supposed to be sailing with the bullion to Sydney.'

'Good.' Kellerman placed his swagger cane on the desk and lifted the phone off the hook. 'What's the home number of your chairman?'

'87114,' Hammond said. 'But you'd better let me talk to him first.'

The nearest thing to a licensed brothel, the Roxy Hotel was usually open twenty-four hours a day; but now it looked as though the inmates had suddenly gone on strike. The windows on the ground floor were shuttered on the inside and the double swing doors in the entrance were bolted top and bottom. Peering into the lobby, Bramwell saw a crack of light under a door at the far end of the passageway beyond the reception desk and pressed the button set into the wall on his left, which he assumed was supposed to summon the night porter. Nothing happened. He tried it again, but it seemed that either the buzzer was out of order or else the night porter was determined not to hear it. Never one to give up easily, Bramwell told his Chinese driver to use his truncheon on the plate glass.

Several hammer-blows later, the door at the far end opened and a thin figure hurried towards them, waving both arms in protest, until he noticed the police constable standing next to Bramwell. Then the arm-waving stopped abruptly and the Chinaman unbolted the swing doors.

'About time,' Bramwell said and shouldered past him into the lobby.

He made straight for the Reception Desk and turned the hotel register towards him; then, borrowing the constable's flashlight, he checked the entries on the last page. King George the Sixth, Winston Churchill, Genghis Khan and Franklin Delano Roosevelt; faced with that limited choice, it wasn't difficult to guess which pseudonym Waldron would have used when he'd checked in.

'The man who was in Room 105,' he said slowly and distinctly. 'What time did he leave?'

The Chinaman stared at him for a few blank seconds, then delivered a long speech in Cantonese. Unable to understand more than about one word in ten, Bramwell turned to his driver.

'What was that all about, Sammy?' he asked irritably.

'This man is the desk clerk, sir. He says the hotel is closed and everybody has gone home.' The constable cleared his throat noisily. 'He also says that if you want a girl you must come back tomorrow.'

'Did he now,' Bramwell said grimly. 'Well, you inform this bloody little pimp from me that unless I get some straight answers to some straight questions, I'm going to lock him in a cell and throw away the key. Then tell him I want to know exactly what happened when Sergeant Lee was here earlier this evening.'

'Yes, sir.'

'And just this once, try to look as though you're angry, Sammy.'

The constable nodded, then rounded on his fellow country-man, his voice sounding untypically harsh to Bramwell. For good measure, he repeatedly slapped the palm of his left hand with the truncheon in a way which suggested he would be only too delighted to use it on the desk clerk if he gave him any nonsense. What followed was a protracted and voluble exchange that lasted all of ten minutes. At the end of it, Bramwell learned that Lee had left the hotel at six-forty-five, shortly after Katherine Goddard had departed and some ten minutes before Waldron did.

'Bullshit. He's lying in his teeth.' Bramwell jabbed the desk clerk in the chest. 'Look at the little bastard, Sammy, he's sweating like a pig.'

'Yes, sir.'

'It's warm in here, but I'm not sweating and neither are you, yet it's dripping off him. Something happened here that scared him witless, and I mean to find out just what it was.' Bramwell moved behind the reception desk, trained the flashlight on the board and removed the keys to the rooms which King George the Sixth, Winston Churchill, Genghis Khan and Franklin Delano Roosevelt had allegedly occupied on the first floor. 'Meantime, you stay here and keep a firm grip on this creep. I don't want him vanishing into the night the moment my back's turned.'

Bramwell walked across the lobby, found the light switch at the bottom of the staircase and went on up. Three of the four bedrooms he checked out all told the same story; the sheets thrown aside, the wardrobes hanging open, clear signs the occupants had left in a hurry. The exception was 105, the room Waldron had rented. Instead of chaos, there was order, the bed still made up, the curtains drawn and the wardrobe locked.

Bramwell didn't know what to make of it. According to the desk clerk, Lee and Waldron had left separately, and judging by the state of the room, it didn't appear they'd had an argument. Maybe the American had bribed the sergeant to let him go? But if that was the case, why had the people in the adjoining rooms departed in such obvious panic? Closing the door behind him, he moved back to the staircase.

It was then he noticed that a large sliver of wood had been gouged out of the handrail on top of the banisters. There was also a peculiar smell, one he couldn't identify until he touched the scar and found the wood was still tacky. Somebody had stained it with varnish in a crude attempt to make it appear that the damage had occurred some time ago. That same somebody had also filled in a hole with putty high up on the far wall, before distempering it over. Measuring the distance by eye from Room 105 to where he was standing, Bramwell figured the angle was about right, that a bullet striking the handrail would have ricocheted into the wall. He could understand now what had prompted the exodus from the Roxy Hotel. However, as far as he knew, Waldron was unarmed and Lee had certainly left his revolver in the armoury. So who had fired at who? Deep in thought, he descended the stairs to the lobby.

'Did you find anything, sir?' the constable asked him.

Bramwell nodded emphatically and pointed to the desk clerk. 'You can tell that little shit he's under arrest, Sammy.'

'Yes, sir. What are we charging him with?'

'Obstructing the police in the course of their duties will do for a start. By the time you've got him handcuffed and into the car, I dare say I'll have thought of several other offences.'

Leaving Sammy to cope with the formalities, Bramwell walked towards the swing doors. For a few moments there was total silence; then in a high-pitched voice, the desk clerk began to lodge a long and agitated protest. Listening to the caterwaul behind him, Bramwell wondered if Katherine Goddard would also raise Cain when he told her she would have to accompany him to Nathan Road.

The Peninsula Hotel was invariably quiet on a Sunday night, but never more so than on this occasion. At five-past nine, the vast and near-empty lobby reminded Katherine Goddard of Euston Station in the small hours of the morning after the last train had departed. Four card-players seated round a table, the dowdy companion of the hotel's eldest permanent resident and Ramon, the Filipino barman; in view of the warning she had received from Frank, she could have wished for a larger gathering of people.

'Another Scotch on the rocks, Miss Goddard?' Ramon asked.

Katherine stared at the crushed ice melting in the bottom of her glass and wondered how many she'd had already. Three? Or was it four? No matter, she was still stone cold sober. 'Why not?' she said, and pushed the glass towards the barman.

In the cathedral-like hush, the sound of measured footsteps on the marble floor echoed through the lobby. One of the card-players looked up frowning, his concentration momentarily disturbed by the rhythmic *click-clack* of steel-tipped heels.

'I'm afraid I shan't have time for another drink after all,' Katherine said to Ramon in a low voice.

'Oh, why's that, Miss Goddard?'

'Well, it looks like I'm wanted elsewhere. That gentleman you see coming towards me is Superintendent Bramwell.'

'Is he a friend of yours?'

'Not exactly, but I'd like you to meet him.' Katherine uncrossed her legs and slipped off the bar stool. 'Good evening, Superintendent Bramwell.' She smiled and waved a hand at the Filipino barman. 'I don't think you know Ramon, do you?'

'No, I don't,' Bramwell said curtly.

'Ramon never forgets a face.' Katherine opened her handbag and took out a small notebook. 'Or a name,' she added.

'Neither do I.'

'That's something you have in common, then.' Katherine tore a page out of the notebook and handed it to the barman. 'This is the telephone number of my solicitor, Ramon,' she said. 'Perhaps you would be kind enough to ring Mr Macdonald and tell him that Superintendent Bramwell has taken me to Nathan Road.' She turned to face Bramwell. 'I presume we are going to Nathan Road, aren't we?'

'We are.'

'Good. Mr Macdonald would be more than a little upset if he had to spend the rest of the night looking for me.'

'I'm not about to cross swords with him again.' Bramwell placed a hand under Katherine's elbow and steered her towards the arcade.

'I gather he's already been in touch with you, then?' she asked.

'We had words earlier this evening. He thinks Waldron is in police custody and threatened to obtain a writ of Habeas Corpus unless I produced him forthwith.'

'Was this before or after your men tried to kill him?'

'Men?' Bramwell halted in mid-stride and spun her round to face him. 'What men?' he snapped.

'Two of your police officers,' Katherine said angrily. 'According to Frank, Sergeant Lee gave them the key to his room.'

'These men – were they Chinese?'

'British.' Katherine paused, then said, 'I think I should warn you that Mr Waldron will have made a full statement to my solicitor by now.'

'Thanks for the tip,' Bramwell said dryly. 'At least now I know where to find him.'

Adams turned off Waterloo Road into Argyle Street, drove slowly past the Kowloon hospital and drew up outside the block of flats where he lived. Shifting the gear stick into neutral, he applied the handbrake and switched off the ignition. Then he stretched both arms above his head and yawned, a nervous mannerism which Thirsk had learned to recognize over the years.

'You know something?' he said morosely. 'I reckon we've lost the bastard.'

'That's a glimpse of the blindingly obvious.' Thirsk explored the lump on the back of his head and examined his fingertips to see if there was any blood on them.

'Time's running on,' Adams continued in the same monotone. 'It's almost nine-thirty.'

'So?'

'So what are we going to do? I mean, should we phone Ramsay and let him know the score?'

'What good will that do? George can't go looking for Waldron. He's got enough problems to deal with as it is.'

'I'm not denying that, but I don't think we should keep him in the dark. The fact is, there's been a fucking cock-up and the whole sodding deal is now in jeopardy.' Adams turned to face him. 'Don't you see, there's no way we can lift the bullion while he's loose.'

'What are you trying to say, Derek? That the merry-go-round is out of control and you want to get off before it blows up?'

'Hell, no. I was just trying to put myself in Ramsay's place and look at the situation from his point in view.'

'It's far too late in the day for second thoughts.' Thirsk smiled in the darkness. 'That's what George would tell you.'

Adams was a blow-hard, all mouth and no backbone. The ex-military policeman was very good at beating the shit out of some undersized Chink suspect, but he was always the first to want out when the going got rough. You couldn't depend on him in a crisis – the way he'd lost his head after Waldron had caught him napping was proof of that. Trying to gun the Yank down in the hotel was easily the most stupid thing he could have done in the circumstances, and as a result, he'd had to waste precious minutes scaring the living daylights out of the desk clerk in order to make sure he kept his mouth shut. By the time he'd rammed that simple message into the man's thick skull, Waldron had vanished, and they'd had to spend the last three hours looking for him, driving round and round in circles and busy getting nowhere.

'I suppose you're right,' Adams said reluctantly after a long silence. 'All the same, I still think Waldron could make a lot of trouble for us.'

'That's where you're wrong,' Thirsk told him firmly. 'He'll lie low and do nothing. As far as he's concerned, the police are all tarred with the same brush. He won't risk getting his head shot off a second time. Besides, you've got to remember, Waldron didn't escape from military custody because he wanted to paint the town red.'

'The FBI.' Adams laughed and pounded the steering wheel

with a clenched fist. 'Jesus Christ, I'd forgotten the FBI were after him.'

Some of his lost courage had returned, but Thirsk reckoned it still needed bolstering with the Dutch kind. 'Have you got any of the hard stuff in your flat?' he asked him.

'You name it, I've got it,' Adams said cheerfully.

'Good. Why don't we have a quick one before we report to the bank? We're not due there until ten o'clock.'

'That's the best idea you've had tonight,' Adams said, already halfway out of the car.

Jill Hammond lay motionless on the bed. The Irishman who called himself Inspector Donaldson had promised her that everything would be all right provided David followed his instructions, but much as she wanted to believe him, the nagging doubts persisted and grew stronger by the minute. How could he afford to let her go when she had seen his face and could describe every line, every contour? And what about the other man, the one who had told her that David had fractured his wrist? He had been here in this tiny room, had cleaned her up when she had vomited; she'd heard the Irishman call him George. Both were gone now, but she wasn't alone. There were two Cantonese guarding her, and although their sing-song voices had been silent for what seemed an age, she knew they were still there. Her ears had become her eyes, and she could hear their shallow breathing.

'They've kept me blindfolded and I'm terrified of what they may do to me.' Those words she had spoken to David were beginning to sound like her epitaph.

CHAPTER SEVENTEEN

Richard Jervis was a good head shorter than Ramsay, had thin, receding fair hair and a long, narrow aristocratic-looking face which was complemented by a somewhat aloof manner. His voice was both languid and plummy, and he had a habit of saying 'orf' instead of 'off'. First impressions were, however, deceptive, and despite the indolent air which Ramsay suspected he assiduously cultivated, Jervis had a quick and incisive brain. Although he'd had no idea why he had been summoned to the bank, it had taken Kellerman hardly any time at all to brief him, something which hadn't pleased Hammond one bit.

'Are you sure we've covered everything, Richard?'

It was the second time Hammond had asked him virtually the same question, and Ramsay thought he was beginning to sound a mite desperate.

'I think so, David.' Jervis smiled patiently. 'As you know, I'm as familiar with "Sovereign" as you are. In fact, you could say it was originally my brainchild.'

'Yes, so it was.' Hammond bit his lip. 'Well, in that case, I suppose I'd better be on my way,' he said reluctantly.

'Quite.' Jervis shepherded him towards the door and opened it. 'Try not to worry,' he said. 'The police know what they're doing. I'm sure Jill won't come to any harm.'

Ramsay met Hammond's gaze, then slowly looked the other way. Jervis had all the makings of a politician, and could make the most banal platitude seem like a pearl of wisdom; but evidently the irony of his pious hope hadn't been lost on Hammond. Contrary to what Ramsay had expected, however, there was no last-minute barbed remark, only a sharp click as the door closed behind him.

'Do you really have any evidence that these people are watching the bank, Commissioner?' Jervis returned to the desk, emptied Hammond's ashtray into the wastepaper bin and sat down. 'Or is it merely supposition?'

'It depends what you mean by evidence,' Kellerman said. 'But from other cases we've dealt with, I'd say this is the standard *modus operandi*.'

Ramsay chipped in. 'Of course, no two crimes are exactly alike, but it's usual for the kidnappers to keep the victim's close relatives under observation. The delivery and collection of the ransom money is always the trickiest part of the whole operation, especially if we've been called in. That's why ninety-nine times out of a hundred, the relatives are instructed to keep the police out of it.'

'This usually happens soon after the victim has been kidnapped?'

'Within a matter of hours, Mr Jervis. Mind you, there are no hard-and-fast rules; sometimes they'll allow the relatives to stew for a while, particularly if the victim is a child. It's one way of convincing the next-of-kin that it's not a hoax when they finally get in touch with them. It also makes them much more compliant.'

'Quite.'

It seemed to Ramsay that Jervis used the word 'quite' in much the same way as Kellerman was apt to say 'I see' when he felt out of his depth.

'What if this ruse of yours doesn't work and there's no response from the kidnappers?'

Ramsay glanced at the Assistant Commissioner. Jervis, meanwhile, was gazing into space, his eyes focused on the office safe midway between them. It wasn't altogether clear who was supposed to answer him.

'It would certainly raise a number of doubts in my mind,' Kellerman said presently.

'What sort of doubts?'

Kellerman mulled it over, seemingly reluctant to answer the question. In the silence, Ramsay heard a low murmur of voices in the main hall and looked up at the clock. One minute past ten; that meant that Donovan, Thirsk and Adams had arrived to relieve Talbot's shift. The next few minutes could be very tricky; but if Kellerman did ask him why those three were on duty together, he was ready with an explanation. It wasn't as solid as he would have liked, but the Assistant Commissioner had plenty of other things on his mind and it would probably be good enough to satisfy his curiosity.

'What sort of doubts?' Jervis repeated.

'Well, I might begin to wonder if Mrs Hammond really had been kidnapped. After all, we've only got Hammond's word for all this. You heard him yourself: he said Chief Inspector Ramsay wasn't present when his wife spoke to him on the telephone.'

'Are you implying that this whole thing is an elaborate hoax?' Jervis stared at him, then continued, in a voice that was ice-cold. 'Because if you are, it's the most ridiculous assertion I've ever heard. You only had to look at David to see how upset he was.'

'I'm not denying that; but it doesn't necessarily follow that his wife has been abducted.' Out of the corner of his eye, Ramsay noticed that Kellerman's face was turning brick-red, the flush spreading from his neck up. 'I'm told Mrs Hammond is a very attractive young woman,' he went on, 'and I dare say she's not short of admirers. You know how it is in Hong Kong; with their husbands on such high salaries, young women like Mrs Hammond can afford to employ a small army of servants to look after the house. As a result, they've nothing to do all day. After a while they get bored with the same old social whirl, the morning coffee parties and the afternoon bridge sessions with other wives, and they're ripe for an affair.'

'You think it's possible Mrs Hammond may have run off with another man?'

'She wouldn't be the first wife to do so,' Kellerman said stubbornly. 'Maybe that's what the telephone call was all about. Maybe Hammond simply panicked; he couldn't bring himself to admit to Ramsay that his wife had walked out on him, so he invented the story that she'd been kidnapped.'

'I don't think we can be talking about the same man, Commissioner. David would never do a thing like that. Besides,

I happen to know Jill Hammond rather well, and I can assure you she's not at all the type to run off with another man.'

'You're probably right, sir,' Ramsay said diplomatically, 'but it's our job to consider every possibility, no matter how remote it might seem.'

'Quite.'

There was that all-embracing word again, but to Ramsay's ears it had a slightly different inflexion this time. Jervis was old enough to be Jill Hammond's father; he probably had a soft spot for her and didn't like to see her reputation smeared. Ramsey went on. 'That's why I've been thinking this whole problem through. I'm just wondering if there isn't some way we can hoodwink the opposition and move the bullion to the dockside without them knowing it.'

'How?' Kellerman demanded. 'You said yourself they'd have the bank under observation.'

'Oh, I'm sure they've got the front and rear entrances covered, but I very much doubt if they're watching the Peninsula Hotel. If the worst came to the worst, we could park the trucks in Hankow Road and trundle the bullion through the lobby.'

'It'll never work,' Kellerman said. 'For one thing, those military vehicles will look completely out of place.'

'I'm not so sure. The ground floor of the Peninsula Hotel will shortly become a First Aid Post, and the civil defence people are planning to use all sorts of vehicles as emergency ambulances. Nobody will give the trucks a second glance if we chalk a few Red Cross symbols on the canopies.'

As a further precaution against snoopers, he suggested that they should place a diversion sign at the junction of Hankow and Middle Roads. A burst water-main would be a good enough reason to close the road to traffic, and the Public Works Department could help with the deception. 'The trucks should move into position as soon as possible, so that people can get used to seeing them parked outside the hotel.'

'What about the drivers and their escorts? They're locally enlisted personnel.'

Kellerman had sounded a cautionary note, but otherwise he was not unreceptive; a little flattery and he'd buy the whole idea. 'You're right, sir, they could be a security risk.' Ramsay paused; one more 'sir' and he'd have the fat little fart eating out of his hand. 'Suppose we told the drivers to immobilize their vehicles, sir? Then they could wait inside the bank where we can keep an eye on them.'

'Yes, that should solve the problem.' Kellerman turned to Jervis. 'What about your chairman? Do you think he would have any objections?'

'I'm sure he wouldn't. In fact, I know he'd back the plan to the hilt.'

'I do have one other suggestion to make,' Ramsay said coolly. 'Under the present arrangements the bank is responsible for loading the bullion on to the trucks, and ten of their British employees are due to report here at 0300 hours tomorrow morning. I don't know what you think, sir, but in my view they could give the whole game away.'

'I agree with you,' Kellerman said.

'So why don't we stand them down? The two till ten shift is still here and if I hold them back, we'll have enough manpower to do the job with the locally enlisted military personnel.'

'It makes good sense to me,' Kellerman said, 'but I can't answer for the bank. It's up to Mr Jervis to give you a decision.'

The question hung in the air for just thirty seconds; then Jervis said he would clear it with the chairman and Ramsay knew he'd got it made. Hiding his elation with difficulty, he left the office to warn Talbot that his shift would have to stay on duty until further notice.

Bramwell read his copy of Waldron's statement a second time and then placed it on one side. It had been a rush job and the typing wasn't up to the usual standard, but there were no factual errors that he could see. No doubt if he had missed any, either Waldron, Macdonald or Katherine Goddard would soon point them out to him.

'There are a large number of spelling errors, Superintendent.' Macdonald wrinkled his nose. Without actually saying so, he managed to imply that his secretary would never be allowed to get away with such a slipshod piece of work. 'Otherwise,' he added, 'it's a true copy of the original.'

'I'm glad to hear it.' Bramwell glanced at Waldron. 'Perhaps you'd sign all four copies?' he said.

'Sure. Can I borrow your pen?'

Bramwell uncapped his Swan and placed it on top of the second copy. Collecting the other two copies from Macdonald and Katherine Goddard, Waldron scrawled his signature on each one.

'I presume you don't want a statement from Miss Goddard?' Macdonald said.

'I don't think it's necessary. Mr Waldron has given us a very full account.'

'Good. In that case, Superintendent, I'd like to retain one copy of his statement in addition to the one you're about to give Mr Waldron.'

'We don't intend to bring any charges against your client,' Bramwell said, temporizing.

'Then I take it he's free to leave?'

'I didn't say that. Surely I don't have to remind you that Mr Waldron is wanted by the FBI?'

'I think you're being very foolish, Superintendent,' Macdonald said coldly. 'I've had a long talk with my client, and it's very clear to me that the whole matter of his extradition has been handled in a most improper manner.'

Bramwell sighed. There was some substance to the allegation, and Waldron and Macdonald had had plenty of time in which to prepare their case before he'd arrived at the solicitor's house in Waterloo Road. Waldron had not been legally represented and had not appeared in court; the FBI had cabled the Royal Canadian Mounted Police and the War Department in Ottawa; they, in turn, had passed the request for his extradition to the Hong Kong Police Force, and some faceless civil servant in the Attorney General's office had rubber-stamped it. He didn't need Macdonald to tell him that there had been a first-class administrative cock-up. But there was no stopping the solicitor; he had prepared a speech and he was going to deliver it, come what may. Wearing a suitably grave expression, Bramwell sat back and waited for him to run out of steam.

'. . . In my view, the police have behaved in a most sinister fashion,' Macdonald said, finally drawing to a conclusion. 'I am of course referring to Sergeant Lee and the two British officers who arrived on the scene later.'

'Yes.' There wasn't much else Bramwell could say in the circumstances. Waldron had made a number of serious allegations against the Force, and he just wished he could pass the buck to Kellerman, but the Assistant Commissioner was still down at the bank, or so he'd been told.

'I assume there will be an official inquiry, Superintendent?'

'I imagine a full report will be submitted to the Commissioner of Police. The rest is then up to him.'

'And Mr Waldron? What do you intend to do about him in the meantime?' Macdonald wagged an admonishing finger. 'I hope you don't think you're going to take him into custody?'

Bramwell frowned. It was heads-I-win, tails-you-lose. If he did put Waldron inside, the writs would start flying and he could find himself up shit creek without a paddle. On the other hand, Kellerman wouldn't be best pleased if the American failed to appear in court when the extradition proceedings got under way. Both men could make life decidedly unpleasant for him. But on balance he thought Macdonald was probably the more formidable opponent.

'I was planning to leave him in your charge,' Bramwell said coolly. 'Naturally your client will be required to report to the police every day until he appears before a magistrate.'

'When is that likely to happen?'

'I think we can arrange a preliminary hearing for the day after tomorrow.' Bramwell pushed his chair back and stood up, hoping the others would follow suit. 'That's not too soon for you, is it?' he asked.

'Oh, no, we'll be ready for you, Superintendent.' Macdonald

smiled and pointed to the typed copies of Waldron's statement. 'May I have two copies?'

'Do you really need them? I mean, the question the magistrate will be considering is whether or not the FBI has produced sufficient evidence to justify their request that your client should be deported to the United States. That being the case, I can't see how this particular statement can be relevant.'

'I can,' Macdonald said. 'You see, I intend to fight you all the way.'

He would, Bramwell thought, he bloody would. Macdonald specialized in conveyancing, and as far as he was concerned, this was a once-in-a-lifetime opportunity to make a name for himself.

Hammond fixed himself a large whisky and soda and collapsed into a fireside armchair. Even now, as he sat there in the lounge with Jill gazing down at him from a silver-framed photograph on the largely decorative baby grand piano, he still couldn't understand how Ramsay had managed to outmanoeuvre him. But the bastard had – and he'd recruited some unlikely allies along the way. The Chairman of the Hong Kong and Shanghai Bank, Kellerman and Richard Jervis; they'd all sided with him. Of course, Kellerman was the one who'd tipped the scales in Ramsay's favour; once he'd swallowed his cockeyed theory, it had all been over bar the shouting, and there hadn't been too much of that. The Chairman had listened to Kellerman, and accepted that the Triad could be using his chief security officer as a lever.

'I'm going to instruct Jervis to relieve you, David, and I don't want any argument about it.' Those were the Chairman's final words. Of course, all that gup of his about how his first concern was to effect Jill's speedy release was so much bullshit. The truth was that the old miser was frightened he wouldn't have the bank's interests at heart when it came to a showdown. And he was right: there wasn't anything he wouldn't do to get Jill back. If necessary, he would even help Ramsay carry the bullion out of the vault and load it on to the trucks.

Hammond downed the whisky in one go. He would go mad if he had to sit around here much longer waiting for the telephone to ring. He had to do something. But what?

Supposing he were to ring the Chairman and tell him exactly why he believed Ramsay was masterminding the whole bloody operation? No; the old man would merely conclude that he was overwrought and the next thing he knew, old Dr Munroe would be on the doorstep, ready with the tranquilizers. Kellerman, then? The Assistant Commissioner was no friend of Ramsay's, but this time round he'd need to be a damn sight more direct. From bitter experience he'd learned that subtle hints were lost on him.

Leaving the empty glass in the hearth, Hammond walked over to the phone and lifted the receiver. A faint click after the dialling tone told him that the line had already been tapped. No two ways about it, he thought, the Assistant Commissioner had certainly pulled out all the stops. It was then he noticed the name Jill had scribbled on the message pad. He put the phone down, his mouth suddenly dry. Somebody had phoned her and she had walked out of the house and into a waiting car and had not been seen again. Jill had believed that somebody was Kellerman; the proof was there in her handwriting, with a couple of exclamation marks after the name.

Kellerman was tired and irritable. Ramsay had turned him into an errand boy and he had spent the better part of the last two hours conferring with the Commissioner of Police, the Managing Director of the telephone company, the head of the Public Works Department and the chief transport officer at Fortress Headquarters. A lot of time and energy could have been saved if he'd been able to use the telephone, but Ramsay had persuaded him it wasn't secure and he'd agreed they couldn't take any chances. He had returned to Nathan Road needing a cup of strong black coffee and several aspirins to relieve a splitting headache; but instead of the few minutes' peace and quiet he'd been looking forward to, he had found Bramwell waiting for him. And just to cap it all, the statement he'd asked him to read was badly typed and trying on the eyes.

'Here, you read it to me,' he said testily, handing the statement to Bramwell. 'Starting from paragraph three on page two.'

'Yes, sir.' Bramwell found the place, then read out, '"Two men got out of the car and walked into the courtyard at the back of Kaznovetsky's restaurant. Some five or ten minutes later, they re-appeared and crossed the road. It was obvious they were making for the Roxy Hotel and I had a nasty feeling that Sergeant Lee had given them the key to my room. I left the light off and lay down on the bed".'

'Waldron isn't the only one who's had a tiring day,' Kellerman said.

Bramwell nodded. 'He goes on to say, "Presently I heard footsteps in the corridor and moments later a key slotted into the lock and unlatched it. The door flew open, the light came on and two men entered the room. One was on the short side and pear-shaped, the other was lean and tall with a hard-boned face. Both Englishmen were armed and said they were police officers".'

'Did they now?'

'Yes, sir.' Bramwell cleared his throat. 'The descriptions could fit Adams and Thirsk,' he ventured hesitantly.

'They're down at the bank.' Kellerman drummed the thumb and fingers of his right hand on the desk. 'Does Waldron say when this incident happened?'

'He wasn't wearing a wristwatch, so he can't be definite, but he reckons it was approximately seven o'clock.'

'I see.' Thirsk and Adams had come on duty at ten. Unless they had an alibi, Kellerman thought they could well have been the two officers who'd visited the Roxy Hotel. 'What else is there?'

'Not a lot. Waldron decided to get the hell out of it and one of the men fired a shot at him as he ran down the corridor. I've been down to the hotel and I know that's true.'

'It's beginning to look as though Sergeant Lee set him up, but for what reason God only knows.' Kellerman rubbed his eyes.

His head was still throbbing and he was finding it difficult to concentrate. 'I think we ought to bring him in for questioning.'

'That's another strange thing, sir. He seems to have completely vanished. I sent a constable round to his flat in Shamshuipo, but his wife claims she hasn't seen him since he left the apartment early this afternoon.' Bramwell turned to the last page of the statement. 'I don't know whether this is significant, but Waldron made some crack about Kaznovetsky's being a popular haunt with the Kowloon Division. When I asked him what he meant, he said that apart from Lee and the two Englishmen, one of our senior officers seemed to be a regular patron there. From the description he gave me, it sounded as if he was referring to George Ramsay.'

Jill Hammond had been kidnapped, Sergeant Lee had disappeared and Waldron had alleged that one of his officers had tried to kill him. Kellerman's tired brain couldn't begin to sort it out, but nonetheless he wondered if there was a connection. 'What have you done with Waldron?' he asked presently.

'I let him go, but I know where to find him. He's staying the night with his solicitor.'

'You'd better get round there,' Kellerman said. 'I want him to walk into the bank dressed in army uniform. Tell him he's not to do anything heroic, but I want to know if he recognizes anyone.'

'Yes, sir.' Bramwell moved towards the door, then stopped. 'What if he refuses to cooperate?'

'Try a little gentle persuasion. Meantime, I'm going to have a word with Mr Hammond.' Kellerman pushed back his cuff and glanced at his wristwatch. 'Five minutes to twelve,' he grumbled. 'With any luck, I should be back around two.'

He glanced longingly at the camp bed made up in the corner of his office, then followed Bramwell out of the room.

CHAPTER EIGHTEEN

Macdonald's house in Waterloo Road lacked a woman's touch, but that was hardly surprising in view of the fact that his wife had been packed off to Australia in June 1940, along with all the other official evacuees who'd failed to convince the authorities they were engaged on essential war work. From his own choice, his social life during the past eighteen months had been virtually non-existent and Macdonald had become something of a recluse both in and out of office hours. He no longer entertained at home and he disliked people dropping in on him, particularly those who woke him up in the middle of the night, as Bramwell had just done.

'This is nothing less than police harassment,' Macdonald said for the second time in as many minutes. 'My client has already given you a very full statement and any questions you wanted to ask him should have been raised at the time.'

'There have been further developments since then,' Bramwell said cautiously.

'What sort of developments?'

'We think we've traced the two men who went to the Roxy Hotel.' Bramwell turned to Waldron. 'We'd like you to identify them.'

'Sure.' Waldron smiled. 'Are you going to put them in a line-up?'

'Not exactly.' Bramwell paused, uncertain just how much he should tell the American. 'As little as possible' had been Kellerman's advice during a last-minute briefing on the stairs, but that was easier said than done. They would be asking Waldron to walk into a potential hornet's nest, and he had a right to know the score. 'This may sound a little crazy,' he continued, 'but we have a hunch that the men who tried to kill you may also have been involved in the kidnapping of a young woman called Jill Hammond. She happens to be the wife of the chief security officer of the Hong Kong and Shanghai Bank, and we think they mean to lift the two and a half million pounds' worth of gold bullion which is currently lodged in the vaults of the Kowloon branch. In your money, that's about ten million dollars.'

'That's one hell of a grubstake,' Waldron said quietly.

'It certainly is.' Bramwell cleared his throat. 'However, the bullion won't be there much longer. It's being shipped off to Australia. The two men we're interested in are down there now at the bank.'

'Yeah?'

'In our view, it's likely their confederates wouldn't hesitate to kill Mrs Hammond if we attempted to bring them in for questioning. We have to tread warily, and that's why we'd like you to go down there and see if you can recognize these men.'

'You want me to walk into the bank?'

'Yes.'

'Oh no, I'm not having that.' Macdonald slapped the dining room table with the palm of his hand to drive the point home. 'I won't allow you to place my client in jeopardy.'

'Your client is quite capable of making up his own mind, Counsellor,' Waldron told him firmly.

'Does that mean you're willing to cooperate?' Bramwell asked.

'I'd like to know exactly what's involved first.'

'We wouldn't ask you to do this unless we thought the risks were negligible. As I see it, we'll drop you off near the Peninsula Hotel; you'll then walk round the corner into Hankow Road and go through the arcade into the lobby. There are eight plainclothes men on duty at the bank, and once you've seen their faces or spotted either one of the officers who were at the Roxy Hotel, you'll turn around and walk straight out again. We'd like you dressed in army uniform; that should prevent you looking too conspicuous. As an additional safeguard, we'll wait twenty minutes and if you're not back by then, we'll come in and get you.'

'When does all this happen?'

'Around 0230 hours,' said Bramwell. 'That's when they'll start loading the bullion on to the trucks.'

'There's only one problem. I don't have a uniform.'

'The Canadians have left a small rear party at Shamshuipo barracks. I dare say they can fit you up.'

Waldron thought it over, then smiled wryly. 'I don't know why I should help you guys,' he said, 'but I guess you've talked me into it.'

Ramsay walked through the arcade and on out into the street. Two Fordson trucks with Red Cross symbols chalked on their canopies were parked outside the Peninsula Hotel, and diagonally across the road from the army vehicles, three workmen from the Public Works Department had erected a canvas shelter near an open manhole. The flood-tide from the supposedly burst water main had drained away some time ago, but the workmen were still down in the sewers and would remain there until he told them to quit. Twenty yards farther on, a barrier had been placed across the road and a winking diversion sign directed oncoming traffic into Middle Road.

The stage had been set and the curtain was about to go up for the last act, but even so, the whole show could still fold if the walk-on players weren't standing by in the wings. His pulse beating faster than normal, Ramsay strolled up Hankow Road and on past the junction with Peking Road. The warehouse, a large brick-built godown with a corrugated-iron roof, was situated just round the corner from the T-junction at the top of the street. Ignoring the main entrance, he walked down the narrow alleyway beside the building and rapped on the side door, tapping out the letters 'R' and 'S' in morse. Repeating the signal thirty seconds later, he got an answering knock and a slim Chinaman, smartly dressed in army khakis, opened the door to allow him inside the shed. The door closed behind him, the overhead lights came on and Ramsay found himself facing three men armed with rifles. Slowly, almost reluctantly, they backed away from him and withdrew into a dark corner of the warehouse.

The two Fordsons were parked side by side, opposite the main entrance, their tailgates hard up against a loading ramp. Beckoning the Chinese soldier to follow him, Ramsay climbed the short flight of steps, walked along the ramp and looked inside the back of each truck. Both vehicles were loaded with steel boxes bearing the same serial numbers as the bullion stored in the vaults of the Kowloon branch, which he'd copied down from the appendix attached to the "Sovereign" file. Not wanting to break the seals, he tried lifting up a few boxes at random, to satisfy himself that they had been filled with ballast. Then, taking a stick of chalk out of his pocket, he stood on the tailgate of the left-hand vehicle and drew a large red cross on the canvas roof.

'You get the idea?' Ramsay said, addressing the soldier in Cantonese. 'I want them on both sides and on top of the cab.'

'The same with the other truck?'

'You bet.' Ramsay pushed his cuff back and showed him his wristwatch. 'My friend, Mr Donovan, will be here at seven-thirty, and I want you to be ready to move off as soon as he arrives. Understood?'

'We'll have the engines running.'

'That's the style.' Ramsay clapped him on the shoulder, jumped down from the ramp and let himself out of the go-down.

The Fordsons would come down Hankow Road and follow the diversion sign into Middle Road. Turning right on Nathan Road, they would then drive past the front entrance of the Peninsula Hotel and swing right again into Salisbury Road. One more right-hand turn and they would pass through the dock gates and on to the wharfside where the *Delphic Star* was berthed. As soon as they were out of sight, the two bullion trucks would pull away from the side entrance of the Peninsula Hotel, turn left into Salisbury Road and then head straight for the disused laundry belonging to the Yam Kwong brothers near

Kai Tak airfield. The basic concept was simple enough, but Ramsay knew it would only work if he succeeded in creating an atmosphere of total last-minute confusion.

Ramsay turned into Peking Road, walked past the Roxy Hotel and entered the courtyard at the rear of Kaznovetsky's restaurant. Unlocking the back door with the key Donovan had given him, he stepped inside the kitchen, waited for his eyes to become accustomed to the gloom and then moved towards the staircase. He went on up, slowly and quietly, testing each step before putting his weight on it, to make sure it didn't creak. A light was showing under the door leading to the private dining rooms on the second floor, and in the stillness he could hear Larissa Kaznovetsky mumbling to herself.

So far so good, Ramsay thought, but the really tricky part was still to come. During the 1914–18 War, he had seen a friendly incoming patrol badly shot up, when a jittery sentry armed with a Lewis gun had lost his head; he wasn't about to take any unnecessary risks. Pausing at the top of the staircase, he called out the recognition phrase in a low voice and kept on repeating it until he got an acknowledgement from one of the Cantonese guards inside the small back room.

The door opened slowly, and a short, thickset man stepped out into the corridor. Ramsay nodded, pointed to the office at the far end of the landing and signalled to the Cantonese to lead the way. Following on behind, he glanced at the lavatory where Donovan had hidden Lee's body and surreptitiously tried the door to make sure it was locked. Then he joined the guard in the office.

Satisfied that the blackout curtains had already been drawn over the venetian blind, Ramsay switched on the light, found Larissa Kaznovetsky's private ledger in the pending tray and told the guard to sit down behind the desk. Handing him a pencil, he then dictated a message to Hammond which eventually filled one and three-quarter foolscap pages with Chinese characters. That done, he made him read the ultimatum aloud and timed it, mentally counting off the seconds. Even without any interruptions, the message took slightly over four minutes to deliver, and he knew that was more than enough time for the phone company to trace the call.

'You did just fine,' Ramsay told the guard. 'Now, the number you have to dial is 135462, and I want the call put through at exactly seven-twenty-five. One hour later, you will phone the Taipan's house again and repeat the message.'

'And then what do we do?'

'Nothing,' said Ramsay. 'You and your friend just walk out of here.'

The lie came with practised ease, so did the final handshake. There was no way the two Cantonese guards would leave the restaurant alive. The second phone call was simply a means of ensuring they stayed around for the shooting match. Leaving the office, Ramsay went downstairs and checked out the private dining rooms on the second floor.

He found Larissa Kaznovetsky stretched out on a chaise longue, her bare legs protruding from beneath a thin blanket covering the upper half of her body. A bottle of Courvoisier stood on the small dining table, along with a brandy glass smeared with lipstick and an ashtray brim full of cigarette ends. Her cheongsam, slip and silk stockings had been left in an untidy heap on the carpet, and as he moved closer to the chaise longue, her eyes opened and stared blankly at him.

'Oh, it's you, George,' Larissa said finally, her voice slurred. She raised herself up on one elbow, the blanket sliding from her shoulders. 'What time is it?'

'One-fifteen.' Ramsay smiled at her. 'Sorry if I woke you.'

'God, I feel terrible.' Larissa explored her mouth and lips with a tongue that was furred with sputum. "Is that woman still here?' she croaked.

'Don't worry your head about her any more. She'll be gone very soon now.' Ramsay perched himself on the edge of the chaise longue. 'Everything's coming along nicely,' he said in a voice that was meant to be soothing. 'A few more hours and it'll all be over.'

There had been a couple of disturbing hiccups along the way with Lee and Waldron, but Thirsk was right about the American: he was scared of his own shadow and was unlikely to cause them any further trouble now.

'I want that woman out of here, George.' Larissa glared at him and raised her voice. 'Right this very minute.'

'Yes.'

'This very minute,' she repeated, and flopped back.

'Whatever you say, Larissa.' Ramsay leaned across her, removed the cushion from under her head and plumped it up. 'You look exhausted,' he murmured. 'It's been a long day and you need your sleep. We can't have you looking jaded tomorrow, now can we?'

He raised the cushion as though to place it under her head, then slammed it down on her face and held it there, his right knee pressing into her stomach until her legs finally stopped thrashing and she went limp. After a while, there was no pulse, no heartbeat that he could detect, and removing the cushion from Larissa's face, he placed it under her head again and straightened the blanket. She looked, he thought, like a fractious child who had suddenly fallen asleep in the middle of a tantrum. Then, without a backward glance, he walked away from her, switched out the light, locked the door behind him and pocketed the key.

Hammond gazed at Kellerman, wondering if the Assistant Commissioner had believed a single word he'd said about Ramsay. Kellerman had called round ostensibly to let him know what progress the police had made with their inquiries, but within minutes of his arrival, it had turned into a question-and-answer session with Hammond doing most of the talking. For a solid hour and ten minutes he had related every single thing that had happened, from the moment he'd tried to ring Jill shortly after nine-fifteen on Sunday morning only to discover that both phones at the bank were out of order. Looking at Kellerman now, it seemed to Hammond he might just as well have saved his breath. The Assistant Commissioner had listened to him attentively, but nothing he'd said appeared to have made the slightest impact on him. Kellerman hadn't so much as raised an eyebrow when he'd showed him the memo pad with his name scribbled on it in Jill's handwriting.

'You say Ramsay was constantly in and out of the bank yesterday?' Kellerman said, breaking a long silence.

'That's right.'

'To your knowledge, did he at any time visit Kaznovetsky's restaurant?'

'I don't think so. But I know he lunched there on Friday.'

'I see.' Kellerman pursed his lips. 'Do you recall meeting Sergeant Lee? He's Chinese and about five foot four inches tall.'

'I remember seeing him at the bank on Saturday morning.' Hammond frowned. 'Why do you ask?'

'No special reason, except that he's another police officer who seems to patronize Kaznovetsky's.'

'How can Lee afford it on a sergeant's pay?'

'That's a good question.' Kellerman launched himself from the armchair. 'We've no proof that he's one of the kidnappers, but we're keeping an open mind.'

'You're leaving?'

'You've been very helpful, Mr Hammond. That may sound a little trite, but I really am most grateful . . .'

'And rest assured we'll leave no stone unturned,' Hammond said, finishing the sentence for him.

Kellerman shrugged and edged his way into the hall. 'We're doing everything we can, Mr Hammond.'

'I'd expect you to say that. But what am I supposed to do in the meantime? Sit here twiddling my thumbs while I wait for a phone call from the kidnappers which we both know they'll never make?'

'I don't know anything of the kind. Time is running out for these people, and if they want the bullion to stay put, they've got to come out into the open and say so within the next four to five hours.'

'The bloody gold, that's your chief concern, isn't it?' Hammond said angrily. 'You don't give a damn about my wife.'

'That's not true.' Kellerman opened the front door, stepped

out on to the porch and began sidling towards the car parked in the driveway. 'You're understandably overwrought, Mr Hammond, and you can't see things in perspective. It's going to be a long vigil for you, and I don't think you should endure it alone. Isn't there somebody who can keep you company? A close friend, perhaps?'

Hammond opened his mouth to pooh-pooh the idea, then changed his mind. 'I suppose I could always ask Tom Blakeney to drop round,' he said slowly.

'You do that.' Kellerman opened the door of the Humber saloon, got in beside the driver and wound down the window. 'Goodnight, Mr Hammond,' he said politely.

The driver started the engine, shifted into first gear and let the clutch out. Tyres crunching on the gravel, the car swung out of the drive into Macdonnel Road.

Hammond watched the masked tail lights fade into the distance and then went back inside the house. He would ring Blakeney and invite him round, but there would be no fireside chat. He just wanted somebody to mind the phone while he went out on the prowl.

Cottis turned over on to his left hip and stared at the luminous hands on the clock, his mind dully registering the fact that it was almost five minutes to two and that the alarm would start ringing at any second. Yawning, he reached out and pushed the button down; then, throwing the blanket aside, he rolled off the camp bed and stood up. Still yawning, he buckled the web belt and pistol holster around his waist, retrieved the paperback he'd been reading from under the pillow and remembering to take his portable radio with him, ambled into the ops room of Fortress Headquarters.

The duty watchkeeper was agreeably surprised to see him arrive a few minutes early and wasted no time in bringing him up to date with the latest entries in the log. That done, he vacated the chair, wished him the best of luck and departed.

Cottis sat down, made a space on the table for his portable

and switching it on, tuned in to Radio Tokyo. Then he opened the paperback and renewed his acquaintance with Hercule Poirot.

CHAPTER NINETEEN

Waldron walked past the front entrance of the Peninsula Hotel and turned the corner into Hankow Road. The army uniform provided by the Canadian rear party at Shamshuipo barracks fitted him reasonably well, but unfortunately the only weapon they'd been able to give him for the pistol holster on the web belt around his waist was a skeleton action Webley .455. That was fine for instructional purposes, but damn all use in an emergency. He just hoped Bramwell was ready to move in fast should he run into trouble.

Two Fordson trucks were parked outside the arcade, and three men in shirtsleeves were busy loading steel boxes on to the leading vehicle. Drawing nearer, Waldron noticed that all three were armed with .38 calibre revolvers carried in hip holsters. Even without their sidearms, he would have known they were police officers by their general appearance and bearing; but he had never seen their faces before. Aware that they were watching him, he turned into the arcade and subconsciously quickened his stride. Two Chinese soldiers wheeling baggage trolleys loaded with steel boxes passed him going in the opposite direction, but to his relief, the hard-nosed British police officer armed with a Thompson sub machine gun who was standing near the reception desk made no move to challenge him.

Four card-players were seated round a table in the lobby and a girl in nurse's uniform was sprawled in an armchair nearby. Waldron had never seen Katherine Goddard in her working clothes before and at first he didn't recognize her. It worked both ways, and she also stared blankly at him for some moments. Then her jaw dropped and he saw a questioning look in her eyes. He signalled Katherine to stay put, hoping she would catch on that he wanted her to ignore him, but she was already halfway out of the chair. Worse still, the British police officer on duty near the reception desk had moved into the lobby, and Waldron didn't like the way he was staring at the pair of them. No two ways about it, the bastard was suspicious and he'd have a hard time convincing him he was there on official business. Or would he? Glancing at the four card-players, he noticed that there was a steel helmet and respirator on the floor by each chair and guessed they were members of the civil defence organization. Deciding the emergency first aid post would need a despatch rider, he moved purposefully towards them.

The revolving door in the side entrance had been dismantled and the bullion transfer was progressing better than Ramsay had anticipated. Even so, moving the gold ingots out of the vaults was no easy task. The steel boxes had to be lifted down from the stack and loaded on to a baggage trolley, which then had to be dragged up a short flight of steps before it could be wheeled through the main hall into the lobby of the Peninsula Hotel. The problem didn't end there; each box weighed eighty pounds, and a team of three was needed to lift the containers on to the Fordsons and stack them neatly in the back. Subtract Talbot, who was on guard at the reception desk, and Thirsk, who was covering the main hall, and he was left with a working party of six, four of whom were locally enlisted army personnel.

There were a hundred-and-sixty-eight boxes in all, and he had calculated that two containers was the maximum anybody could handle at one time. That meant each man would make twenty-eight round trips before the task was complete. So far, they'd averaged three apiece in less than half an hour. The pace was bound to slacken as fatigue set in and he would have to relieve them in due course, but the way things were going, it still looked as if they would finish ahead of schedule.

Ramsay looked up from tallying the check marks on his millboard and stared at the soldier approaching the four card-players in the lobby. There was, he thought, something vaguely familiar about him; then he heard a muttered 'Jesus Christ' from Thirsk, and the penny dropped.

'*Waldron.*' Ramsay swung round to face Thirsk. 'Move yourself,' he snapped. 'Get down into the vaults and make sure Adams stays there with you until I give the all-clear.'

Just what the American was up to and why he was in army uniform was immaterial. The answers to those questions would come later. Right now, he had to be neutralized and it would have to be done discreetly, otherwise all hell could break loose. There was, however, one point in their favour; from the way Talbot was closing in on Waldron, it looked as though he'd recognized him from the APB. Moving into the lobby, Ramsay dumped his millboard in a chair and came up behind the American.

'Surprise, surprise,' he said, tapping him on the shoulder. 'We've been searching everywhere for you.'

Waldron jerked his head round and stared at him, his eyes narrowing for a split-second. He knows me, Ramsay thought. I've never met him before, but he's seen me somewhere and remembers my face.

'Who the hell are you?'

'We're police officers,' Ramsay said, indicating Talbot. 'And you're Frank Waldron.'

'So what?'

'So you're under arrest.'

'You're making a big mistake,' Waldron said in a loud voice.

'That's what they all say.' Ramsay was suddenly conscious that they had become the centre of attention for the four card-players and the nurse with the dark brown hair. Taking a firm grip on Waldron's left arm, he started to steer him out of harm's way. 'Let's you and I take a walk,' he said quietly.

'He's right, Officer, you're making a big mistake.'

Ramsay eyed the nurse warily. 'What's your name, Miss?' he asked.

'Katherine Goddard. I'm the resident nurse here and this gentleman is a friend of mine.'

'Oh, really. Well, let me give you a piece of advice, Miss Goddard. Obstructing a police officer is a serious offence; I think you should remember that, and let me handle this affair.'

Ramsay tugged Waldron away and signalled Talbot to grab his other arm, but as they hustled him out of the lobby and into the bank, he heard Katherine Goddard say something about phoning her solicitor. Ignoring Talbot's questioning look and Waldron's voluble protests, he lifted the counter flap, steered the American into the chief cashier's office and pushed him up against the wall. Then he told him to spread his arms and legs.

'Aw, for Chrissakes,' Waldron said, 'this is plain stupid. Why don't you stop acting like the Gestapo and call your people at Nathan Road. They can soon put you straight about this whole deal.'

Ramsay sensed he was heading for trouble and acted fast. Spinning Waldron round, he jabbed a fist into his stomach and then chopped him down with a rabbit punch to the neck.

'What the hell's the matter with you, George?' Talbot said hoarsely. 'He wasn't giving us any trouble.'

'I don't know what got into me.' Ramsay gnawed his bottom lip. 'When he accused me of behaving like the Gestapo, I just saw red. Who does he think he's talking to anyway? I spent three years in the trenches in the last lot while he was still wetting his nappies.'

'You don't have to justify yourself to me, George.'

'Kellerman's going to love this. It's his big chance to break me, something he's been longing to do ever since he was made Assistant Commissioner.' Ramsay shook his head. 'You'd better phone him and break the good news.'

'If it's any help, George,' Talbot said, poker-faced, 'I never saw you hit Waldron.'

'Thanks.' Ramsay smiled. 'Thanks a lot. Maybe I'll be able to do the same for you one day.'

'I hope not,' Talbot said.

Kellerman leaned both elbows on the desk and gazed at the street map. Bramwell had the front and side entrances of the Peninsula Hotel under observation from the railway sidings, and one of his sergeants was watching the rear of the building from near the Post Office in Nathan Road. But somehow Kellerman still felt uneasy. Although he couldn't fault the surveillance plan, he still had a nagging doubt that some vital factor had been overlooked. He couldn't think straight, that was the trouble. Nodding to himself, Kellerman began to massage his temples.

The street names gradually became a blur, and presently he closed his eyes and allowed his head to droop. Then, just as the splitting headache which had plagued him all day was beginning to ease, the telephone shrilled at him and the top of his skull felt as though it had lifted off. Answering the call, he found it was Talbot on the line. Evidently his idea of using a sprat to catch a mackerel had backfired. Given Talbot's photographic memory and the fact that Waldron's description had gone out in an APB on Wednesday night, he supposed it was inevitable that Talbot should have recognized the American the moment he walked into the lobby. The setback might not have occurred had the APB been cancelled, but there was no way Bramwell could have done that without alerting Adams and Thirsk.

'What have you done with Waldron?' Kellerman asked him eventually.

'We're holding him in the chief cashier's office.' Talbot cleared his throat, making a noise in Kellerman's ear which rivalled a dumper truck tipping a load of gravel. 'There's one small problem, sir,' he continued. 'It appears Waldron is friendly with Miss Katherine Goddard, the resident nurse at the Peninsula Hotel. She was downstairs in the lobby when we arrested him and I gather she intends to phone her solicitor.'

Kellerman closed his eyes and held back a sigh. So he could look forward to another acrimonious conversation with Macdonald, and no doubt the solicitor would have plenty to say about police inefficiency. 'Thanks for the tip, Inspector,' he said dryly. 'Forewarned is forearmed. Meantime, I'll arrange for somebody to collect Waldron.'

'Yes, sir.' There was a brief pause, then Talbot said, 'I think Chief Inspector Ramsay would like to have a word with you.'

He would, Kellerman thought, and steeled himself for an acid exchange.

Ramsay said, 'Good morning, sir. I couldn't help overhearing what you just said to Inspector Talbot. Of course, I'd like to get shot of Waldron, but I wonder if that's altogether wise in the circumstances . . .'

Kellerman pinched his eyes. Ramsay's words were open to all kinds of interpretations, and he couldn't see the wood for the trees. He didn't like Ramsay, nor did he trust him, but he had never been able to prove the Chief Inspector was corrupt. One thing was very clear; he couldn't allow an ingrained prejudice to affect his decision. He had to be guided by the facts, and they were simple enough. Jill Hammond had been kidnapped, both telephones at the bank were probably tapped, and the bullion was now being loaded on to the trucks parked in Hankow Road. He could forget the bullion; Bramwell had the trucks under observation and would soon report any unusual occurrence. Adams and Thirsk had every reason to fear Waldron, but the American was unlikely to come to any harm, if only because too many people knew he'd been arrested. No, Jill Hammond was the only one whose life was in jeopardy, and her well-being had to be his main concern.

'I take your point, Ramsay,' he said tersely. 'Waldron had better stay where he is for the time being.'

Kellerman put the phone down. Whether or not he'd made the right decision, Bramwell would have to be warned in good time, otherwise there'd be another cock-up. Leaving his office, he went downstairs to the information room and called Bramwell up on the radio.

Hammond left the shop doorway and crossed the road. For more than an hour now he'd been keeping the restaurant across the way under observation, and he thought it was about time he took a closer look at the place. Opening one of the double gates, he entered the courtyard in the rear of Kaznovetsky's and craned his neck to look up at the small back room on the top floor.

His eyes hadn't deceived him; the blackout curtains had been drawn and there was a light burning in the room. Of course, there would be a rational explanation for that; he and Jill had gone to sleep with the light on any number of times, but invariably one of them had woken up sometime during the night and switched it off. Still not wholly convinced that his theory was altogether valid, he stared up at the darkened window and wondered if the gut-feeling that Jill was there was simply wishful thinking on his part. The fact that Kaznovetsky's was almost directly opposite the bank and Ramsay was known to frequent the restaurant was hardly conclusive proof, but it was all he had to go on. Besides, this was no time for having second thoughts.

Walking on tiptoe, Hammond crossed the yard and tried the back door. Although it was locked, there was a certain amount of give – a sign, he thought, that the door hadn't been bolted top and bottom on the inside. If he used his shoulder as a battering ram, he could probably force the lock, but it would be a noisy business and if the steel bars inside the kitchen window were anything to go by, there was a chance he'd set off a burglar alarm in the process. There were no windows open on the floors above that he could see, and though he could climb up the drainpipe, he'd still have to smash a pane of glass to get inside the building. There was, however, a double trapdoor to his left, which suggested to him that there was a cellar beneath the kitchen.

Moving towards the trapdoor, Hammond saw that it was secured on the outside with a padlock and hasp. It was obvious that he'd never be able to prise the padlock open in a month of Sundays, but he thought the hasp looked a good deal less resilient. Scouting round the yard, he found a rusty steel chisel amongst the junk near the dustbins and inserting the tapered end under the hasp, he exerted all his strength and heaved upwards. With the veins standing out on his forehead and his hands beginning to tremble under the strain, he felt the hasp give. Taking a deep breath, he attacked it with renewed vigour until finally he was able to drag it out by the roots like a bad tooth.

Pausing only to make sure the flap of the holster was buttoned down over the .455 Webley revolver, he then opened the left-hand trapdoor and lowered himself down into the dark cellar.

Cottis yawned, stretched both arms above his head and then suddenly froze; the dance music on the radio had faded out, and an excited announcer now came on the air to broadcast a warning to all Japanese nationals living abroad that war with Great Britain and America was now imminent. The prediction he'd made so often in the past had finally come true, but the knowledge that he'd been vindicated at last gave him no satisfaction. Lowering his arms, Cottis glanced at his wrist-watch, saw that it was 0445 hours and noted the time down in the operations log. Then he roused the other watch-keepers on duty in Fortress Headquarters and alerted the garrison. Fifteen minutes later, the preliminary demolitions at Lo Wu were blown and the covering force up on the frontier withdrew to Tai Po.

CHAPTER TWENTY

When Ramsay heard the telephone ringing in the manager's office, he felt his stomach lurch. Kellerman, Jervis and the Chairman of the Hong Kong and Shanghai Bank had all agreed there should be no incoming calls until the kidnappers estab-lished contact, and he'd given that Cantonese goon strict instructions to ring Hammond at exactly seven twenty-five. For some unknown reason, the stupid bastard must have jumped the gun and put it through damn nearly two hours ahead of time; this must be Kellerman phoning now to give him the good news that the telephone company had traced the call to Kaznovetsky's restaurant. Sick with anger, Ramsay went into the office, slammed his millboard down on the desk and lifted the receiver.

A crisp voice said, 'Mr Hammond?'

'I'm afraid he's not available.' It wasn't Kellerman after all, but the voice at the other end of the line was somehow familiar. 'Is that you, Ralph?' he asked.

'George?' Cottis said tentatively.

'Yes. Can I take a message for David? He's busy right now.'

'We're at war with Japan.' There was a longish pause, then Cottis said, 'I thought you should know.'

'Thanks for telling me.'

'Their infantry crossed the frontier half an hour ago. Judging by what I heard on Radio Tokyo, it looks as though the Yanks will be in it too.'

'I'm glad we're not alone, Ralph.'

'So am I, George,' Cottis said and hung up.

Ramsay felt like laughing out loud as he put the phone down. Thanks to the Nipponese, he'd get all the last-minute confusion he'd wanted – and more. Somehow he managed to wipe the smile from his face; then, wearing a suitably grave expression, he left the office and went down to the vaults to break the news to Jervis.

The cellar was roughly forty by thirty feet and was considerably larger than the kitchen above. Beyond the maze of wine racks, a flight of wooden steps led to a solid teak door fitted with two burglar-proof locks, but the frame was made of softer wood, something Hammond had discovered early on when he'd tested it with the chisel and decided to dig the hinges out. The Webley made a useful hammer and to muffle the noise, he'd removed his khaki shirt, ripped the tail off and wrapped the cloth round the revolver butt and the chisel head.

He'd tackled the bottom hinge first, reasoning that it was better to work on his knees in a cramped position while he was still fresh. In the event, the job had proved far more difficult than he'd supposed, and with precious little room to get any leverage on the chisel, it had turned out to be a long and frustrating business. Although the upper hinge had been less troublesome to dig out, his problems hadn't ended there, and he'd had to hack a good two inches off the frame before he could get his fingers round the door and pull it back against the double locks. It had then taken him some considerable time to open a gap roughly four inches wide between the door and the frame.

Hammond switched off the cellar lights and peered through the crevice. He had forgotten to wind his wristwatch and the damned thing had stopped at four twenty-one, but just how long ago that had been was difficult to guess. There was, however, sufficient daylight for him to see the vague outline of a staircase to the left of the cellar door, and since dawn had obviously broken, he reckoned it was now somewhere around six. Grim-faced, he tried the same old combination of brute force and energy; then, still making no headway, he chipped away the frame around the double locks; but obstinately, the lugs held fast and the door refused to budge another inch.

Frustrated at every turn, Hammond cast round the cellar in search of any kind of implement that would enable him to exert greater pressure on the locks. A few minutes later he found a two-foot-long steel claw, which he surmised was used to prise open the wooden crates the bottles of wine were packed in when delivered to the restaurant. It was, he thought with exasperation, just the kind of tool he could have done with a few hours ago. Inserting the claw between the door and the frame, he braced his legs and heaved.

Waldron stared at the dark-haired, softly-spoken Irishman who was keeping him company and wondered if he was any different from the others. There had been some pretty strange characters in the ranks of the NYPD when he was an Assistant District

Attorney, but the Hong Kong Police had them licked to a frazzle. No two ways about it, they certainly had a formidable number of oddballs: Sergeant Lee, Inspector Talbot, Chief Inspector Ramsay, never mind the two slobs he'd met at the Roxy Hotel . . . He doubted if Bramwell was in the same category, but it was evident the Superintendent was no ball of fire, or he wouldn't be sitting here now in the chief cashier's office with his wrists tied behind his back with a leather bootlace.

'How much longer are you guys going to keep me here?' Waldron asked.

'What's the matter, don't you like this place?' Donovan grinned. 'I'll tell you one thing, my friend, this office is a hell of a lot better than a prison cell.'

'Try telling that to Macdonald.'

'Who's he?'

'My lawyer,' said Waldron. 'By the time he's through, you'll be glad to see the back of me.'

'I can't wait for that,' Donovan said dryly.

'Yeah? What time is it?'

'You're a great one for asking questions, Waldron.' Donovan pushed his cuff back to expose an expensive-looking time-piece. 'I make it six forty-seven. Seems to me your Mr Macdonald is a real deadbeat. He's not exactly in a hurry to spring you, is he?'

'Somebody up high must be stalling him.'

It was the only explanation Waldron could think of. Macdonald was not the kind of man to drag his feet when his professional reputation was at stake, and there was no way Ramsay could have prevented Katherine from contacting him unless he'd grabbed her too – and he was unlikely to have done anything so rash as that in the presence of four witnesses.

'You're barking up the wrong tree,' Donovan told him. 'We've been at war with Japan for the past two hours; that's why nobody gives a damn about you.'

'I don't believe it,' Waldron said in a low voice.

'The Japs crossed the frontier at five o'clock this morning.

That's official from Fortress Headquarters. They also told us America is in it as well.'

'Now I know why you guys are sweating.'

'What?'

'The bullion.' Waldron smiled. 'You were all set to grab it, but now it's beginning to look as though the Japs will beat you to the finishing post.'

There was a brief moment when he could have heard a pin drop; then the Irishman laughed derisively and told him he was crazy. But it wasn't a convincing performance; Waldron knew he'd guessed right, knew also that at least four police officers were involved in the heist. It wasn't a very comforting premise for him. He just hoped Bramwell was on his side.

Hammond bent down, unlaced his boots and pulled them off. It had taken a lot of time, sweat and energy, but he'd finally managed to open a gap wide enough to squeeze through. He certainly wasn't about to undo all his good work by advertizing his presence. Holding in his chest and stomach, he pressed his back against the frame and gradually eased himself out into the hall.

There were two doors on the right side of the passageway and it seemed only a wise precaution to check out the kitchen and the main dining salon on the ground floor before going any further. That done, he went on up the staircase, pausing every now and again to listen intently. Nothing disturbed the almost uncanny silence and by the time he reached the first landing, Hammond was beginning to wonder if the light he'd seen in the small back room on the top floor hadn't been left on by mistake. The doubt was removed moments later, when a door opened and he heard the sound of footsteps above his head.

Hammond froze. The footsteps were too heavy for a woman and whoever it was was moving away from him towards the front of the restaurant. Another door opened and closed at the far end of the landing above; suddenly Hammond realized that if Jill really was up there, he'd better take advantage of the fact that one of the kidnappers was no longer guarding her.

Disregarding the private dining rooms on the second floor, he moved on up.

A narrow corridor stretched before him at the top of the stairs with two rooms on the left and a third at the far end. Hammond tried the first door, found it was locked, and edged up to the next, his back to the wall. He glanced at the Webley revolver in his right hand, wondering if he should thumb the hammer back; then, deciding even that might make too much noise, he reached out and gently closed his other hand round the door knob. He turned it swiftly to the right, threw the door open and went into the room fast.

Jill was splayed out on the bed, her eyes blindfolded, a gag rammed deep into her mouth. A gaunt-looking Chinaman in a black pyjama suit gaped at him and started to rise from the chair. He was still in a crouching position, his legs not fully straight, when Hammond grabbed his jacket to hold him steady while he raised the revolver and smashed the barrel down on his skull. The hammer-blow opened a long, deep gash and the blood welled out of the furrow, seeped through the black hair and ran down the left side of his face. Dragging the unconscious Chinaman across the room, Hammond lowered him on to the floor near the window; then, closing the door quietly, he moved to one side of it and pressed himself against the wall.

Jill lay still, scarcely breathing, her body tensed, her head turned in his direction as though straining to see through the strip of dark green cloth over her eyes. She was only a few steps away and he longed to go to her and cradle her in his arms, but the man in the front room was a latent threat he couldn't ignore.

'It's me – David,' he whispered. 'Everything's going to be all right, Jill. I'm here now and nobody is going to hurt you.' He wondered if she had heard him and was about to repeat his words when Jill nodded her head and visibly relaxed. 'That's the style,' he went on. 'Lie still and be patient just a little longer. I'll have you out of here in no time, darling – no time at all.'

Jill nodded twice, the movement of her head slow and very deliberate. She understood, Hammond thought – but no; she was doing it again, once, twice, two separate and emphatic movements. Was she trying to tell him something? 'Are you saying you've only heard two men?' he whispered. Again there was an answering nod, and Hammond told her he understood. He would have to remain silent from now on.

The seconds ticked away and multiplied into minutes, the seemingly endless passage of time grating on his nerves, until at last he heard the sound of footsteps in the corridor. Then the latch turned, the door opened inwards and a short, thickset man entered the room. Timing it to perfection, Hammond came out of his hiding-place and struck hard and fast, wielding the revolver like an axe to lay his head open to the bone. One blow would have been sufficient, but releasing all his pent-up emotion, he hit the Cantonese again, breaking his neck as he lay face down on the carpet.

Jill had told him there were only two men, but hearing was one thing, seeing quite another. Cocking the trigger back, Hammond left the small back room, ran down the corridor and stormed into the office at the far end, only to find the room was empty. A bound ledger, lying open on the desk, caught his eye and he bent forward to take a closer look at the Chinese characters that filled one and three-quarter foolscap pages. The threat to kill his wife was there in the opening sentence and was repeated in greater detail halfway down the first page and again right at the very end.

Kellerman would have to be informed that they'd intended to steal the bullion, but there was no urgency about that. Right now, Jill was the one who mattered most of all. Easing the hammer forward, he shoved the revolver into the holster on the web belt around his waist and returned to the small back room.

First Ramsay had kept him company, then the soft-spoken Irishman and now he had Talbot, who hadn't said a word to him from the moment he'd walked into the office a good ten minutes ago. The strong silent type, Waldron thought, the kind of man you'd hate to be marooned with on a desert island.

'A penny for them,' he said abruptly, hoping to draw Talbot out of his shell.

'What?'

'Your thoughts,' said Waldron.

'They're not worth it.'

'Really? I figured you were planning how to spend your share of the two and a half million.'

'My share?' Talbot repeated uncomprehendingly. 'I don't know what you're talking about.'

'Don't give me that. I've been sitting here for hours listening to those baggage trolleys going back and forth. We both know that any minute now the Hong Kong and Shanghai Bank can kiss their gold bullion goodbye, because it'll never reach the dockside.'

'You're mad. Stark, raving mad.'

Talbot wasn't acting, of that he was sure; his reaction had been spontaneous and genuine, and that meant he wasn't in on the heist. Now all he had to do was hit the sceptic with a few solid facts and he might have a welcome ally.

'Bramwell thinks Mrs Hammond was kidnapped to facilitate the robbery.'

It was the perfect opening punch-line and Waldron could tell from the expression on his face that Talbot was hanging on his every word. But just as he reckoned he'd got him hooked, the telephone rang in the office next door and Talbot ran out of the room to answer it.

Seven-thirty: the moment of truth. Donovan nodded to the Chinese driver sitting next to him in the cab of the Fordson and the soldier shifted into first gear, let the clutch out and built up the revs. As they rolled out of the godown and began to turn left, Donovan glanced into the nearside wing mirror and saw that the second truck was practically nosing their tail. Turning right at the T-junction, they came down Hankow Road at a steady twenty-five and swung into Middle Road. He caught a brief glimpse of Ramsay's Chevrolet parked outside the rear entrance to the bank and smiled knowingly; then they hit Nathan Road, turned right again and went past the front entrance of the Peninsula Hotel. Another right-hand turn brought them into Salisbury Road and on past the railway station and the Star Ferry terminal, and suddenly there were the dock gates looming up in front of them.

Bramwell was still down at the railway sidings and had seen both vehicles from the moment they'd appeared in his field of vision and driven past the front of the Peninsula Hotel. As he observed their progress towards the docks, he wondered what on earth was going on and went over to the car to raise Police Headquarters on the radio. The instant he picked up the mike and gave his call sign, he realized that the transmit switch was malfunctioning and Nathan Road couldn't hear him.

Once again Ramsay asked Kellerman to hold one minute and cupped his hand over the mouthpiece of the telephone. Talbot was busy posting his detail on the second floor of the Peninsular Hotel to cover the front of Kaznovetsky's restaurant across the street; Adams and Thirsk were running through the lobby towards the bullion trucks parked in Hankow Road, and it was vital he delayed Jervis for at least another three minutes.

'I think we should handle these people with kid gloves, sir,' Ramsay said, continuing from where he'd left off. 'We have to bear in mind they've got a trump card in Mrs Hammond.'

'I'm aware of that,' Kellerman said tersely. 'The question is, what do we do now?'

'I don't believe we should discuss that over the phone. However, Talbot knows my views and he could brief you.'

'You'd like me to come down there?'

'I reckon it would be worth your while, sir,' Ramsay said guardedly.

'All right,' said Kellerman, 'I'll be there in five minutes.'

Ramsay heard a loud clunk and put the phone down. Kellerman had bought it, the whole load of bullshit, and from now on it was going to be plain sailing.

'Can we go now?' Jervis demanded impatiently.

'We certainly can.' Ramsay grabbed his arm and steered Jervis out of the manager's office and towards the rear entrance of the bank. 'My car's parked outside,' he said, anticipating the inevitable question.

Ramsay opened the door, bundled Jervis across the pavement and into the Chevrolet, then ran round the front and got in behind the wheel. He fired the engine into life, slammed the gear lever into first, released the handbrake and deliberately jumped the clutch, stalling the car.

'For Christ's sake,' Jervis exploded, 'get a move on.'

'That's exactly what I'm trying to do.' Ramsay cranked the engine again and took off smoothly. 'You know the old proverb,' he said calmly, 'more haste, less speed.'

The diversion sign had now been removed and he turned into Hankow Road and drove past the side entrance of the Peninsula Hotel.

'The trucks have gone,' Jervis said uneasily.

'Don't worry,' Ramsay told him, 'we'll soon catch them up.'

He turned into Salisbury Road and went up through the gearbox into top. Tyres screaming on the tarmac, he turned right again, shot past the Star Ferry terminal and sped through the dock gates, lights flashing, horn blaring.

'See?' Ramsay took one hand off the wheel and pointed to the trucks a hundred yards ahead. 'Didn't I tell you there was nothing to worry about?'

Swerving to the left, he pulled up alongside the two Fordsons and scrambled out of the car. The bullion detail, a lieutenant and twelve men from the Royal Rifles of Canada were in position on the rooftops of the adjoining warehouses, the four bogus Chinese soldiers were guarding the trucks, and the First Mate of the *Delphic Star* was down on the quayside, talking to an official from the Dock Labour Board and a group of stevedores. Donovan moved towards him, his eyes smiling triumphantly. Then suddenly the Irishman stopped dead in his tracks and stared mutely into the distance, his left arm a signpost pointing towards the sky.

Ramsay turned slowly about, saw a column of black smoke rising above the airfield at Kai Tak and noted, almost absentmindedly, that a stick of bombs was falling from a single-engined dive bomber. Offshore, the Pan Am flying boat was burning fiercely, and three fighter planes were strafing the oil storage tanks at North Point near Victoria across the bay. As he looked towards Kai Tak again, a plane roared low overhead and raked the bridge of the *Delphic Star* with machine-gun fire. It happened fast, so fast that the danger was past before he had time to throw himself flat on the ground.

'I guess this is what you would call last-minute confusion,' Donovan said, grinning at him.

Ramsay nodded. If he'd planned it himself, the Japanese could not have intervened at a more opportune moment, but he hoped they realized the Portuguese freighter berthed opposite the *Delphic Star* was a neutral ship. At the end of the day, half a million pounds' worth of diamonds would be so much junk if he was unable to leave Hong Kong. Closing his mind to the possibility, he went over to Jervis.

'Are you okay?' he asked.

'I think I'm still in one piece.' Jervis finished brushing the dirt from his trousers and straightened up. 'That was a close call,' he said, his voice still shaky.

'You can say that again.' Ramsay jerked a thumb over his shoulder at the two Fordsons. 'You don't want me to hang around while they're being unloaded, do you?' He paused, then played the trump card. 'I mean, Mrs Hammond is still in danger and I don't want to wait here a minute longer than I have to.'

'Yes, of course.' Jervis smiled and stuck out his right hand. 'Thank you for everything you've done, Chief Inspector,' he said solemnly. 'The bank owes you a great deal.'

'I was only doing my job.'

Somehow Ramsay managed to keep a straight face as they shook hands. Then he turned about and signalled to Donovan to follow him.

Adams held the shotgun across his lap, his finger curled round the trigger, the barrel pointing at the Chinese driver in case he gave any trouble. Not that Adams believed he would, for although the driver had been puzzled as to why they weren't going to the docks, he'd obeyed his instructions to follow the leading vehicle up Nathan Road and into Waterloo Road. Now, less than ten minutes later, both trucks were heading east on Boundary Street towards the disused laundry. They were practically home and dry.

Or were they? Adams leaned forward and stared at the huge column of black smoke on the horizon. At first, it looked to him as though it was merely an isolated building on fire, then he heard several distant crumps and knew different when he glimpsed a plane skimming the rooftops.

'Holy Christ, it's the Japs,' he said in an awed voice.

It was the last statement he was destined to make. Above and behind him, a marauding Zero spotted the two military vehicles moving in tandem and came in low to rake the Fordsons with cannon and machine gun fire. In the last few seconds that remained to him, Adams saw Thirsk's truck swerve off the road, mount the pavement and plough through a hedgerow into the front garden of somebody's house. He was also aware that his own vehicle was heading straight for a lamp post; then the pain in his back and chest became intolerable and he slumped over the dashboard, a trickle of blood oozing from his open mouth.

Bramwell had started to shadow both vehicles shortly after he saw them turn into Nathan Road and was approximately half a mile behind them when the Zero pounced. By the time he arrived on the scene, only the Chinese corporal in charge of the escort was still alive and he died while Bramwell was applying a tourniquet to the bloody stump of his right leg.

Waldron gave the door another savage kick and yelled a string of obscenities at the top of his voice. The raid appeared to be tailing off, and though he could still hear a couple of planes machine-gunning Shamshuipo barracks up the road, he didn't understand why the people in the office nextdoor couldn't hear him. He kicked the bottom panel again and cracked the pane of frosted glass above. Then a voice said, 'All right, all right, I'm coming,' and Talbot finally unlocked and opened the door.

'You took your time,' Waldron growled. 'What kept you?'

'Didn't you know? There's a war on.' Talbot unslung the Thompson sub machine gun he was carrying over his right shoulder and leaned it against the wall. 'If you turn round, I'll cut you loose.'

'Thank God for that,' Waldron said. 'Make it fast, will you?'

'I'm trying not to hurt you – your hands are badly swollen.'

'Yeah? Well, by the time I've finished with Ramsay, his neck will be in much the same condition.'

'You're out of luck,' Talbot said. 'He left with the bullion twenty minutes ago.'

'Which way did they go? Along Middle Road?'

'Why the hell would they do that? The trucks were parked outside the arcade.'

'Ask Ramsay,' Waldron told him. 'Maybe he can tell you. All I'm saying is that two vehicles went by a short while back, and I know an army truck when I hear one.'

'You think the bullion has been lifted from under our noses, don't you?'

'Right first time.'

'Wrong,' Talbot said. 'It's down on the dockside. Word came through from Fortress Headquarters a few minutes ago.'

'Yeah?' Waldron massaged his wrists, trying to restore the circulation to his hands. 'Has anyone thought to look inside the steel boxes?'

Talbot stared at him and slowly shook his head. 'You've got a fixation about Ramsay, haven't you?'

'I've no reason to love him,' Waldron said dryly.

'Okay, so he roughed you up a little, but hell, you asked for it. Right now, Ramsay is out there risking his neck to save Mrs Hammond.'

'What do you mean, out there?'

'Kaznovetsky's restaurant,' said Talbot. 'That's where she's being held. We aim to cover the front while Ramsay goes in the back way.'

'Whose bright idea was that? Kellerman's?'

'The Assistant Commissioner would like to think it's his plan, but it was Ramsay who suggested it to me in the first place.'

'I might have guessed.' Waldron paused, wondering how he could convince Talbot that the bastard had fooled everybody all along the line. Then, in a quiet voice, he said, 'I suppose you do realize that if you don't stop Ramsay here and now, she'll never come out of that place alive?'

'Oh, Christ,' Talbot said in disgust, 'I was right – you are stark, raving mad.'

There was, Waldron decided, no point in prolonging an argument he couldn't possibly win. Moving swiftly, he kneed Talbot in the groin, grabbed the Thompson sub machine gun and ran out of the office. Somebody called after him as he left the bank, but he ignored the angry voice and kept on going across the street, the boot with no lace chafing the heel of his right foot.

Both doors in the entrance to Kaznovetsky's restaurant were locked, and he had to smash the plate glass with the butt of the sub machine gun before he could gain entry. From then on, Waldron adopted a more cautious approach, checking out the main dining salon and the kitchen at the back, then starting slowly up the staircase.

A tall, fair-haired man was waiting for him on the top floor, and the Webley revolver he held in a double-handed grip was pointed straight at his chest. It took him some considerable time to convince Hammond that he was on his side.

Ramsay crouched beside Donovan in the doorway of the silk emporium adjoining the Roxy Hotel in Peking Road. It had taken them longer than he'd anticipated to work their way through the back streets behind the docks, but it seemed the unexpected delay was about to work to their advantage.

'Hear that?' he said, nudging Donovan in the ribs. 'Sounds as though the second wave is coming in.'

Donovan poked his head outside and looked up at the sky. 'I can hear them,' he said, 'but I don't see them.'

'You will soon enough,' Ramsay told him.

'That's what I like about you, George. The eternal optimist.'

Ramsay grunted and looked at his wristwatch. 'It's eight thirty-five,' he announced calmly.

'So what?'

'So our Cantonese friend should be talking to Hammond again.' He reached inside his jacket, drew the Colt .45 automatic from the shoulder holster and pulled the slide back to chamber a round. 'I think we should go in through the kitchen and pay him a visit.'

'Maybe we should shoot the lock off first to make it look good?'

'We can do that later,' Ramsay said, 'after we've set fire to the place.'

'All right,' Donovan said testily, 'let's get it over with. Waiting here is giving me the creeps.'

Ramsay grinned at him. 'Why so glum, Bill?' he asked. 'You know, this is our lucky day.'

Then he started across the road towards the courtyard in rear of Kaznovetsky's restaurant, the Irishman close behind him.

Half the Jap air force seemed to be overhead, but above the noise of their radial engines Waldron thought he could hear somebody moving along the landing on the floor below. Glancing at Hammond, he raised a quizzical eyebrow and got an affirmative nod in return.

'Are you sure you know how to handle that thing?' Hammond whispered.

'Sure,' Waldron murmured. 'You just push the safety forward to automatic and squeeze the trigger.'

It suddenly occurred to him that Talbot was unlikely to have cocked the Thompson; sure enough, checking the ejection slot, he saw the breech block was still forward. He swore under his breath. The intruders were just one flight of steps away and it was too late to do anything about it now.

Then Ramsay's head and shoulders appeared in view, and Hammond said, 'Hullo George, fancy seeing you here.'

Ramsay turned and looked up, a disarming smile gradually appearing on his face. 'I could say the same, David,' he said, and fired from the hip.

In that same instant, Waldron cocked the Thompson and loosed off a long burst. The sub machine gun kicked high and to the right, and a line of bullet holes appeared in the opposite wall. As he brought the butt up into his shoulder to take a more deliberate aim, Hammond squeezed off two shots in quick succession and hit Ramsay in the chest and between the eyes. Then Waldron leaned over the banisters and emptied the rest of the magazine into Donovan.

POSTSCRIPT

CHAPTER TWENTY-ONE

The Gin Drinkers Line was expected to delay the Japanese for at least a week, but with only three infantry battalions available to hold a frontage of eleven miles, the defenders were necessarily very thin on the ground. The key position of the Shingmun Redoubt was garrisoned only by one under-strength platoon of the 2nd Royal Scots. Their approach march concealed by a layer of thick fog, the 3rd Battalion of Colonel Doi Teihichi's 228th Imperial Japanese Infantry Regiment attacked the isolated Redoubt on the night of the 9th December at 2300 hours and in bitter hand-to-hand fighting in the underground tunnels, succeeded in annihilating the tiny garrison before midnight. Forty-eight hours later, the Gin Drinkers Line irrevocably broken, the three battalions on the mainland were evacuated to Hong Kong.

There was only a handful of anti-aircraft guns on the island and the Japanese had achieved total air supremacy on day one, when the two Walrus amphibians and three ancient Vickers Vildebeest torpedo bombers were destroyed on the ground. The Japanese also possessed overwhelming artillery firepower, two factors which enabled them to bombard the island at will for the next seven days and nights while they prepared to execute an amphibious landing.

The night of the 18th December was exceptionally dark, the sky was overcast and there were frequent showers of rain. The weather conditions could not have been more favourable to the invaders, and despite intense machine gun fire from the beach defences, the Japanese managed to put two regiments ashore, the 228th between North Point and Taikoo Docks on the north side of the island, and the 229th at Lei Mun on the east coast.

The following night, the Second Motor Torpedo Flotilla

made a determined attempt to prevent the Japanese landing additional reinforcements, but of the six boats involved in the action, two were sunk, one was badly damaged and beached and a fourth was holed above and below the waterline. Further attacks were considered suicidal and thereafter, Major General Sano was able to ferry the remaining units of the 38th Division across to the island. Better trained and better equipped, the 38th Division then proceeded to pulverize the six under-strength and widely-dispersed battalions defending the island with the Hong Kong Volunteer Defence Corps. Short of water, their ammunition practically exhausted, and having suffered three thousand five hundred battle casualties including more than two thousand killed in action, the tiny garrison finally surrendered on Christmas Day.

David Hammond and Ralph Cottis were among the survivors who were eventually herded into a POW Camp at Shamshuipo, where they remained for the next nine months, existing on a starvation diet consisting of two bowls of watery soup per day, supplemented by whatever stray cats and dogs that happened to wander into the camp. On the 27th September 1942 they were transferred to Japan in the holds of the *Lisbon Maru* along with eighteen hundred other British prisoners. The ship was armed, and in addition to carrying a draft of Japanese troops, there were no distinguishing marks to show that she had POWs aboard. Four days out from Hong Kong, the *Lisbon Maru* was torpedoed by the USS *Grouper*. Cottis was one of the eight hundred and forty-three men who were drowned at sea, but Hammond managed to swim five miles to the nearest of the Sing Pang Islands off the coast of Chekiang Province. He was recaptured three days later and sent on to Japan, where he spent the rest of the war working on the docks at Kobe.

Kellerman, Bramwell and Talbot were interned at North Point. Kellerman died from the ravages of malnutrition and dysentery in March 1943 and Talbot was murdered some eight months later by one of the Formosan guards, who beat him to death with an iron bar because he failed to bow to a senior NCO.

Bramwell survived the war and went on to become an Assistant Commissioner of Police in Kenya before retiring in 1961 to settle in Dorset.

Jill Hammond, Tom and Rhoda Blakeney, Malcolm Vines, the gossip columnist of the *South China Morning Post*, Spencer Jarrold, the American Vice Consul in Hong Kong, and Harold Quarrie of the *Chicago Herald Tribune* were all interned at Stanley on the southern tip of the island. Although the Geneva Convention specified that civilian prisoners were to receive 2400 calories a day, their diet only averaged 850 for the first three months. Thereafter there was a slight improvement, mainly due to the fact that the internees cultivated every bit of arable land within the camp perimeter and grew their own vegetables. Spencer Jarrold and Harold Quarrie, together with three hundred and forty-eight other American civilians, were repatriated in 1942, sailing from Hong Kong on the 29th June in the *Asama Maru*. Jill Hammond, Tom and Rhoda Blakeney and Malcolm Vines were still behind barbed wire when Japan surrendered on the 15th August 1945. David and Jill Hammond were reunited three weeks later, meeting by pre-arrangement in the bar of the Gloucester Hotel. Both had lost considerable amounts of weight during their captivity and it was some moments before they recognized one another.

There were two escapers and one evader. The evader was Inspector Yeuh-Shen, who disappeared the night before the mainland was evacuated, to re-emerge in February 1942 as the leader of a guerrilla band operating in the Canton Province, where he subsequently remained after the war. The escapers were Katherine Goddard and Frank Waldron. In fact, Waldron never went into the bag. Much against his will, he left Hong Kong on the night of the 10th December 1941 in a light aircraft belonging to the Volunteer Defence Corps which had been concealed from the marauding Zeros in the disused laundry Ramsay had been planning to use. The Colonial authorities appeared to think it was vital Waldron returned to Washington to testify before a Congressional Committee, but in the event, he never progressed beyond Chungking. Commissioned in the field, he was assigned to the Judge Advocate's Department attached to General Chennault's 14th Air Force.

The true escaper was Katherine Goddard, who was interned at Stanley along with the other civilians. On the night of the 19th April 1942, she crawled under the barbed wire and persuaded a friendly Chinese fisherman to take her across to the mainland. Moving only at night, she then made her way through the New Territories and crossed the frontier into China near Sha Tau Kok. Passed from one guerrilla band to the next, Katherine finally reached Chungking in August 1942 where, on the 22nd September, she and Frank Waldron were married by an Army Air Corps chaplain.

Ramon Garcia was killed during an air raid on Christmas Eve but his patron, Li Ho Chung did rather well out of the war. Aside from his Black Market activities, he organized a chain of couriers to supply essential foodstuffs and life-saving drugs to the POWs and civilian internees. Although it could be said that he was simply backing every horse in the race, his services were recognized and he was awarded the OBE in 1946, a stroke of irony in view of the fact that he had provided the financial backing for the robbery.

The bullion was recovered from the wrecked trucks in Boundary Street and as the *Delphic Star* had been badly damaged by a two-hundred-and-fifty-pounder in a subsequent bombing raid, it was transported back to the island. At one stage it was thought HMS *Thracian* might take the bullion to Australia, but the old 'S' Class destroyer was considered indispensable and, in the end, the gold was returned to the Hong Kong and Shanghai Bank in Victoria. It was still there on the 16th August 1945, the day the bank staff returned. However, when the steel boxes were unpacked, it was discovered that two gold ingots were missing. To this day, they have never been recovered.